AUTHOR
ON THE RUN

VICKI EIDE

Copyright © 2014 Vicki Eide
All rights reserved.

No part of this book may be reproduced, stored in a retrieval system, or transmitted by any means without the written consent of the author.

ISBN: 1490594868
ISBN 13: 9781490594866

Library of Congress Control Number: 2013915982
CreateSpace Independent Publishing Platform
North Charleston, South Carolina

Printed in the United States of America

This is a work of fiction. Names, characters, places and incidents either are the product of the author's imagination or are used fictitiously, and any resemblance to actual persons, living or dead, business, companies, events or locales is entirely coincidental.

Thank you to all my family and
friends who gave encouragement and support

*To: Jan & Jim,
Thank you for
your support -
Enjoy the read -
Best Wishes Always
Vicki Eide
2014*

Previously Published:

Victoria Place

CHAPTER 1

"**M**s. Noble."

I had retained my maiden name, "Although I'm completely sympathetic and understanding with your issues in this divorce, it is unfortunate the most I can offer you is a police escort for the removal of your belongings. I am ordering Mr. Aston to remain off the property during this time. I suggest you have friends help you get in and out of the home as quickly as possible. You will have two hours for the removal of your personal property. If you discover any damage or missing items from your belongings, notify the court immediately and it will be dealt with accordingly. Good luck, Ms. Noble."

We sat in the courtroom as the judge read the final settlement of the divorce and placed a temporary restraining order on Trevor. I could see out of the corner of my eye he was seething with rage and hate. That look brought chills up my spine. I grabbed my attorney's arm, he patted my hand and whispered, "It's okay, Wendy, he can't hurt you."

"Mr. Aston, you have heard my decision. You have thirty days to make all the appropriate transfers related to this divorce settlement. In addition, I am ordering that you enter into an Anger Management and a Parenting Program and you have sixty days to complete both programs. I suggest you do this immediately. Your case will be turned over to a case worker with the Children's Services Division. I am hopeful that I will not see you again in my court. Good luck, Mr. Aston."

As we left the court room, Trevor rushed by me, taking a moment to whisper in my ear, "We are not done. I'll see you dead." He gave me a sick fake smile and rushed out. My heart stopped and I thought I was going to be sick.

Sitting near the back of the courtroom, waiting for their trial coming up next, Detective Brenda Lou Davis leaned over to her husband, Detective Sam Davis, and said, "Did you hear that? He just made a life threatening remark to that woman. What an asshole. I hope we won't be reading about her in the obits."

Sam replied, "Yah, I did, but then so did her attorney so I'm sure he will deal with it. Arrogant men like that need to be strung up."

The Davis's came to Boston after a wild chase of hide and seek with a child molester who had kidnapped an eight year old little girl in Seattle and run with her to Boston. They had chased Loren Pratt and little Mia across the states and SWAT apprehended Loren in a motel with the traumatized Mia in Boston. Mia's parents flew to Boston and then returned to Seattle where she would undergo much therapy. Sam and Brenda Lou would testify to the details of the case to put Loren Pratt behind bars.

I was in such a state of terror and depression, and horrified when my attorney informed me that even the simplest, uncontested divorce could take up to eighteen months before it would be final. All I wanted to do was run away as far as I could get from Trevor.

I had been so in love with Trevor that I never saw the subtleties of abuse until they became so strong that I feared for my life. I had to get out as quickly as possible.

Having stayed with friends during the divorce process, and even though they tried their very best to make me feel safe and welcome, it was difficult not to feel like an intruder. I will be forever grateful for their support. As the days grew near for the court date, I was getting more and more anxious to leave Boston. I didn't have a plan or destination, I just knew I had to leave and get away from Trevor Aston.

Although, Sheila and Billy, Trevor's two children, were now thirteen and fifteen, I regretted not having the opportunity to tell them goodbye. It was probably better for all of us and it would've been extremely devastating for them. I seemed to be the only stability in their lives and the only one that showed love and caring. I did love those two.

Most of my friends were associates through Harvard while I was working on my Master's Degree. Some of us kept in touch, but I never developed a real closeness with any one of them. Gradually, we all moved on, especially after Trevor and I were married.

My childhood friend, Allison, came for the divorce trial to spend time and help me to be strong. We had gone through all four years of high school together and then went our separate ways for college, but we always kept in touch. Allison definitely was an extrovert and truly a party girl. I liked to party as well, but I drew the line much faster than Allison. She was on her third marriage and had two beautiful daughters who were presently in college. Allison met Matt, the love of her life, five years prior to Trevor and me meeting. Matt had been a great substitute father to the girls and treated them as though they were his own. Although Matt had three sons of his own, I never knew what had happened to their relationship, but according to Allison, he was not in good standing with his boys. I didn't know anything about them; no one ever volunteered any information and I never asked.

It was a nasty divorce. Allison and friends were willing to take the risk to help me even after Trevor threatened them a number of times. I thought it was strange that Matt was not around to help, but then I remembered Allison telling me every time they moved, he was always unavailable to help, seems he was either out of town or had a very important meeting to attend. She got used to it and would hire movers and Matt paid. It worked for her.

All I could think about and was completely obsessed to getting out of Boston. I didn't have one close supporting friend that I felt I could trust one hundred percent, but friends willing to give me sympathy and advice of should do's and should not's. I just wanted to get away from all of that, try and start my life over and get back to writing again. There was so much I had missed out on during the years of our marriage and I wanted to recapture me, I needed to recapture me.

Everything I owned was in storage, added to my parents' stuff that had been stored for over twelve years. I hadn't taken time to go through it after their death. All I had was clothing, a laptop computer and personal items. I closed my checking and savings account, for now, cash was not a problem. Credit card use was out of the question and I purchased prepaid cell cards.

CHAPTER 2

Detective Brenda Lou Davis, she still found it hard getting used to her new last name, even though she'd been married just over a year.

Brenda Lou and Sam Davis are a detective team, formerly from San Diego, currently working out of Seattle. The Davis couple had worked together for about five years, as partners, before they were married. But the last case ended with both of them being shot, Sam more seriously with a long recovery. Brenda Lou closed the case and brought down two corrupt police officers with the San Diego Sheriff's Department, an embezzling blackmailing minister, as well as an unsolved twenty year old hit and run.

This particular case had taken a toll on them both physically and emotionally in addition to the struggle of an off again on again relationship.

Brenda Lou Weathers had graduated from college in Boise, Idaho, taught school for a couple years, then married a doctor and moved to San Diego. It was there she discovered her husband was having an affair with a nurse at the medical clinic of his practice. Teaching jobs were hard to obtain in California, so Brenda Lou made a career change and attended the Police Academy. Her ambition and drive to succeed, to be the best officer she could be, took only a few years until she had worked her way up to sergeant detective.

Sam Davis had been a detective with the Sheriff's Department until his wife of fourteen years became ill with cancer and he took a leave of absence to take care of her. Linda's illness took a rapid turn for the worse and she passed away in less than thirty days. Sam was suddenly a single parent of Sean – twelve, Sara – ten and Sandy is eight. Devastated at the loss of his wife, Linda, and overwhelmed with the sudden responsibility of three kids, Sam went into a deep depression and became nonfunctional.

Several months of therapy, support from his parents and a sister, Monica, who was bound to whip Sam into shape, he finally got back to reality for his kids. Monica interviewed several nannies, and hired Sylvia to move in and help out for a while. Sam returned to work after six months.

Sam was assigned to partner with Brenda Lou, which neither one was happy about. Sam was not in favor of a female boss and Brenda Lou wasn't sure he was ready to get back on the force.

Brenda Lou and Sam became an excellent detective team and worked many cases together over the next five years. During that time, they got involved in an intimate relationship, which was against department policy and Brenda Lou periodically tried to squelch their affair.

They maintained a working relationship while Sam continued to pursue Brenda Lou romantically. He was in love with her and even though she cared deeply for Sam, she just wasn't ready to give up her career and become a Mom of three children. She internally struggled with her emotions and feelings for Sam, but was bound to follow the department policy on employee cohabitation. However, in the end she caved, let her heart rule over department rules and accepted Sam's proposal.

After Sam was severely injured from being shot, Brenda Lou took a leave of absence to care for him and his three children. During Sam's recovery, they made their wedding plans, as well.

They all made the adjustment very smoothly with the new marriage. However, when Sam and Brenda Lou decided to move to the Seattle area to be closer to Sam's aging parents and continue their work, the idea of moving didn't go quite so well with the kids. End results were they moved that summer.

CHAPTER 3

When I left Boston, my first stop was a small town in Connecticut. There, I found a beauty salon and changed my hair from long dark brown to a bobbed, highlighted auburn. The style was really quite cute, and with my olive complexion it looked pretty natural. As a published author and my picture on the back cover of every book I had published, I needed to change my appearance and hope it worked.

I continued driving and by late evening, I decided I had better start looking for a motel room. My plan was to stay off the main freeways and thoroughfares. I rented a dumpy motel room in a dumpy little town in Pennsylvania. I had such a sick feeling in the pit of my stomach that Trevor was going to find me, I could hardly sleep.

Up early the next morning after a fitful night's sleep, I headed out again with no destination in mind. I just kept driving south on back roads. I picked up a map at one of my gas stops - I certainly didn't want to get lost. But how would one get lost when there wasn't a particular destination in mind, only the southern direction. The country was beautiful, but I kept my eye on the rearview mirror.

In West Virginia I stopped at a quaint bed and breakfast and checked in for the night. The owner, Mrs. Keller, was so sweet and accommodating and somehow recognized me as a troubled woman. She kept coming to my room with one excuse after another, bringing fruit, then the newspaper, offering a cocktail or glass of wine and finally insisted I go down to the sitting room and watch TV with her. She was so nice I found it hard to decline her invitation and I joined her. After a while I convinced Mrs. Keller I was tired and going up to my room and would be leaving early in the morning. She assured me she would have breakfast ready before I left.

While I was eating, she chatted nonstop, asking questions why I was traveling alone, it wasn't safe. Where I was going? If I had a family? All the usual questions. Finally, I told her I didn't have a family and was an artist just looking for someplace nice and quiet to paint. Another lie, hopefully this would throw off any connections if someone were to inquire about me. Author to artist? I think I can make it work.

Mrs. Keller got so excited and enthusiastic about me wanting a quiet place, she was beside herself. She had a friend that had the perfect place for me. She made a phone call and confirmed her friend would let me rent their casita. Mrs. Keller gave me the phone number to call her friend, Cecelia Downs, when I got to Lexington, Kentucky.

I felt rather uneasy that Mrs. Keller would pass me on to her friend when she knew nothing about me. I certainly wasn't accustomed to Southern hospitality.

With the directions I needed I was on the road again. I told Mrs. Downs I wouldn't arrive for a few days, I wanted to take my time along the way and she assured me it was not a problem

When I got to the outskirts of Fayette, West Virginia I checked into a motel for a week. I mailed myself a couple of letters under my new name. I picked out the name Alicia Browning. I have no idea where I came up with that name; it just came out of nowhere. I applied for a new driver's license and was amazed how easy it was. No one questioned that my wallet, holding my entire ID, was stolen. Hoping a new identity was my fresh start to a new life. Yah, right.

Forging Trevor's signature on the car title, I traded it in for a Chevy Blazer. This was going way too easy and I was terrified something was going to go wrong. That old saying, 'When things seem to be too good to be true, they usually are', and that was my fear. I obtained insurance in my new name and I was good to go. I went back to the motel and after only four days, it was time to move on before anyone got suspicious and my plans backfired. Paranoia was setting in; actually, I don't think it ever left after I met Trevor.

Driving back roads, I stayed in some of the most horrible motels one could imagine. With all the threats Trevor had made, and I truly did believe him, I knew I had to stay out of sight. I stayed a night here, a couple nights there and definitely was not making a pattern, just being extremely cautious. I have no idea how long I thought I was going to hide or what even made me think I could. So far it was working. The further I got from Boston, the safer and more relaxed I felt. I also knew, deep in my heart, I would probably never be safe.

Midafternoon, I stopped at a road side café for a late lunch. There were only two other people in the place, so I got the best seat in the house, a table in the back, near a big window with a view of the rippling river drifting by. It was hypnotic and relaxing, if only for a few moments.

My thoughts quickly went back to Trevor and his controlling ways and that sickish nauseating feeling of fear came over me again. What had happened behind closed doors in our home was never known outside those doors. My only confidante was my best friend, Allison, who lived on the West coast. She and her husband, Matt, had insisted I should go west and hide out with them, but I knew that would be the first place Trevor would look. I did not want to put them in jeopardy.

Trevor was a very successful attorney in a large law firm, in the suburbs of Boston, who represented a huge investment institution. I knew nothing about Trevor's clientele or the kind of investments he made, not only because Trevor chose not to talk about his business and was quite secretive about it, but because he had made it very clear he never brought work home. I was busy running the house, taking care of his two children, Sheila and Billy, and struggling to find time to write without upsetting the apple cart. Which, in the end, I just gave up writing. I couldn't concentrate and it became too stressful.

Matt introduced Trevor as an old acquaintance he happened to run into at the bar. Trevor was such a charming man, so smooth and so gentle and when our eyes met I knew it was love at first sight. He treated me with the utmost respect, wined and dined me at some of the most elite and expensive restaurants in Boston. Trevor showered me with gifts and flowers that embarrassed me to be spoiled by a man I barely knew. We spent a few afternoons together with his children on Sundays in the park and I was intrigued by how well-behaved they were for an eight and ten year old. I thought it was extremely abnormal to be so polite and proper. They didn't go play with other children, didn't bring games to play with each other, instead they very quietly sat at the picnic table.

When I remarked about his children being so quiet, he snapped at me that 'children were to be seen and not heard' and he laughed with a chilling tone. I soon learned that was exactly the way Trevor treated Sheila and Billy, even in their home. They loved their Dad, but were terrified of him at the same time.

Shaking my head and coming back to the present, "You have got to quit thinking about this man, it will only drag you down further and nothing will ever change what happened." I said out loud.

"Excuse me. I'm sorry I didn't hear what you said. Do you need something else?" The waitress asked.

Startled, I realized I was talking out loud, I was embarrassed. "Oh, no thank you, I just need my bill." Well that was cute, now I'm talking to myself, out loud and in a public place at that. I paid my bill and headed for Lexington.

CHAPTER 4

Calling Mrs. Downs as I approached the outskirts of Lexington she gave me directions to a shopping mall. We met in the parking lot of the mall and after short introductions; I followed her out of town to the most amazingly beautiful farm country and a simply stunning plantation estate. This was way beyond a farm and indescribably picturesque-gorgeous.

Driving onto the plantation gave me such a feeling of safety and peace. We drove around the back of the main mansion to a much smaller house. Mrs. Downs stopped in front and got out of her car, I sat in my car mesmerized over the beauty.

"Wow! This is a beautiful place." I exclaimed. Mrs. Downs smiled, then helped me with my bags and gave me a tour through the house, then we walked outside to the patio.

"Mrs. Downs, this is far more than I expected. I can't thank you enough for allowing me to stay here. This is going to be perfect for me to write, that is, if I can concentrate and not be distracted by all this."

"You are so welcome," she said smiling. "When Jean called and told me about you, we both agreed this would be perfect for you. But I thought she said you were an artist? I must've misunderstood, it doesn't matter. Anyway, Jim and I don't have anyone to use this house anymore since my mother passed away. It will be a delight to see some activity around here again. I'll let you finish getting settled and if you need anything at all, please don't hesitate to call. I showed you where the intercom is, so use it."

Crap, I was caught in my first lie. I needed to get my story straight. "Thank you so much. Actually, I do both write and paint. I like to take pictures and paint later, but I write occasionally, nothing to brag about. This will be just perfect." Mrs. Downs got in her car and drove to the mansion and I walked out on the patio and continued to admire the view before going back inside.

I had stopped and bought a few groceries and a couple bottles of liquor before meeting Mrs. Downs, so I was good in that department. I finished putting stuff away and poured myself a drink. This was going to be just what I needed, I could live here forever. I sat out on the patio and got lost in the view.

It had been a couple years since I had been able to sit down at the computer and concentrate on writing. My life with Trevor that last year and a half had been only a means of survival and trying to maintain a semblance of normalcy for Sheila and Billy. I loved those two kids as though they were mine. My heart was breaking knowing I had to leave them and I didn't get a chance to tell them goodbye. It was such an ugly parting for Trevor and me; I wouldn't have wanted Sheila and Billy to experience any of it anyway.

I hadn't talked to Allison since I left Boston, so when I phoned, she answered and was thrilled to hear my voice and started in with an abundance of questions. "Oh, my God, Wendy, are you okay? We have been so worried about you. I've tried your cell phone several times; did you change your number?"

"I'm doing okay and yes, I did change my cell. I bought one of those pay as you go cell phones so it can't be traced. You won't believe this but I cut my hair and am now a highlighted redhead."

"You are kidding me, the same color as mine?"

"Kind of, a little more on the auburn side. Have you heard from Trevor?"

"Oh yah. He is sure you are here and is obsessed with trying to find you. Don't even tell me where you are; just be sure you keep in touch. Are you being careful and keeping yourself safe?"

"I think so. I've changed everything. I traded in the car and got new ID. I can't believe how easy it was to get a new driver's license and insurance."

"Good girl. Are you okay on money? You aren't using your credit cards or check book are you?"

"No, I'm not using any of them. I told you I had been taking little bits of cash and stashing it when things started going south. I closed my checking and savings accounts and took a bunch of cash out of our joint account before Trevor closed it. One more reason he's so furious with me, among many others."

"Just remember our plan when you start getting low. We're here for you, Wendy, and we are both so worried about you. Matt won't let me talk to Trevor whenever he calls, you wouldn't even believe how obnoxious Trevor has been. Well, I guess you would, you had to live with it for the last few years. I don't know how you did it. I'd have killed him or pulled a Lorena Bobbitt." We both laughed.

"Sweetie, I better get off here. I just wanted to let you know I'm okay. I'll call you again real soon. I'm planning to stay at this place for a month and see if I can get going on this book. I can't quite get my head into this one."

"It's not as though you've had anything else going on in that head of yours. It'll come to you. Hang in there and be careful. Keep in touch with us. We love you."

CHAPTER 5

White fences and beautiful horses so peacefully grazing, the babies running playfully, kicking up their heels and green hills rambled on for as far as I could see. What more could one ask for? Just below the guest house, my residence, was what I thought to be a nursery or garden of sorts. I couldn't tell what was growing in there, but I was sure I would find out. There was a smaller house off to the right in a setting among some tall trees. I had no idea what that house was, but I would find out about that as well.

With my note pad in hand, I continued to sit out on the patio and jot down ideas for a new book. My mind was a blank. I was so lost in the scenery, I couldn't think. Then it hit me. Why not write a mystery love story and life on a plantation?

I started making a character list and giving them names, I came up with a different town other than Lexington, but this place was implanted in my head and it was going to be very hard not to use all this in my story. I could use all the descriptive adjectives I needed to bring my readers right here with me.

I'd ask Mrs. Downs about her life on the plantation, and if I played my cards right, I might even get acquainted with some hired hands and get information from them.

And so I started my notes and outline: ***The owners of the place would be a middle aged couple and a first marriage for him and second for her with*** *a troublesome son. When her husband mysteriously and suddenly dies, the hired manager tries to warn the wife of suspicious behavior from her own son. She finds the accusations positively absurd and refuses to listen to him.*

When she has an automobile accident, and is in critical condition for several days and not expected to survive, the hired man refuses to leave her side. This only creates an angrier and more vindictive son and the temperament between the two men gets increasingly worse.

She finally starts to make improvement and, with a fulltime nursing staff, is allowed to go home. The hired man is emphatic with the staff that her son is never to be alone with her. In the meantime, he continues to work with investigators in determining the cause of the accident. He still has not given up the idea that his boss had been murdered and the number one suspect is the wife's son, in his opinion.

Several months go by and the hired man is slowly but firmly falling in love with her, but with the friction between him and her son, she doesn't recognize love over his attitude towards her son.

So the investigation continues and everyone is careful that she is not involved as she slowly starts to recover from her many injuries and the possibility she may never walk again.

My book was laid out and I had a beginning and ending plan. Now I just needed to figure out the in between. A flash of light caught my eye; I watched what it could be until I saw it was a vehicle on the side of the hill off in the distance. My first thought was Trevor had somehow found me. But how could that be, I just got here. I watched as it continued winding down the road and getting closer and closer. I picked up my note pad and quickly went in the house and watched out the window. It was one of the ranch trucks.

The question came to me as to how long it was going to take before I got over the fear Trevor was going to find me? How long was it going to take before I quit looking over my shoulder and in the rear view mirror every place I went? Or was this going to be my life until Trevor did find me and he got his wish, "I'll see you dead"?

CHAPTER 6

Early one evening I decided to be brave and take a short walk while there was still plenty of light. It was a beautiful evening and the weather was perfect. The further I walked the more little roads there were that kept branching off to other parts of the fields. It was like a maze.

Thinking I had better start back - suddenly I was confused as to where I was in this field. I had walked and walked, made turns right and left and I knew I was lost. I came to a clearing directly in front of a house that sat among a grove of tall trees, a very pretty setting.

This must be the house I could see from the patio at the guest house. It was much larger than what I had observed and thought maybe it was the original plantation home. It was two stories with a huge wraparound porch and there were no lights on so I thought it was empty. I wished I had my camera, then, I laughed at myself. Why would I want a camera, I'm not a photographer. I was beginning to believe my own lies. How funny was that?

I started to walk away and heard someone behind me, "May I help you?"

Startled, because I thought I was alone out there, I turned to see a man standing on the porch of the house I had been admiring.

"Oh, I'm so sorry. I didn't know anyone lived here. I'm staying in the Downs' guest house. I'm afraid I got lost in the fields; it's kind of a maze in there. I didn't mean to intrude."

"No intrusion. Josh Townsend, here, and you are?"

"We………Ah, Alicia."

He stepped forward and extended his hand, "Nice to meet you, Ah, Alicia. What brings you out here to the Downs' Ranch?"

Shaking hands, I knew I was caught again. Damn, I had to get my shit together and keep my stories straight. "I'm just traveling around looking for quiet places to take pictures and paint. This place was recommended to me, and I can certainly see why, it is beautiful. And what do you do here?"

"I'm the foreman. I've been with the Downs since I was a young boy and I love it here. They're great people, Cecelia and Jim. How long do you plan to be here?"

"I'm planning to stay a month. So what does a foreman do?" I really wanted to get the subject off me. My new identity was way too new and I wasn't used to telling the lies, hopefully, that was going to come with time. I just didn't want any red flags going up or suspicions of my presence anywhere I stopped. I had to be careful and so far I was failing.

He laughed at my question, "I guess the better question would be what I don't do. I oversee the crew and set schedules, make sure everything goes according to whatever is needed for a successful crop all the way to harvest. And I supervise the training and care of the race horses."

"Wow. That sounds like quite the responsibility and demanding job. What kind of crop is this?"

"In this field, we are growing red grapes for cabernet wine and the field further back is white grapes for chardonnay. I've done this job for so many years that it's become as automatic to me as breathing."

"Really? I didn't know there were vineyards or wineries in Kentucky."

"Oh yah. We have several vineyards around here and at least four big Wineries right here in Lexington."

"Thanks, didn't know that."

"So what does a picture taker and painter do when stuck out here in the middle of nowhere?"

"Take advantage of the solitude and take pictures along the way to paint later. This is a beautiful place to do just that. Is this the original plantation house?"

"Yes, it is. Jim and Cecelia built the big house about fifteen years ago, then the guest house seven years ago for her mother to live in. She passed away a year ago and it has sat empty ever since. Oh, occasionally friends have come to visit and stay there, but not too often. You'll love it here."

"I already do. Well, I had better try to find my way back. Any suggestions to make the trip shorter?"

"Sure, hold on a second, I'll get the ATV and give you a lift back." He turned and walked towards the house.

"Please, I don't want to bother you. I can walk back; in fact I can see the house from here."

"No bother, just hold your horses. I'll be right back." And he disappeared around to the side of the house.

Pretty soon here he came around the corner with the muddiest four wheeled thing I'd ever seen. "Sorry, I didn't know I was going to be chauffeuring such a beauty today or I would've taken it through the car wash and had it detailed." He smiled at me, "Climb on and hang on tight."

When he took off, it was with such a jerk that I thought I was going to somersault off the back, which only forced me to wrap my arms around Josh and really hang on for dear life. "Now that's better." He said laughing.

Pulling up to the guest house, he smiled and said, "How's that for front door delivery ma'am? Josh Townsend at your service, if I can be of further assistance, please, don't hesitate to call."

"Why thank you, Josh Townsend, I'm quite sure this will be sufficient for the time being. The pleasure has certainly been all mine." We were both laughing as I extended my hand, "Seriously, thank you very much for the lift, and yes, it was a much faster trip than had I walked. Although, I thought for a second there I was going off the back of this thing. Guess you meant it when you said hang on tight."

"Yep, I sure did. If you decide you want another tour of the property for pictures, let me know and I will take you out evenings after work. There are some real pretty sights up there in the hills. I better get over to the big house and check in with Jim on things to do for tomorrow. It's been a pleasure meeting you Ah…..Alicia." He smiled and took off.

Josh seemed like a very nice man, a genuine man. About 5'11", medium built and very muscular, I detected that when I wrapped my arms around him. Josh wasn't what I would consider a handsome man, but he had such a pleasant persona about him, it was extremely cute. I know, men aren't supposed to be cute, but to me Josh was cute. He sure didn't have that smiling charm like Trevor, I soon learned was fake. "Quit doing comparisons, there won't be anything become of Josh." I thought to myself.

CHAPTER 7

The first two weeks at the plantation were wonderful. I was feeling safe and secure, rested and relaxed in my hideaway.

I had settled into writing and felt my story was starting to flow. I would sit for hours outside on the patio enjoying the sun and surroundings and write. I could stay here indefinitely.

Josh had stopped by several times to let me know he was going to town and offered to pick up anything I needed. He took me for rides on the ATV all over the plantation. Of course, I took my camera hoping I was portraying a successful artist. It was magnificently beautiful on top of some of those rolling hills and the view was stunning. I wished I knew how to paint pictures; I could make a fortune on the beauty.

We had spent quite a bit of time together. Josh took me to the barn and showed me the prize race horses and I got to help brush and wash them down. He took me into the winery and explained the process from grapes to bottle. Certainly, there was a lot more to making wine than I ever thought and sampling the wine was an added benefit.

I had been at the ranch almost three weeks when Cecelia came over one afternoon with a plate of cookies and it was obvious she wanted to visit because she lingered on the steps until I invited her in.

"Hi, I was just checking to be sure you were alright. We haven't seen you out much."

"That is really sweet of you, but I'm doing just fine. Josh has been really great to take me around and show me the place. Most of the time I've been sitting out back on the patio because the weather is so nice and the view is spectacular. When I first got here, I ventured out on a walk one evening and got lost in the maze of the field. I practically walked into Josh's house by mistake. He came to my rescue and brought me back. I wasn't sure it was going to be a rescue or hospital recovery when he first took off with that four wheeler." We both laughed.

"Yes, he is quite the speed demon with that thing. Josh is a great guy. He's been with us for a lot of years. Jim would be lost if he ever left, and he is rather smitten with you, I might add. Every time he stops by the house he has more questions to ask about you. You certainly got his attention."

"Yah, I know, he asks me a lot of questions too. There's nothing special about me or anything very interesting to know. Just a 'plain Jane' that bums around taking pictures. Can I get you something to drink? We could sit outside on the patio, it is lovely out there and you can tell me about life on a plantation."

"I don't mean to interrupt you if you are busy."

"No, not at all. I would love to hear about the plantation."

"Then iced tea it is if you have some. And actually we don't really have plantations anymore. This is just a ranch."

Smiling, I said, "Oops, that's right, Josh already told me this was a ranch and not a plantation."

We must have sat out on the patio for an hour and a half. I hit on a topic that Cecelia loved talking about and she gave me a good insight of life on a ranch of this size. She also talked about Josh and revealed that his wife and both daughters had been killed in an accident when she had gone to visit her parents during a spring break. Apparently, a semi-truck driver had fallen asleep, crossed over into their lane and killed them. She said they had a rough year with Josh, but he slowly worked himself back on track. It had been over three years since the accident.

Cecelia finally stood and said, "I had better get back to the house and let you back to your projects. Oh, by the way, we are having a small dinner party tomorrow evening and we'd love it if you would join us. Nothing fancy, it's a pretty casual group. Say about six o'clock?"

"Oh man, thank you very much, but I think I will decline. I'm not real good at socializing. Besides, I won't know anyone there. I think I'll just stay in."

"Come on, it will be good for you to take a break, besides, you know Josh and he could use the company."

"We'll see what tomorrow brings, but don't count on me. Thank you anyway." After Cecelia left, I went out to clear the dishes from the patio and sat down for minute. Shit, I think she is setting me up for a date with Josh, or had he put her up to it? What the hell am I going to do now? Guess I had better make some plans for tomorrow afternoon and evening. Maybe I should go shopping, grab a bite and go to a movie. Yah, that would work, just sneak out mid-afternoon and not be here. Good idea.

Even though Josh and I had spent quite a bit of time together, it had been strictly a casual friendship. I didn't want it to be anything more. Going out on a date could change everything.

I was feeling guilty enough taking up so much of Josh's time, plus, he seemed to be more attentive than I wanted. I can't get involved with him with all my baggage. Being friends was good enough for me.

Early the next morning I started pecking away at the computer. My story was coming right along and the plot was thickening with **the hired man continuing the investigation and finally getting cooperation from law enforcement.**

I spent time with Josh, picking his brain and what it was like to be a foreman, and details about the vineyard and harvest and all about the horses. The information I got was filling in my story very nicely.

So far, my new book *The Plantation* was progressing, but I was going to have to change the name of the book from *The Plantation* to *The Ranch*. However, *The Ranch* sounded rather boring; I needed to come up with a more catchy title.

Wow, I looked at the clock and it was already eleven thirty. If I left around two, I could shop in the mall where I'd met Cecelia, get a quick bite to eat and catch the movie right there. I hadn't been to a movie in years, so I had no idea what was out there.

I had just gotten out of the shower, dressed and was finishing putting on my makeup, when the doorbell rang. As I came around the corner, I could see out the side window, it was Josh.

I opened the door, "Hi there, what's up?"

"Well, I hear we have a date tonight. I just thought I'd stop by and let you know I'll pick you up a few minutes before six. Supposed to rain later this afternoon, don't want you getting wet now." Josh had such a pleasant smile with a dimple on one of his cheeks.

"Thank you, Josh. That is so nice of you, but I already told Cecelia I wasn't going to the party."

"What? Now you can't go doin that to me. Besides, I just helped Jim bring the tables and chairs up from the basement and Cecelia already has your place card next to mine at the table."

"Josh, please. I'm really not good at socializing and I don't know any of these people. I was just getting ready to head into town to do some shopping and see a movie."

"Ah, come on Alicia. I even polished my boots and bought a new shirt for tonight. You've been holed up here in this house sitting in front of that computer now for three weeks. It'll be fun and you need to get out. I am one stubborn son of a bitch and won't take no for an answer. See ya at six." He stepped off the porch and headed back to his truck.

"Josh." I hollered at him.

He just turned, smiled and waved, "Six it is," And drove away.

Now, what the hell am I going to do? My plan was not working. Guess I'll go to town and shop for a new outfit and the movie is definitely out. I had not a clue what I should buy, Cecelia said casual, but what is casual to her could be evening wear to me. Crap, I really don't want to go. I'm still not comfortable with my new identity and can't keep my stories straight in my head. I suppose I'll have to play the part of a bashful and very timid artist, which I am not. Ordinarily, I love socializing with people and mixing around and getting involved with different conversations. However, it is a different story when one is living a lie and hiding out. I just hope I can pull it off.

So, I'm going to a party.

CHAPTER 8

Driving into town I was hoping I could remember how to get there and back, I found the mall without any problems. I started at one end of the mall, in and out of every store on one side and then back up the other side. I was beginning to believe there were absolutely no stores for anyone other than teens or very young adults. I felt like the elderly generation according to the styles I saw, and I wasn't even forty.

Noticing a boutique, I was intrigued by the display in the window, lo and behold, a clothing store just for me. And shop I did, filling two shopping bags. I laughed at myself. This was all for a dinner with people I didn't even know and a date I didn't want to go on. But, I was ready for my date and the party, attire wise anyway.

When I got home, I threw all the new clothes in the washer and set up the ironing board. Even though I didn't want to admit it, I was really getting excited for my date with Josh. He was such a sweet, unpretentious and humorous man, not at all the arrogance of Trevor. I had all my new clothes pressed, hanging up and was trying to decide which outfit to wear. I turned the stereo up, mixed a drink and was singing and dancing around as I got ready.

It suddenly occurred to me I hadn't been in such a happy mood for several years. Instead, I lived in a very stressful environment and then it was fear. I made up my mind it was going to be a nice evening with Cecelia and

Jim and their friends and nothing more. I couldn't let anything more than just being friends with Josh, become of the evening. I would only be here another week or so and then would be moving on to parts unknown, other than I knew I was going south. I had to make damn sure I didn't let this wonderful feeling overcome my sensibility.

∽

At 5:45 I refreshed my drink to take the edge off and heard a knock at the door, of course, it was Josh. "And good evening to ya ma'am." He said with a big smile and tip of his hat, "You are lookin mighty pretty, Ah….Alicia."

"Why thank you sir", and I made a curtsy. "And you are lookin pretty handsome yourself. Please do come in."

Josh took his hat off and hung it on a hook next to the door, and then handed me a beautiful bouquet of fresh cut spring flowers.

"Wow, now why did you do this? They are very pretty and thank you, but you shouldn't have. I don't even know if there is a vase here. But I'll figure something out." I looked through some of the cupboards and found a quart jar. "This isn't very fancy, but it will work. Since you are a bit early and I just freshened up my drink, may I get you something?"

"Yah, that would be great, what do you have?"

Laughing, I replied, "I'm afraid my bar is pretty limited. I have beer, chardonnay and vodka with water for a mixer. Sorry."

"No problem, I'll have a beer, sounds good."

We took our drinks out on the patio. It was a nice evening and the sun was starting to drop toward the west. Clouds were starting to move out and it looked like it might clear up after the earlier rain.

"Tell me, Ah……….Alicia, what's your story? We've never really talked about you. You seem to manage to change the subject."

"What do you mean what's my story? And why the 'Ah' every time you address my name?"

"Everyone has a story. Where ya from, married, single, kids, what ya do and where ya goin, ya know, just your story?"

"My story is pretty boring, just *plain ole Jane* me. Let's see in order of questions - from up north, single, no kids, don't do much, take pictures and paint and heading south. Now what's with the "Ah" before my name, I know you don't stutter."

"Well, Alicia, I think you are hiding from someone, I don't believe your name is Alicia and I think you're on the run. And the "Ah" was not my stuttering, but yours'. The first time I met you I knew you were lying about your name because it was you that couldn't quite get your name out there without hesitation."

"Whoa! That is quite an accusation for someone who knows nothing about me. So let's try this one on for size in order of questions: from out west, a polygamist, twenty-five kids, axe murderer of men only and heading south to the border. So how's that story? I guess you can take your pick, and if you don't like that one, I'll see if I can come up with another one. Where the hell do you get off with thinking you know so much?"

"Sorry, didn't mean to get you all riled up. It's only a personal observation and body language, nothing more. Let's change the subject, okay? Hey, really, I'm sorry and it is none of my business. Let's drink up and go have dinner. Cecelia is one good cook."

"Ya know Josh, I have suddenly developed a headache. I think I better just stay in and take a couple of aspirin and go to bed. You go ahead and give my apology to the Downs."

"Ah shit! Alicia, please don't do that. I promise it will never come up again. Come on, let's go over to Cecelia and Jim's. If you don't go with me now, they will chew my ass out and give me chicken shit house duty. Please, I said I was sorry."

Josh had such cute puppy dog eyes and dimpled smile, I couldn't stay mad at him. Besides it wasn't Josh's fault, but my own blunder. It was me I was mad at.

"Okay, fine! But I don't want to stay too long. I need to get back soon after dinner. Is that alright with you, Mr. Know-It-All?"

"No, no, no, no," he said wagging his finger at me. "Now I promised I would never bring it up again! So you be good! And whatever you say ma'am, you just give me the word. Your request is my command."

CHAPTER 9

It appeared most of the guests had arrived and were mingling with drinks and appetizers in hand or sitting at tables scattered around. It was a beautiful setting and nicely decorated with soft music playing in the background.

Josh took my arm as we started up the steps to the deck. As soon as we were in the lights, all eyes turned on us and the guests became silent. I suddenly felt like we had appeared 'stark ass naked'.

Cecelia and Jim came from the middle of the guests, "There you are. Please, come let me introduce you to our guests." We wandered in and out of various groups, meeting everyone. I was quite amazed at the variety of people, some with titles (doctor, dentist, lawyers), but mostly so and so that lives across the road, so and so that lives up the road a couple miles at the bluegrass farm, so and so that has the vineyard down the road, and it went on.

One couldn't tell from the attire everyone was wearing if they had a title, were grass farmers, pig farmers or horse breeders. But, they seemed to be quite the close knit group of friends.

Josh and I mingled for a little while then went back out on the deck. It was a very warm evening after the afternoon shower, the air was so fresh, and the sunset beautiful. We were standing off to the side admiring the view and making small talk about the setting. I started asking Josh more questions about his jobs on the ranch.

It wasn't long until a couple spotted Josh and me standing alone and ventured towards us. I was dreading the one on one conversation, because I knew what the questions would be and I was not the least bit disappointed.

Tom and Rachsel reintroduced themselves as the bluegrass farmers up the road and described their friendship with Jim and Cecelia. I tried to steer the questions to them and their farming, but I only got a couple questions out when they turned the conversation to me. The usual interest: where I was from, married/single, kids, what I did and how I arrived at the ranch?

I answered as casually as I could but with very careful thought. Rachel seemed interested in my paintings and if I had any here with me, I of course, told her I didn't. At this point, I was just taking pictures and would be painting later. Josh tried to interject into the conversation that I was also a writer, and that turned out to be a big mistake. Rachel was an avid reader and I reminded her of an author of several books she had read. I tried to laugh it off that I was not a published writer, just played around with it.

Oh, shit. That's all I needed, some busybody that thought she recognized me and made a big deal of it. I was going to try and convince her otherwise and maybe just blow it off as one of those, 'it was a mistake'. That fearful and sickening feeling hit the bottom of my stomach.

Fortunately, Cecelia hailed us all in for dinner. As we found our place cards at the dinner tables, I was relieved we were not seated next to Rachel and Tom. Instead, we sat next to a couple that owned the vineyard down the road, Fred and Elaina.

Dinner was wonderful. Cecelia had set up four tables with two couples at each table. Much to Josh's surprise, they had the dinner catered and what a delightful display it was. We started with a pumpkin soup served in hollowed half pumpkin shells, followed by a Caesar salad with small chunks of fresh apple and dried cranberries. The entree was a chateaubriand with béarnaise sauce, asparagus spears topped with butter and fresh grated parmesan cheese and garlic mashed potatoes. They served a couple different kinds of wine, cabernet and chardonnay, both from their wine cellar, from grapes grown in their vineyard. The wine and conversation relaxed me and I ate until I thought I was going to explode.

It reminded me of parties Trevor and I used to attend. But it never occurred to me until that moment that we never did have guests in our home or couples in for cocktails. We always went to other's homes or out to elite restaurants. There were lots of thoughts coming to surface that I chose to ignore during my marriage to Trevor.

I'll never understand why I waited so long to leave. I was afraid to stay, yet I was more afraid to leave.

After dinner and visiting around the tables, everyone eventually walked back outside to either the upper deck, lower patio, or strolling around admiring Cecelia's yard and flower gardens. Josh and I chose the latter. We each had a glass of wine as we walked around and admired the surroundings.

I broke the silence first by asking, "So, Josh what is your favorite part of this ranch, the horses or the vineyard?"

"Well, I really take care of the horses, but I manage the vineyard. I make sure the vineyard is on schedule with pruning, weeding, spraying, fertilizing and keeping it mowed. I have a real competent guy, Manuel, who keeps the crew on top of it all and then he reports to me, but I love the horses. We have some real high quality race horses and some upcoming potential racers. Jim and I work pretty close together with them and during the racing season we do a lot of traveling from track to track."

"Do you ever get time off and go out on your own?"

"I suppose I could, but I don't have any need to. Jim and Cecelia are about the best family anyone could ever ask for."

"What about your parents or siblings? Do you have family around here?"

"Oh, yah. My parents live on the other side of town, so I see them pretty often. My sister is married and lives in Dallas and my little brother follows the rodeo circuit and stays wherever he can find shelter. He's really good at what he does, but I sure couldn't live out of my truck and camper most of the year."

Cecelia had told me about Josh losing his wife and two little girls in a tragic auto accident, but I did not want to bring that up to him. I did not want to bring that pain back and I really didn't know what to say. I know the pain I went through when my parents were killed and that feeling never leaves. So I tried to switch the subject back to the horses and learn as much as I could about them.

"Tell me more about the horses, how many are there? I love watching them running and playing out there in the pasture. Those babies are so cute running and kicking up their heels." Alicia inquired.

"Yah, they are fun to watch. We have four champion racers and they demand a lot of attention. There are twenty mares and one Jim uses for stud service. But he brings in a stud when it's time to breed a mare. I love it and have learned a lot from Jim."

"I'm fascinated with the beauty of the horses and really enjoyed working with them, brushing and washing them down the other day, it was fun. Plus, I'm still in awe by the scenery of this whole place."

"I know exactly what you mean. I live here and I never get over the beauty. But, I rarely take time to slow down and admire it all." Josh replied.

Behind us I heard Rachel, "There you are. I hope we aren't interrupting anything?"

"Oh no, we were just talking about the horses and the setting here at the ranch. Looks like Cecelia pulled off another one of her dinner parties, wouldn't you say?" Josh answered.

"Absolutely, she always does. First time I think I've ever known Cecelia to have a party catered. But it's also the first time I've actually seen Cecelia able to join in the party and be so relaxed. She deserves it, she works too hard. I'm fifteen plus years her junior and she can work circles around me on any given day." We all laughed. "Alicia," Rachel continued, "What brings you to the ranch? How long have you known Jim and Cecelia?"

"I just needed a break from the trials of the city, so through connections I was able to rent the house for a while and enjoy the solitude. And I'm finding it to be perfect and just what the doctor ordered."

"I still can't believe how much you resemble Wendy Noble, the author. You could be her twin, except for the hair. But then twins don't always keep the same color of hair either." Rachel continued.

"I don't know this Wendy whoever, guess I just have one of those faces. You know the kind – one size fits all." I said smiling to Rachel. "I really don't want to be rude, but Josh, it is getting late and I think I've had enough wine that I would like to call it a night. I can walk from here. You stay and enjoy the rest of the evening."

"Nah, I have to be up early in the morning, your timing is perfect and I'll drive you. I hope you don't mind, but duty calls bright and early." Josh said to Tom and Rachel.

"I agree, we have an early day as well. It was nice meeting you, Alicia, hope we see you again while you are here. How long will you be staying?"

"I'll be here another week. It was nice meeting both of you. Shall we?" I said and turned to Josh.

"You got it. Night you two." And we walked out towards the truck.

The conversation and prying from Rachel was making me nervous and I couldn't get away from them fast enough. I was terrified Rachel was going to pursue the author topic and I had to get out of there. Josh had a puzzled expression on his face as we walked to his truck. Even though he said nothing, I knew he was full of questions. He was already suspicious of my name and had made issue of it. I just needed to say good night and regroup.

CHAPTER 10

When we got back to the house and I started to get out of the truck, Josh reached over and put his hand on my arm. "Just hold on there, ma'am. A gentleman always helps his lady out of the truck and walks her to the door."

I smiled and waited for Josh to open the truck door and walk me to the house. "Thank you Josh, I am glad I went this evening. This was far better than staying in. I had a great time meeting all the neighbors and friends of Jim and Cecelia's."

"I'm glad you came with me. It was a nice evening and a lot more fun for me to have a date rather than mingle around as a single, thank you. How about a quick nightcap, would you mind?"

"Josh, I don't have nightcap drinks, my bar is really limited. Maybe another time."

"I have just the ticket for a nightcap. How about a little Grand Marnier?" And he walked to the truck and under the front seat he pulled out a bottle and held it up. "A good Boy Scout is always prepared."

I laughed, "You are a hard one to turn down, and you are now two up on me. I'd better get my game going before I'm a total loser."

"You'll never be a total loser, Alicia. Trust me on that. Let's go in and see if we can find a couple snifters in the cabinet."

I made coffee to go with the Grand Marnier, and then we went out on the patio to sit in the moon light. The earlier showers had totally let up, but rain still remained on the lounge chairs. I wiped them dry and grabbed a couple afghans from the sofa to take some of the chill away. I was so relaxed and at ease in Josh's company that I leaned my head back in the chair and stared into the night. For a little while, I forgot I was on the run and living under false pretenses.

"Rachel made you a little nervous tonight, didn't she? I'm sorry she was so persistent, that's just Rachel. She's kinda a busybody around the neighborhood."

"Every neighborhood seems to have one," I said and laughed. "I just don't know that Wendy Aston, she was talking about."

"I thought she said it was Wendy Noble?"

"Whoever, I still don't know her. So, what is on your agenda for tomorrow, the horses or the vineyard?"

"Alicia, I'm a good listener and your secret is good with me. Would you like to talk about it? Everyone needs a shoulder at some time in their life and I do have broad shoulders." Josh poured more Grand Marnier in my glass.

"Josh, please don't push me. I'm fine and just needed a break from life, and this is the perfect place for just that."

"I'm not a judgmental person, maybe I can help you. Ya know, everyone needs a friend they can trust and I could be that friend, if you wanted."

Fidgeting in my chair and not at all comfortable with where this conversation was going, I guzzled the remainder of my drink. I didn't even notice Josh was filling it again. The next thing I knew or I think I remember, I was pouring my guts out about the last four years of my life. I must've talked non-stop, because I don't remember Josh saying a word. He was a good listener. I looked at my watch and saw it was two a.m., when I tried to stand up; I staggered and decided I'd better sit back down before I fell down.

"Whoa, how many of those things did I drink? Did you try to get me drunk and take advantage of me?" I said and laughed.

"Not at all, and I wouldn't do that. I'm so sorry you had such a rough time in your marriage. You didn't deserve that kind of treatment, no one does."

"Well, I guess I'm lucky I got out physically unscathed and only emotionally traumatized. But I'm tough, I'll get over it. I think I'd better go to bed and let you get home. You said you had an early morning and I've kept you up way too late as it is."

"You're probably right. Let me pick this stuff up and get it in the kitchen and then I'll help you into your bedroom. Just sit tight." When Josh came back I must have fallen asleep, or passed out, which is more like it. He walked me into the bedroom and turned down my bed and found my nightshirt under the pillow. He took my shoes off and told me to get out of the rest of my clothes and into my gown (what did he know?) and he stepped out of the room, I guess. Josh came back in and swung my feet on the bed and pulled the covers over me. He leaned down and gave me a gentle kiss on the forehead and said, "Sweet dreams little one, I'll catch you tomorrow."

I don't know what possessed me to put my arms around his neck and pull him down to me, and plant a big kiss on his mouth, "You have been a good friend, more than you know."

Josh sat on the edge of the bed and returned my kiss ever so gently. I didn't want to let him go. I felt so hungry for tender loving that I clung to him. Josh tried to pull away, "Are you sure you want to do this?"

"I am, I need you Josh." And with that he removed his clothes and got in bed with me. It felt so good to have Josh holding me. I pulled my nightshirt off and threw it on the floor and snuggled right in. Josh was rubbing my back and down my legs and back again and I started kissing his neck and chest and up to his lips and the heat was starting to rise in both of us. It didn't take long until the passions between us got out of control. Josh tried to remain calm and caress me with tenderness, but I had lost it. All I wanted and needed at that moment was total and complete love making. When Josh was finally inside me, I was thrusting at him like a mad woman. I had lost all control of myself and sensibility. After we had simultaneously climaxed, we fell back onto the pillows. Josh rose on his elbow and was staring down at me.

"I'm so sorry; I should never have let this happen. I think I did take advantage of you, Alicia."

"Not at all, Josh. It was my idea, but if you don't mind, I think I will excuse myself to the bathroom. Let yourself out, please." And with that, I made a mad dash for the toilet. I swear to God, I threw up everything I had eaten in the last week. It was not a pretty sight. There is nothing attractive about a nude woman sitting on the bathroom floor with her head in the toilet throwing up her guts. This was not a pretty picture. I know better than to mix drinks - vodka, wine followed by Grand Marnier. Not too smart.

Josh found my robe and put it around me along with a cold wash cloth for my face. "Can I do anything for you?"

I assured him, "I'm quite alright, please leave. I'll talk to you tomorrow. Thank you for the nice evening. Night Josh."

CHAPTER 11

When I woke the next morning I was flabbergasted to see it was 11:30, and then I had to make a mad dash to the bathroom. I could tell immediately this was not going to be a good day. My head was pounding and I couldn't quit throwing up. I finally made my way into the kitchen, put on the coffee and poured a glass of juice. Toast, yah, that's it, I needed toast.

With coffee and toast, I went out to the patio and laid down on the chaise lounge. Admiring the view and watching the colts play out in the pasture, I fell asleep. I was in and out of sleep and vaguely heard the birds chirping in their own choir. The sun beating down on me made it very comfortable to sleep on the chaise lounge.

I was surprised to see Josh sitting in a chair watching me. I was startled and a little miffed until he smiled and offered me a sandwich.

"Did we have too much fun last night, Cinderella?" He said chuckling.

"Oh, my God! How long have you been sitting here? I think my head is the size of a watermelon. How much did I have to drink, anyway?" Then it occurred to me I didn't remember getting into bed the night before. "How did I get into bed last night?"

Josh was laughing at me. "Well, let's see, in order of questions. I have been sitting here about ten minutes. I'm not sure how much you had to drink, I wasn't counting. And last but not least, I put you to bed. You were pretty much a noodle, kind of like a rag doll."

"I'm so sorry; I can't remember the last time I drank like that. And I think I can assure you it is going to be a very long time, if ever, before this happens again. I feel like hell. I think there was more to the night than me getting drunk and you putting me to bed. I apologize for my behavior. Don't know what else I can say."

Still smiling at me, "Well, I can promise you if you eat that sandwich you will feel better. How about a glass of milk to go with it?"

While I ate my sandwich and asked questions about the night before, Josh filled me in on the fact that I had spilled my guts about my life with Trevor and mentioned nothing about our sexual encounter. I was furious with myself, now my cover was gone. I had put myself out there and no longer felt safe. Josh recognized the color had drained out of my face and saw my frustration.

What the hell was I thinking last night. I am losing control of everything. Josh is a super nice guy and I think under any other circumstances I could find myself attracted to him. Now was not the time and I needed to get a grip with reality. My stomach was in a knot, I was panicked that I had spilled my guts to Josh. This was something I could not afford to do and I just had. Shit!

"Alicia, your secret is good with me. I have no intention of telling anyone, not even Jim and Cecelia. I can help you if you'll let me, and I can tell you for sure, so would Jim and Cecelia."

"I can't involve anyone else in this, it is my problem. I need to move on; I can't stay here any longer."

"Alicia, you don't have to do that. You are perfectly safe here, and probably better off than trying to set up somewhere else. You can't keep running without being found, especially, if Trevor gets the least bit of a hint that you are heading south."

"Then, maybe I better change directions. And, with Rachel being so insistent that I look like Wendy Noble, it won't take her long to figure it out and then I will be out in the wide open. Josh I don't have a choice here." I started to shake and tears were welding up in my eyes.

Josh moved over to the chaise lounge and put his arm around me and held me tight. "It's okay, we can keep you safe, I promise. But you have to trust me and Jim and Cecelia. Let us help you."

"Josh, I can't. I'm scared. I need to get out of here, someplace where no one knows me."

"I wish you wouldn't, but I know I can't stop you. Will you at least promise to keep in touch with me? If you need help of any kind, will you promise to call me? Please?"

"We'll see." Josh gave me a pleading look, "Okay I promise."

Josh stood up, "I need to get back to work. Will you have dinner with me tonight? I'm a pretty good cook, if I must say so myself. Say about six, I'll pick you up?"

Smiling at Josh, I accepted.

After Josh left, I went inside, took a shower and immediately started packing. I had made the decision I would leave bright and early in the morning. Sitting down at the computer, I composed a letter to Jim and Cecelia and then one to Josh. I would leave these on the counter. It was already three and I had lots to get done, including cleaning to leave the house as spit polished and shined as it was when I arrived. I carefully stacked suitcases, coolers and other miscellaneous items in the bedroom and started cleaning. By five o'clock I realized I needed another shower and best be getting ready for dinner at Josh's.

Josh had prepared country fried chicken, mashed potatoes and the best chicken gravy I had ever tasted. He had made baking powder biscuits with wild berry jam he claimed to have made. Dinner was absolutely delectable. We had a very comfortable evening and I was beginning to feel sad that I would be leaving the next day. I didn't want to have those feelings because I couldn't allow myself to get involved any more than I had already allowed to happen. I had to move on.

Josh tried to convince me and gave me every reason why I should stay at the ranch rather than move on to parts unknown. I had no idea where I was going other than I was heading south.

In the end, I promised Josh I would keep in touch. With a long lingering kiss, I finally broke away and asked Josh to take me back to the house.

"Alicia, would you please stay the night? I have become very fond of you and I need you to stay and I think you want to. We would be good together."

"Josh, I can't. This isn't fair to you with all my baggage. I need to deal with this and make a new life for myself. I'm sorry about last night, I should've never let that happen. I need to go, this isn't doing either one of us any good. Josh, you are a good man, thank you for caring. We'll be in touch."

After Josh took me back to the guest house, I cried for the first hour. How could I have let my emotions and heart start caring for Josh? I knew he was a good man and could be trusted, and I knew he would protect and care for me. I was too scared to stay and scared to keep running, but I had to.

I started packing the car. I wanted to be out of there in the morning before daylight and before anyone was up. Then I decided, why wait until morning and take the risk of Josh dropping by. I changed the bed, washed all the linen and finished the final touch-ups, leaving the house very clean.

At two a.m., I was done and driving away from the ranch. I couldn't have slept anyway, so why not drive. I was sobbing as I drove away, not only for the sadness of leaving Josh, but because of my anger towards Trevor and the situation he had created for me.

CHAPTER 12

Louisiana? Why was I going to Louisiana? I had no idea. I had never been there and didn't know anything about the state other than it had been hit hard by Hurricane Katrina. I drove the back roads and my intention was to stay out of sight and inconspicuous along the way.

The country was beautiful, everywhere was so green and smelled so fresh. I drove by small family farms, some you could hardly tell the difference from the family home to the dilapidated barns. Equipment sheds had every kind of broken down farming tractors, cars, and pickups imaginable and falling down fences circling the property. Then a mile or so down the road was a beautiful estate sitting on top of a hill with completely manicured yards, color-coordinated barns and equipment sheds, not a vehicle in sight and white upright fences circling the property, just like Cecelia and Jim's place. I was driving through dry lands, swamp areas, along small rivers and back to dry land again. What a contrast.

Parts of the country felt the same as the ranch. I had a sense of loss for leaving Josh and the safety there and now I was back out there, all alone and going into unknown territories again, on the run. Was this ever going to end?

It was slow driving these back roads, but the beauty of the countryside was worth it. I was constantly checking my rearview mirror for a vehicle that might be following me. So far I had no idea what I would be looking for in my mirrors, but I was sure I would recognize something. I was getting that closed in feeling again and a sense of panic. My stomach was churning.

While driving, I had lots of time to think about stories to write. Ideas popped into my head and then another one. I should've been writing these ideas down, but, it's rather hard to write and drive at the same time.

Memphis was my first stop and I was physically and emotionally drained. I checked into a cheap motel and immediately crashed.

The next day I continued on to New Orleans, this was a real cultural shock for me. I was amazed at the devastation left from hurricane Katrina, yet there had been so much restoration. On the other hand, so little had been done in many areas.

I checked into an out of the way motel to give me time to find a new residence. I picked up a few snacks and a couple For Rent magazines from the grocery store across the street. As I was walking out I noticed on a bulletin board a sign – House Sitter Wanted. I copied the number down and went back to the motel and made the call.

"Fredricks' residence." She answered.

"Hi, this is Alicia Browning and I'm calling regarding your bulletin board ad for a house sitter. Is it still available?"

"So far it is. However, I'm meeting with a gentleman at noon today. Can I get back to you?" Mrs. Fredricks asked.

"Yes, of course. I'll talk with you soon. Thank you." I gave her my cell number and waited for Mrs. Fredricks to call.

When the call finally came, I was getting overanxious. "Miss Browning? The gentleman I met is not interested in our place; he thinks it is too far out. If you would like to come take a look, I'll give you directions."

"Yes, I would, Mrs. Fredricks. I can leave now."

She would be driving a Lexus SUV, and gave me directions to meet her at the first gas station on the right, on the other side of Pontchartrain Lake, which took me over a six mile long bridge. I learned later that the lake was only fifteen feet deep in the deepest spot. It was not clean looking water and certainly didn't appear to be a recreational body of water.

"It is so nice to meet you. I can't tell you how much I appreciate this opportunity."

In her southern drawl she responded with a big smile, "It is our pleasure to have someone staying in the house while we're gone. I hope this will work out for both of us. We try to leave several times a year for a month or two and hate to leave it empty. The Sheriff checks on the place for us occasionally, but not very often. So this would be reassuring for us if someone was here."

I followed Mrs. Fredricks on roads along creeks and swampy areas until we came to a clearing where there was a long narrow building and a big sign, SWAMP TOURS. There were three tour busses and lots of people mingling around. She made a sharp right turn, down a little dirt road past one house that was evidence of the Katrina disaster. We parked the cars in back of a huge house on stilts with a deck that wrapped around the entire house. This place was out in the middle of nowhere and right on the river.

Mrs. Fredricks introduced me to her husband, Bob, then, gave me a tour of the eighteen hundred square foot, one level house. She had a 'how to' list already made out - the security system, TV remote (tricky) and places to shop in the next little town.

Walking out on the deck, Mrs. Fredricks gave me a short rendition of the area, "This is the Pearl River, and during Katrina, the water got up to sixteen feet high, just under the bottom of our house. The house to our left was totally under water. Cecil lives in the little trailer now and has been working on restoring the house for the last five years, I don't know if he will ever get it done. It has been a slow and very expensive renovation process for him. That little dingy over there is my husband's." She chuckled as she went on, "He went shopping one day for a sport fishing boat and the next thing I knew he was pulling up in this monstrous shrimping vessel." She laughed and continued, "Anyway, what started out to be a hobby has turned into a job, but he loves it. It gets Bob out of my hair since we are both retired." Smiling, she turned to me, "So what do you think? Is this a place you think you could put up with for a while? I can assure you, you will have your privacy."

"I think this will work just fine for me. Again, when are you leaving for your trip?"

"Like I said, this is short notice. We'll be leaving bright and early the day after tomorrow. We have a condo on Maui and go as often as we can, we love it there. So, are your prepared to stay tonight? You are welcome to stay here."

"Actually, I didn't have any plans. I just found your ad quite by accident at the grocery store and decided to take a chance. And here we are and I am prepared to stay or I can get a motel for the night and come back tomorrow."

"There's absolutely no need for that, let's just get you settled in and we'll have this time to get better acquainted."

CHAPTER 13

We spent the evening talking about life in the swamp lands. They never had children so they both became workaholics. Betty was a retired middle school teacher and involved herself in volunteering and various crafts. Bob was a retired professor of engineering at a college and got bored real fast after he retired, therefore, the hobby shrimp boat. They told so many funny stories about their teaching days, I was laughing until my sides ached. It felt good to laugh again. They had traveled a lot throughout their marriage and had no intentions of stopping now. However, Maui seemed to be their favorite place to go.

Betty fixed a lovely traditional Southern dinner of fried catfish, sautéed shrimp, black beans and rice, collard greens and cornbread. For dessert she made bread pudding with rum sauce. It was all very delicious and I stuffed myself.

After dinner we walked out on the deck to look at the moon beaming through the trees. I was slapping at bugs and Bob said, "I guess we forgot to mention the mosquitoes here, they're big enough to carry you off. They come out in the early evening so you better buy a big supply of bug repellant. The other thing we need to warn you about is the alligators. They are usually very harmless, but they do wander out of the water onto land to sun themselves and warm up. Just watch out for them."

"What's that? Those little lights out there?" I asked.

"Those are lightning bugs. They only come out at night and are really fascinating to watch. They don't bite, they just eat other bugs. Now if you see bigger lights out in the trees, they will be the locals with flashlights hunting for raccoons. Sometimes they are out poaching for deer, which is illegal, but for some families, that is their only meat."

"Wow, it sounds like grand central station out here. I thought I was going to be all alone," I said, sort of laughing. "You haven't mentioned snakes."

Bob laughed at me, "Oh, you'll see one once in a while around here, but they'll run from you. Just watch where you walk. In fact, there is a stick by the sliding door that we take when we go out for a walk. We bring it out here and keep it by the chair in case one of the snakes gets lost. Trust me; you are really quite safe out here. We love it. You will, too. We sit out on the deck at night, wrapped in a blanket, and just listen to all the swamp sounds. You'll be just fine. Tomorrow, I'll take you out in the little boat and give you a tour of the area. That's if you want to?"

"I'd like that if it isn't too much trouble."

"Not at all."

The next morning when I got up, Bob and Betty were having coffee and reading the paper, "Good morning and how did you sleep?" Betty asked.

"Perfect, I didn't hear a sound all night. How long have you two been up?"

Bob replied, "Just a couple hours, you ready for breakfast?"

"Oh, my God, what time is it anyway?"

Betty laughed, "It's only eight o'clock. We always get up at six, habit, have our coffee and read the paper, watch the news and then have breakfast. Your timing is right on."

"What can I do to help?"

"Not much, it's going to be pretty simple. I picked up some cinnamon rolls, going to heat them a bit, pour juice and that will be it. But thanks for asking."

"Are you still up for a swamp tour, Alicia?" Bob asked.

"You bet I am, if you are. What should I wear, warm or light?"

"Um, probably jeans and a light top, tennies and throw in a jacket. That should work."

"Are you going with us Betty?"

"Nah, I have been on that tour more times than I can count. You'll enjoy the ride, and I have plenty to do to get ready to leave in the morning. I'll have lunch ready for you two when you get back."

I returned to my room and got appropriately dressed and threw a jacket and camera in a small duffle bag of sorts. Why the camera I had no idea. We ate and Betty shooed us on our way.

Once we were aboard the small boat, Bob told me about the devastation of Katrina and how the river and land had changed course. There were four homes that were totally destroyed, knocked off their foundations and broken up by the force of the water. One of the homes had stayed intact and floated down the river and ended up stuck in a group of scrub trees. When the water level receded, and calmed, the owners went in by boat and removed what was salvageable from the house. The house remained on top of those trees for the last five years and left to rot away.

Bob pointed out two alligators, "Now these are a couple, Big Al and Cindy. However, Big Al seems to have quite the entourage of girlfriends."

"How can you tell the difference between Big Al and Cindy?"

"Cindy is the one with the mole on her cheek." Bob said nonchalantly with a smile.

"Okay, I see it." Then it dawned on me there were so called moles all over both their bodies. "You got me on that one, Bob." And we both laughed.

Way back in the swamp we saw different species of beautiful birds and visited with one of the guides with a boat full of tourists from the Swamp Tours. Bob explained about the cypress trees that could no longer be cut. They had been over logged and were trying to let them rejuvenate themselves. However, the blown or fallen down cypress trees that were under water were in a preserved state. He went on that frequently people would come in the swamp and pull some logs out and take them to a mill for making exotic furniture.

When we got back, Betty had lunch all ready for us. We chatted about the tour and the people that live in the area. Then I took a book and went out on the deck to stay out of their way while they finished packing. My thoughts wandered off to Josh. I was missing him, but knew better than to do anything about it. I didn't dare call him yet.

⁓

I slept in until ten and I hadn't done that in months, with the exception of the 'morning after the night before' with Josh. I got up and walked around looking at the surroundings. I couldn't even imagine why someone would want to live on a swamp and be so isolated. It was different out here and the destruction was still very evident from the wrath of Katrina.

Placing a call to Allison, using my pre-paid cell phone, I didn't know if I could even get service out here. But the call went through without a glitch.

Their recorder came on so I left a brief message, "Hey there, how are you guys doing? I thought I'd better call and let you know I'm alive and well. I'll give you a call later. Gotta run now. Love ya."

Showered and dressed, I made out a small grocery list and made a run into town to check it out.

A boutique caught my eye so I went in to look around. I got the feeling this was definitely a locals store and not anything like I would buy in the city. Maybe that was what I needed; change my appearance, a little more on the rustic side. Of course, I purchased an outfit, like I needed more clothes.

I finally made it to the grocery store and bought far more than was on my list. At the magazine and book section I picked out a few cheap paperback novels. I did not want to go to the bookstore that I had seen right next door to the grocery market; being recognized would've been a real disaster and I sure didn't need that.

Stopping in at the local café, I had soup and a sandwich and started reading one of the novels. I was distracted and more interested in listening to the locals and the stories they were telling than I was in reading. When I started back to the house and glanced at my watch, I was shocked to see I'd spent almost four and a half hours in this little town. It was a great afternoon.

Driving back to the house I was listening to a blues/jazz station, I turned it up and was singing at the top of my lungs. Then I saw a black car in my rear view mirror and my heart stopped for a second. Now what? The car seemed to be getting closer as I approached the driveway so I decided to drive past it, to where, I had no idea. I sped up and crossed a bridge and finally turned into a driveway of an old farm house. The black car continued on. Turning around and back on the main road, I watched for the black car, but it never appeared. I turned down the driveway and drove faster than I should have on that narrow graveled road, but I had to get inside the house. I carried everything in with one trip and locked the door. I was shaking so hard I grabbed the counter bar to steady myself and then started crying uncontrollably. "What the hell am I going to do? I'm afraid to be by myself and I'm afraid to get close to anyone."

After I put the groceries away I mixed a stiff drink and kept going back to the window to be sure I hadn't been followed. "You are paranoid, Missy." I said to myself. I really wished I had not taken this Godforsaken place out in the middle of nowhere. This is going to be a very long month, if not longer.

I took one of my new books, a blanket and snake stick out on the deck and curled up to read for a while. But the sounds from the swamp kept me distracted and I didn't read a single page. It really was quite peaceful way out here in a scary sort of way. I was staring into the waters trying to find an alligator, but I never did see one. I assumed they were there I just couldn't see them.

Considering there wasn't much to do out here and my intentions had been to get back into writing. I should be trying to come up with some ideas.

So much for reading, I got out my note pad and started jotting down ideas I had come up with.

Allison had convinced me I should take notes of incidents that had happened during the last year and a half of being married to Trevor. When I go back and read it all, I get nauseated and scared all over again. Allison thought it was for my own well-being that I document stuff in case anything ever happened to me, not that it would matter. Who would ever know or care. Alison and Matt might.

I was criticized by most of my friends for staying as long as I did. I was so in love with Trevor that I didn't see anything that should've been so obvious to me, or I didn't want to see the obvious.

Since I had the computer out, I may as well get back to one of my books. I had several going that I would leave for one reason or another and start another then go back. Staying grounded on any one book in particular was a challenge. One hundred pages into writing a story about two children that were victims of physical and mental abuse, I started pecking away. ***Jamie is an eleven year old boy and his sister, Jill, is eight. Their parents are successful in their careers and pay little to no attention to the children. However, when Glen and Marsha do pay attention to Jamie and Jill it is certainly not in a positive manner. Jamie is a smart, quiet, timid, blonde little boy; whereas Jill is a redheaded, freckle faced little girl with thick glasses. Jill, even though she is also very quiet and timid, has a bit of a feisty and inquisitive personality that has caused her a tremendous amount of problems. Jamie tries to protect her and guide her to a different behavior so she doesn't get the rage from their parents. Jill and Jamie attend school regularly and are model students. But, they are very often called into the principal's office and questioned about bruising marks and various kinds of injuries. Of course, they both deny any kind of parental abuse and always had a story to explain the injuries. They also knew what would happen if the parents were called, it had happened before. There is an ongoing investigation on Glen and Marsha, but so far, the authorities can't charge them with anything because Jill and Jamie are so well coached and terrified of their parents.***

I had researched the policy and procedures with Children's Service and had a pretty good understanding of the limitations they are challenged with. Then I tried to come up with someone that could be an advocate for Jill and Jamie.

As the abuse continued in their home, I ventured off on the path of Glen and Marsha's career. I made myself the investigative officer, and then

I thought I could be the advocate, a counselor at school or a close friend to the family.

This story was becoming more depressing and harder to stay with because I let my thoughts wonder back to my own stepchildren, Sheila and Billy. Although Trevor was never physical with them, his verbal attitude of '*children are to be seen and not heard*' was truly displayed in our home.

CHAPTER 14

Two weeks had gone by and I kept at the computer without enthusiasm. Occasionally, I would sit out on the deck during the day and read for a while, then back to the computer. I even resorted to taking the small aluminum boat out in the swamp to explore around. But I was so terrified an alligator was going to appear under the boat, tip it over and eat me, I only did that once.

It made me nervous when the locals came out at night with their flashlights, I would sit in the house with the lights off. I felt like I was living in a fish bowl and the last thing I wanted was one of Trevor's *goons* peering in at me or anyone for that matter. I was beginning to think my idea of solitary living was a real bad idea. I didn't like being alone out there in the swamp at all. Several nights I went to bed as soon as it got dark, which was six o'clock, and watched TV or a movie I had rented. I certainly was not making much progress in writing.

I decided I was going to put Jamie and Jill on hold and start another book. Maybe I could go back and forth, but for now, I had to get away from the children's story.

Ideas to continue the story about the widow and her troublesome son and the hired man were not coming together. So that one went on the back burner as well.

Then I got the idea of writing about a couple on their honeymoon that went on a cruise and the groom fell overboard. I had read about that story in the newspaper, so I thought about making a mystery novel out of it.

Now I was off and running in a different direction. I was doing real well on the story and it was coming along very nicely. My explicit description of the cruise ship, the activities, the various kinds of food, and the fun I was having meeting people would draw my reader's right in as though they were on the same ship. It was fun and refreshing and I was at the computer day and night.

Writing me in as the off duty detective on vacation on a cruise ship, would immediately draw the detective into the investigation.

The detective just happens to meet the newlyweds and occasionally hangs out with them and sees a totally different side to the normal life of a newlywed couple.

The husband is tall and handsome and so charming in a cool sort of way, while the bride is a bubbly, humorous, funny blonde. They are everywhere on the ship, but he seems to have a quiet controlling manner about him. Even though the bride constantly smiles and appears to be having a wonderful time, she also has that look of discontent and a bit of fear about her. As the detective and passenger of the ship, I try to befriend her and see if I can get her away from the groom for ship activities. I give them the name of Pam and Todd and describe them as a Ken and Barbie couple until I get to know Pam better. Ken spends a lot of time in the bar or the casino on the ship and alcohol changes his sweet personality by day to a cruel abusive animal by night.

I soon realize I was writing about my own marriage with Trevor. There are so many unanswered questions during the years I had known Trevor. I was putting all of those questions into my story about Pam and Todd. I hadn't even gotten to the part where the groom ends up overboard and started my investigation, when I close the computer and knew I couldn't go on.

Now I have three stories going, two of which have ended up relating to my life with Trevor. First, Jill and Jamie have become Sheila and Billy; second, Pam and Todd became Wendy and Trevor. Then it hit me like a ton of bricks. Why not write my own story, who best could tell a story of mental abuse to children and a devoted wife?

CHAPTER 15

Picking up my cell phone, then changed my mind and used the pre-paid cell phone, I called Allison. I knew there was no way to trace a pre-paid phone call where a cell phone can be traced. I should've just dumped my cell phone and used only the pre-paid one, but couldn't bring myself to do it.

When Allison answered, I told her of my idea for a new book, "*My Story*". I would write about my life and marriage to Trevor from the day I met him until the day we walked out of the court room. Allison was not at all in favor of my idea. She felt it would just bring back all the pain I had endured. It would be a constant reminder of how miserable I was and in the end, fearful for my life.

I explained to her how I had started three different stories and two of them had walked me right back into my own situation and I didn't even try. I told her I believed this was a story worth telling and maybe in the end would give me better understanding of what really happened. Maybe someone else would read this story and 'get it'. I sure didn't and I'm not sure I have yet, not totally anyway. Maybe I wouldn't be able to finish it, but I could sure get a lot of it off of my chest.

Allison always stressed to me how worried she and Matt were and harped constantly to be careful, and if I needed anything, I should call them immediately. I really loved Allison and Matt, but sometimes she got on my nerves and tried to be my mother. We hung up when there was a knock at the door. Peering out the side window, I was surprised to see a policeman standing there.

As I opened the door, I asked, "May I help you?"

The policeman was smiling, "Sorry to bother you, I am Sheriff Dale Scott, may I come in for a minute?" He showed me his badge and stood there.

"I guess." I said hesitantly and stepped aside. "What can I do for you?"

"Betty and Bob told me they were going to be gone for a month and had someone housesitting for them; however, they neglected to give me your name. Are you housesitting?"

"Yes I am, is there a problem?"

"I hope not. What is your name?"

"I'm Alicia Browning."

"We've received a missing person's bulletin that a Wendy Nobel/Aston has disappeared and could be in this area. May I see some ID?"

"Of course." I went into the bedroom and got my wallet. I took my new driver's license out and handed it to the Sheriff. He looked carefully at the bulletin and my ID picture.

"You're from Pennsylvania?"

"Actually, I'm not from Pennsylvania, I lived there for only a short time. I grew up on the West Coast."

"Oh really? Where on the West Coast? I love it out there, that's my wife's and my favorite place to vacation. We often go to Southern California."

"I've only been to California to go to Disneyland as a child. I lived on Camano Island north of Seattle for a while." I immediately thought I'd just revealed too much information, but I wanted to stay away from Boston.

The Sheriff handed my license back to me, "Thank you for the information. I hope you are enjoying your stay and the locals out here in the swamp aren't bothering you. Some of them can be pests."

"I'm enjoying it here, who wouldn't? And no, no one has bothered me at all. But I do have a question I've been curious about. Occasionally, I've seen men out in boats going from tree to tree in the mornings, and then again in the early evenings just before dark. What are they doing?"

Laughing he said, "Well, they are putting bait in baskets that are in the water and attached to the trees to catch crawfish. Then, in the evenings, they go back and empty the baskets for their catch. Crawfish are very good to eat, have you ever had one?"

"No, I haven't. Guess I've shied away from them and never gave it a thought as to where they came from. Thank you for answering my curiosity."

"No problem. Thank you for your help. Like I said, enjoy your stay." And he left.

I closed the door, locked it and leaned against it and started shaking. I wonder if he really believed me. Now what do I do? Should I leave or will that throw up a suspicious flag?

Returning the call to Allison, I explained what had happened with the Sheriff's visit. Although, I never grew up on Camano Island, my grandparents had acreage and I would visit during the summers and work in their vineyard. I don't see how that could be traced as true or false. Trevor never met any of my family and wasn't particularly interested in any of my prior life. We must have talked for over an hour. Allison has always been such a wise and methodical friend. She makes me think about all angles of any given situation and offers advice I can either take or leave. The conclusion of our conversation was I should go ahead with my idea of the book telling *"My Story"*. I always felt so refreshed after talking with Allison. She was such a great mentor.

The computer was becoming my worst enemy. After saving the three stories, I went into the file of 'Trevor notes' and printed them all. I was surprised I had so many pages. Now I needed to put them in chronological order and decide on my plan.

And so it goes:

Born 1972 in Seattle, we lived in the Federal Way, WA area while Dad was in the Navy. When he was discharged, he became Fire Chief in Renton, which was not far from Federal Way.

Dad went back in the service when I was three and we traveled from base to base until I started school. My years in grade school led me to live the lifestyle of a gypsy. I never finished one grade in the same school until I was in the sixth grade. I was bounced back and forth from my parents to my grandparents who lived on Camano Island. They had a vineyard and I loved spending time out there working with Grandpa. The years spent on Camano Island are so vivid whereas most of my childhood is somewhat hazy.

After high school graduation, I moved away and went to college. I didn't know what I wanted to be so I just mottled through and ended up graduating with a teaching degree in English, Literature and Journalism. I taught for five years in a small town in Washington. Then my parents were killed in an automobile accident and I was devastated.

I took a year off from teaching to take care of the estate issues and get my head on straight. Mom and Dad were so young and had done so well financially; they were workaholics and never had time to spend their money. So, when they were killed, they left me a large amount of money. With the settlement of their estate and property, I invested it all with the same financial institution they had used. My parents had managed their parents' estate which had been left to me as well and I didn't want to touch it. It was invested well and I made the decision to leave it alone with the exception of a comfortable withdrawal while I attended college to get my Master's Degree.

Writing, suddenly made me realize how much I missed my parents. Even though I had taken the year to get their estate settled, I had moved on at such a rapid pace that I never looked back. And now, it has been almost ten years since their death. I can't even remember the date they died. Wow! How time has flown by. I started crying and wished they were here, I needed them to talk to. I missed them and was terribly lonely. I was Daddy's little girl and he always gave me such good advice. I know he would've hated Trevor and would've done everything he could to talk me out of that marriage and I'm sure I would've listened. "Oh, Daddy, you were my rock and I miss you so much." I cried even harder.

Applying at Harvard and accepted, I entered their Master's program and graduated with honors. At that point in time I knew I didn't want to teach anymore. I wanted to become a published author. Having already written three books, I pulled them up on my computer and started re-editing for publication. With the advice and suggestions from one of my professors, he thought they were publishing worthy. He gave me the names of a couple agents and told me to meet with them and give each a book and see what they could do with it. I did just that.

The next four years just flew by. I dated occasionally and friends were constantly trying to set me up with blind dates. I couldn't get interested in any of the guys and was trying my best to discourage my friends from their mission to get me married off. I was perfectly happy the way things were going at the present time.

Pumping books out right and left, they were being published at the same rate. Every book signing I set tables up in front of Faneuil Hall in downtown Boston. Supplying finger foods and wine for the occasion seemed to draw a reasonably large crowd. It was fenced off so people had to go through a gate to get in and could purchase the book at a 25% reduced price. It was word of mouth that sales seemed to increase.

Then there he was. Trevor. He was so charming and good looking and swept me off my feet at first sight. We dated for six months and I was so in love with Trevor I couldn't concentrate on my writing. He wined and dined me, showered me with so many gifts and flowers I was embarrassed to be so spoiled. When Trevor asked me to marry him I was shocked. Even though I knew I loved Trevor I really felt it was a little soon. But he insisted and thought we should get married right away.

I tried to convince Trevor to wait for the wedding a little while to let his children and I get better acquainted. But he wouldn't hear of it and said his children would get used to me as I would with them. At the time I thought it to be a rather cold remark to make, but quickly put it out of mind.

My friends were all excited and anxious to help with the wedding. We hadn't been able to socialize too much with my friends. It seemed with

Trevor's schedule and business meetings and socializing with his associates and friends, there wasn't time for my friends.

Wow, I had forgotten how much fun my girlfriends and I had shopping, going out for lunch and helping me with some of the wedding plans. I only had a few friends that had stayed in the Boston area and only a couple of those that we stayed in fairly close contact. None of my friends had met Trevor and periodically one of them would make comment to his absence. I tried to be convincing that he was extremely busy and there would be plenty of time after we got married and I could have them over to the house. Of course, that never happened.

Closing the computer, I had to take a break. I was beginning to rethink my idea of writing about my past. I kept remembering things I didn't want to remember and other stuff that was too painful to write about.

CHAPTER 16

I turned on some music, grabbed one of my books and curled up on a chaise lounge to read for a while. I don't think I read more than a couple pages and fell sound asleep. I woke up with a start from the horn of the Swamp Guide boat. I went down the ramp to greet them. "Haven't seen you around so thought it was time to make noise and say HI! How ya been?" Gregg asked.

"I've been just fine. Lovin this weather for sure." We chatted for a few minutes and off down the river they went. I watched till they were out of sight and went back in the house.

I hadn't written for several days and I was still finding it hard to get back into it. I decided to go into town and see a movie and have dinner. It was a real nice break and when I got back that evening I settled into watching television and went to bed. Surprisingly, I slept well.

The next morning I got up refreshed, the first in a very long time. I went back and caught up where I had left off, starting again on *'My Story'*.

I bought a simple white wedding dress, called a couple catering services and floral shops to get an idea of prices. At the stationary store, I signed out one of their invitation books and took it back to my place. With the invitation list of my closest friends and Allison and Matt, it was going to be very small. But I still needed Trevor's invitation list.

Planning dinner that evening for Trevor, I hoped we would discuss the wedding. I hadn't found the church or where to have the reception, but I knew that was something Trevor could handle, or at least give me some suggestions.

I was not prepared for Trevor to explode into a temper tantrum. I sat at the table speechless and totally in shock, I couldn't even respond.

Trevor went into a horrible rage about how stupid I was to think he would have any part of being the laughing stock to his friends and be on some kind of joking display. I broke into tears.

Then, like he always did, he put his arms around me and turned on the charm and gently told me he didn't want to share our special day with anyone else. We could go to Las Vegas to get married and then stay for a couple days and honeymoon.

Trevor was so sweet that it was easy for me to understand his feelings about it all and with his busy schedule, I agreed to a Las Vegas wedding.

When I called Allison and explained the wedding plans had changed, her reaction wasn't at all surprising. She gave me as many arguments why this was a bad idea as she could come up with, and all in one breathe. Was I sure I wanted a quiet Las Vegas wedding? This was my first marriage and she thought this was very selfish of Trevor.

We visited a while longer, or maybe I should say we argued, but I could tell Allison was not happy about the wedding, but the decision had been made.

My apartment was pretty crowded with furnishings, most of which I kept from my parents. There were some real special pieces I couldn't bear to part with. I had always thought I would eventually find a house and then it would all fit perfectly. But that was one of those things I never prioritized.

Trevor didn't spend much time at my apartment and only occasionally did he spend the night. I knew how busy he was so I didn't take it to be much of an issue. When I spent an evening with him and the kids at his house, it was just that, the evening. The children always seemed to be busy with homework and quiet time before going to bed. It was really hard getting to know them, but Trevor said there would be time after we were married.

As the wedding date drew closer, I started getting serious about the stuff I really wanted to take and what I could get rid of. Trevor had made remarks to the effect that he didn't want this junk in his house.

My feelings were hurt but I was also insulted that Trevor considered these souvenirs from my parents and grandparents as junk. I wasn't about to just discard these as pieces of garbage. However, once again, Trevor turned on the charm that he didn't mean it quite like that. It was that there wasn't any room for all of it in the house. Then he said we would look for a bigger house for all of us, that it would be a nice start to have a new house for our family, the perfect new start.

What a sweet thought. So that made decision making easier for me. It would all go in storage except for my personal things. In the end, Trevor had relented to let me have the loft for my writing room. Loft, as he called it, but I called it more a part of the attic. But it was big and I decided with a little imagination I could make it look nice. Besides, no one was ever in my office anyway, so what did it matter.

The end result was that I packed everything except my personal items, clothes and everything I would need for my writing room. I had wanted to keep out a curio cabinet and some of my mother's trinkets, but it didn't seem to be worth the argument and I stored it all. I still got enough grief about the amount of clothes I had. It was suggested very strongly that I go through them and donate to a Women's Shelter. Actually it wasn't a bad idea, I should've done it months ago.

The weeks before the wedding were extremely stressful for me. I tried to spend time with Sheila and Billy and get acquainted with them before I moved in. That was causing a change in their routine and Trevor became angry with the children. I talked with Trevor about his attitude with me trying to spend time with them, and he got very angry. Then, immediately, he would turn back to being so sweet and apologetic and understanding of my *wanting to be with his kids, and went on to explain, again, there was plenty of time after we were married and we were one big happy family, same ole' line.*

The more I went through my notes, the more things came back to me and I began inserting notes in between notes. I had to take breaks from writing *'My Story'*. It was way too depressing to stay at it for very long.

Walking outside to get some fresh air, I watched the boat guides go by with another tour group. We got in the habit of waving. Gregg, one of the guides, occasionally pulled his boat up close to the dock next to Bob's shrimp boat, cut the motor and asked how things were going. Just small talk for about three to five minutes, tells me a joke, then be on their way. One of those moments I looked forward to, a connection with people. I was beginning to realize how lonely it was out here.

Looking for a quiet, unpopulated place was what I thought I wanted and needed to concentrate on writing and putting the rest of my life behind me. It was starting to give me a feeling of claustrophobia. The quiet was closing in. The loneliness was stifling and my thoughts started drifting back to Josh at the ranch. I had not talked to him since I left. I made the call, but only got the voice mail on his cell phone, so I left a brief message.

As I started to go inside the house, I heard a whimper and stopped, but I didn't see anyone. I listened and heard it again. Around the corner of the house I saw a dog lying on the deck. He was muddy, wet and looked awful. I squatted down closer, "Hey there, what happened to you?" I slowly reached down to pet this dog and he didn't move, just whimpered again. He had on a collar with a tag so I took the collar off and read: My name is Spook. I turned the tag over and there was a phone number. I went back in the house to find a towel to wipe him down and see if I could find any injuries. With wet towels in hand, I started gently going over the dog's body. Ironically, he didn't object, he just laid there. I didn't find any injuries so I went back in and got a bowl of water and took it back out and he drank almost all of it. I coaxed him to get up and go in the house with me so I could see what I had for him to eat. I had part of a chicken breast I cut up, scrambled an egg and added some green beans and he gobbled it up in nothing flat.

Now, I had a problem. What was I going to do with Spook? I looked at the tag again and the area code was not a familiar number. In the phone book I found that the area code was in Georgia. I tried the number and it had been disconnected with no forwarding number. Guess I would deal with it tomorrow. I rummaged around and found an old rug and torn blanket in the garage and made a bed for Spook. He laid down and promptly went to sleep.

An option was to go up to the Swamp Tour and see if anyone had lost a dog when my phone rang, it was Josh.

"Hey there little girl, how are ya? This is Josh."

"I knew who it was the minute the phone rang. How are you Josh? I'm just fine."

"How did you know it was me? Are you psychic?"

"No, I'm not psychic. I called earlier and was going to call you again but got detained."

We talked for about an hour. He filled me in with goings on at the ranch. I filled him in on what all I had been doing and about my new friend Spook. I tried to keep the conversation light, but the longer I talked with Josh the more I realized how much I really missed him. Although we had only been acquainted for a month, our encounters had been more intense than I had given credit.

"How is the book coming along?"

"I suppose, alright. I have started so many and put them on hold for various reasons; if I ever decide to get serious and finish all of them I'll have my own library."

"What are you working on now?"

"I've started my own story about my life and with Trevor, but I can only work on it for a short time then I have to walk away. It's too depressing. And ironically, I keep remembering more 'stuff', and jotting down more notes. This is really turning into a bucket of worms and makes me more nervous the more I write and remember. I'm not sure I'm going to finish it. Right now, I'm on a break from writing."

"Good, then maybe you will be up for company for a couple days. What do ya think?"

"OH, WOW! Josh I don't know. I'm not sure that is a good idea."

"Give me one good reason why not, Alicia. I have missed you terribly and just want to come see you."

And I have missed you terribly too, but I can't say that to you, I thought to myself, "I don't want to start something we can't finish, Josh. We can't get involved in a relationship".

"Who said anything about a relationship, I just want to visit for a few days".

"And who do you think you are fooling?" Oh, man, why can't I just shut up and enjoy his company and quit making such a big deal out of everything?

"I'm not trying to fool anyone. I can take a much needed couple of days off and I want to see you and I thought you could use the company. Do you see anything wrong with that?"

After a lengthy deliberation, Josh finally won out. "Let me see if I can make the arrangements for this weekend. I'll fly in Friday late afternoon and go home on Monday. Okay?"

I agreed I'd pick him up at the airport. Although, I was hesitant about the visit, I had to admit I was looking forward to seeing Josh.

CHAPTER 17

"Well, Spook, I guess we better see if we can find your owners. I sure don't know what I'll do with you if we don't."

I called the Swamp Tours' office and asked if any of the tourists or neighbors had reported a lost German Short Hair. No one had. I called the Humane Society and got the same results, and left information with the house number in case anyone reported a lost Spook.

"Spook, whatever have I gotten myself into and what are we going to do?" He just laid there on the blanket and looked at me with the most forlorn look I had ever seen. I sat down on the floor beside Spook, and as I was petting and talking to him, I had this feeling he was going nowhere.

I made a few fliers to put up about Spook. I had a few groceries items I needed to get if we were going to have company. Main items were dog food, shampoo and flea treatment.

Fliers and grocery list in hand, I started for the door with Spook right on my heels. "Okay, Buddy, you are going to have to stay here. I won't be gone long." I opened the door and he followed me out, which was okay, I had no intention of leaving him in the house. However, I had no intention of taking him to town with me as he jumped in the front seat of my car when I opened the door. "So, I guess we're going to town?"

After dropping off fliers at the Swamp Tours office, a couple gas stations, we went on to the grocery store. Spook sat up in the passenger seat as though that was where he belonged.

When I came out of the store, I saw a man standing near the back of my car writing on a note pad, what I thought might be my license plate number. I stopped very quickly and stepped behind a van, hiding, to be sure it was my car he was paying attention to. He was looking around as though he was expecting someone to show up.

My heart was racing and if I hadn't been holding the sack of dog food and bags of groceries, I would have been shaking like a leaf. I walked back in the store and put all my stuff in a cart and started looking for my keys and cell phone. I found a rack of sun glasses and baseball caps and purchased the cheapest ones and put them on.

Even though I had refused carryout service the first time through checking out, as I was paying, I asked for help to my car. I felt more comfortable having someone with me. I wasn't sure how much protection I was going to get out of Spook, who was still waiting in the car.

I tried to ignore the guy leaning against the shiny black car with darkened windows, two aisles over from mine. Making small talk with the carryout boy, he unloaded my groceries into the back seat where Spook had been laying.

Spook got in the front seat where he sat up tall which gave me a little bit of security. I know a big dog could draw attention to me, but on the other hand I have never owned a dog, so maybe this could be misleading. I got in and started the car, shut the door, thanked the boy and at the same time he shut the back door, I pulled out of the parking lot.

Not wanting to speed and draw any attention, I had a definite desire to get away. I drove a few blocks watching my rearview mirror and, as I suspected, the black car was behind me, keeping a reasonable distance. I made the decision not to go home but didn't have a clue where I was going to go. I knew I had to stay where there were lots of people.

I continued to drive around still observing the black car a couple cars behind me. I finally thought of a dog park, there are always lots of people there with their pets. I pulled into a gas station and asked if there was such a place and the attendant gave me directions that just so happened to be only a few blocks away.

When we got to the park, there was an abundance of people and their pets. I didn't have a leash for Spook, so I took off my belt and looped it through his collar. It appeared to me this was not a new experience for Spook as he was anxious to go play.

Once inside the fenced area, I turned Spook loose and found a group of ladies to join. I hadn't noticed if the black car had followed me into the parking lot or not, but I was sure the guy was still out there, I just didn't know where.

It was getting cool and people were starting to leave. I grabbed Spook, leashed him and we started for the car in the middle of a group of ladies. Scanning the parking lot, I saw the black car parked at the end. I waited until a few cars were ready to pull out and I pulled in front of one, rudely cutting her off, but now I was in the middle of the pack.

I drove as fast as I dared, watching in the mirror I did not see the black car, but I was afraid to get off the main highway and I knew I had to in order to get back home. My whole body was shaking. Why is Trevor doing this to me? What does he want? I just kept driving and watching the mirror and so far I was feeling pretty lucky. Hopefully I had lost him.

The garage was not attached to the house so I had to go through the garage side door to hit the button to open the big garage door. Then I rushed to pull the car inside and quickly closed the door again. I grabbed as many grocery sacks as I could carry and ran out the side door and up the stairs to the house. Once inside the house I started closing all the drapes and double checked the locks on the windows and doors and sat down in the middle of floor and started crying. Spook got on his blanket and stared at me. Pretty soon he slithered towards me and laid his head on my leg. "Spook, what are we going to do?" I laid down beside him and put my arm over his back and continued to cry.

I couldn't for the life of me figure out why Trevor was going to such lengths to make my life miserable. It was only a divorce and people go through those without a glitch every day, well sometimes. There had to be more to it.

Josh will be here in a couple of days. I need to call him and tell him not to come. I don't need him in the mix of this mess. Besides, I've got to figure out exactly what I'm going to do and where I'm going. Somehow Trevor has found out where I am and has his 'goons' watching me.

For the first time reality hit me that Trevor meant what he said in that court room, "We are not done" plus the many telephone threats, "I'll see you dead." Why? There is more to this. He thinks I know something, but what could it be? I didn't know anything about his business because he made sure it was never discussed at home. I only met some of his colleagues at social affairs and he always had a reason why I shouldn't become friends with any of the wives. That didn't bother me because I never felt comfortable around them anyway. Most of them were too high maintenance for me.

One thing I know for sure is I need to leave here and move on. I haven't heard from Betty and Bob since they left so I don't know if they are staying one or two months or somewhere in between. Since I am sure Trevor, somehow, has located me, being so far out and isolated is terrifying me. I need to be around people, a lot of people.

CHAPTER 18

Placing a call to Josh, I thoroughly expected to get his voice message. Instead he answered with an excited tone in his voice, "Hey there, and to what do I owe for this call?"

"Josh, I need you to postpone your trip. Something has come up and I won't be able to pick you up at the airport. I am so sorry, but...." And he cut me off.

He immediately detected a quiver in my voice and pressed the issue. I tried to explain something had come up, then, I changed to the fact I was a guest in the house and should not be having guests. He wasn't buying either story.

Josh did his best to convince me he just wanted to take a break from work and come visit me for a couple days, No strings attached, just a break. I could tell he was getting a bit irritated with me and I didn't want that at all.

It was all I could do to keep my composure and not start crying. I didn't want Josh in the middle of this mess, whatever it was. I was scared to leave the house and be followed again, yet I was scared to stay alone anymore. My idea of traveling and being alone was backfiring, big time.

I finally told him about the two different incidents being followed by a black car. Josh could hear fear in my tone and he didn't try to make light of it. I don't think Josh ever really understood the magnitude of what Trevor was capable of. He encouraged me to stay at the house until he got here.

To keep me busy and my mind off the black car, Josh suggested I check my computer for hidden files that Trevor could've put there to hide. He wanted me to go through all of my files and be sure they are all my entries. Then I should know for sure it is not the computer he wants.

Man, I have really gotten myself in a pickle. I don't want Josh in danger, yet I am now terrified of being alone. My whole plan was not working and I didn't know what to do or where else to go. I had thought New Orleans would be far enough from Boston and densely populated enough that Trevor wouldn't find me. And I still hadn't figured out why he would even want to. That was really my question, why?

Taking Josh's suggestion, I went to my computer and started opening every program I had. Then I opened every file within each program and I didn't see anything other than my stuff. I closed out all the programs and shut it down. Well, that was a waste of time, what next?

I looked at the clock and was surprised it was so late. I had totally forgotten about my new friend, Spook, who was contently lying on his blanket. I got his new dog dishes and filled one with water and the other with dry food. "Come on, Spook, it's dinner time". He got up, stretched and started eating.

While I was fixing a sandwich I turned on the news. The news was as depressing as my life was turning out to be. War in the Middle East countries, and not looking like an end in sight; earthquakes and floods all over the world, Senators and Congressmen in constant disagreement and the President trying to play referee and not winning. Things were looking pretty grim. I changed channels to a music station and sat down to eat.

When I finished and cleaned up the kitchen, I turned to Spook who was very comfortable lying on his new bed and appeared very content with his new home. "Okay, buddy, let's get you cleaned up. It's time for a bath." In the bathroom, tub half full, old towels, dog shampoo and now the dog. Hmmm, Spook had disappeared. Apparently, this is not only a familiar sound to him, but not his favorite thing to do. I finally found him tucked behind the sofa. After wrestling him into the tub, the task was completed. Ironically, I had forgotten that traditionally, after the bath and before towel drying, dogs like to shake. The only good news is that German Short Hairs are just that, short hairs, but can still make a mess. And a mess it was. There was water everywhere.

It only took me an hour to clean up the bathroom and wash all the towels and get them back in their appropriate places. Of course Spook was back on his bed sleeping soundly.

My thoughts go back to my computer and Josh's idea. Considering I'm not very computer savvy, I know just enough to get by. I don't know where to start to find anything that is not one of my entries.

As I open my laptop I heard a noise outside. At the same time, Spook gave a low "Woof" and his hackles came up. I grab his collar and pull him into the bedroom. I have no intention of answering the door. There is only a lamp light on and the TV music is low, so hopefully, whoever is out there will assume no one is home and will leave. We get on the bed and I hold tight to Spook with my hand close to his nose. I do not want him to bark.

We stay hunkered down in the bedroom for what seems like an eternity. I hear footsteps as they walk around the deck with a flashlight trying to look through the windows that have closed drapes or blinds. Then there is a knock on the sliding door by the kitchen. I immediately grab Spook's nose so he won't bark. A few seconds later is another knock.

"Hey, Betty, Bob, you guys in there? This is Cecil, didn't know you were back." There is silence. "You okay in there?" Then I hear him walk off the deck.

Now what do I do? I don't dare turn off any lights or turn on anymore. It is only eight o'clock in the evening. I need to take Spook out to potty, but I'm afraid of being seen by Cecil. Why didn't I just answer the damn door? I've talked to Cecil a couple times, very briefly, and he seems like a nice man.

I peer out all the windows to see if Cecil is still around. I can't see anyone. I decide to take Spook out for a walk and go over to Cecil's to let him know I'm alright. I told him I was asleep and didn't realize it was him until

I saw him leaving. I can create more trouble for myself than anyone I know. Why I didn't answer the door is beyond me. Stupid, just plain stupid.

Spook was nosing around for a little bit until he found the perfect spot to do his business then we went over to Cecil's. When he opened the door he was surprised to see me and said, "Well, Alicia, I thought maybe you had left, I haven't seen your car since yesterday. I thought maybe Betty and Bob were home. I was just over there rapping on the door, didn't you hear me?"

"I'm sorry, Cecil, I had laid down to read and I guess I fell asleep. I thought I was dreaming and didn't realize it was you until after I saw you walking back home. My car is in the garage; I just ran it through the car wash and thought it looked like rain." Now why the hell did I say that? If you look at the car it is obvious it hasn't been through a car wash in weeks, in fact since I bought it. I can't even tell a sensible lie, let alone keep the necessary ones straight.

"That's okay. I was just going to say hello to Betty and Bob if they were home, that's all. Have you talked to them since they have been gone?"

"No, I haven't. They weren't sure if they were going to be gone one or two months or somewhere in between. I hope they are having a good time."

"They always do. Betty loves to golf and is pretty good so I hear. Bob used to golf quite a bit until he bought that *'hobby'* boat and now he is busier than ever. So Hawaii is about the only time he gets out and plays. Let me know if you hear from them, okay? Oh, I'm going home for the week end, I'm getting real tired of this place. I don't know if I will ever get it done and my wife refuses to come out here until it is one hundred percent complete, so it could be awhile or never." He said laughing.

"I better get back over there and thanks for checking, Cecil."

As I turned to walk away, he said, "I didn't know you had a dog?"

Smiling, "Well, I didn't. He came up on the deck and was whimpering, muddy, wet and starving when I found him. I made a few phone calls around and put out several fliers, but no one has responded. I'm still not sure what I'm going to do with him. He seems like a real nice dog, well-mannered and well trained. Guess we'll see. Night Cecil, have a great weekend?"

"Thanks, you too."

CHAPTER 19

When I woke up I felt like I had been run over by a truck. I heard every sound there was during the night, plus I had kept Spook in the bedroom with me. He snored and snorted like a freight train.

Josh will be here tomorrow. Today will be laundry and the domestic crap to get ready for company. Might even do some cooking, nah, I can't get that carried away.

Spook went outside and I was starting to vacuum when the phone rang. Checking caller ID I saw it matched the number Betty had left on the pad by the telephone.

I answered, "Fredricks' residence."

"Hi Alicia, this is Betty. How's it going?"

"Just fine. How's vacation? I suppose the weather has been perfect and you'll be coming home with gorgeous tans." I laughed.

"Actually, the weather hasn't been all that great. It's been alright, but overcast most days, rainy a few days, and it has been so windy it has made it difficult to play golf. Bob is ready to come home. That's why I'm calling you. I know we asked you to stay possibly for two months, but Bob is ready to come home tomorrow."

"Tomorrow!" I exclaimed. "Wow, that's short notice."

Betty laughed, "Alicia, we are not coming home tomorrow, I just said Bob would like to. However, we are planning to leave here by next week end. Our reservations are for next Saturday. We'll fly into LA and spend the night and then home on Sunday. Is that going to work out for you? I'd like to stay awhile longer, but Bob is bored and ready to leave."

"Yes, that'll work out okay. That gives me a week and that is plenty of time. After all, I found you in a day. So unless there are any changes, I'll see you in a week. And Betty, thank you so much for letting me stay here. It was just what the doctor ordered."

"You're welcome, besides you did us a great favor, as well. Talk to you soon. See you in a week."

"Okay. Bye."

"Well crap. Now where am I going to go? Guess I had better get a map out and start plotting my road trip. Spook, what am I going to do with you?" He just lay on his blanket and stared at me as if to say, "Don't know why you're asking me, of course, I'm going with you."

I don't know what brought to my mind then, but it occurred to me someone has recorded my auto license number. I need to get rid of this car before I head out on the road again. Maybe Josh could help me with this.

What an absolute dilemma I'm in. I feel like I should go into the witness protection program. Actually, in a way I guess I already am.

I got on the phone and called Allison. I hadn't talked to her in almost three weeks and I got the reaction I expected.

"Wendy, we have been so worried about you. I wish you would call more often. I don't want to know where you are, I just want to hear from you. How are you?"

"I know I need to call. I'm doing okay. Lots has been going on. I have a new friend that has been here for a couple days. He's a German Short Hair and is a sweet dog. I tried to find the owner but so far no luck. I think I am stuck with him unless I turn him over to a rescue."

"That might not be a bad idea for you to have a dog for company and maybe protection. How's the book coming along?"

"Slow. I can't stick with it for very long. I'm remembering more stuff than I want to. When I pulled up all those notes it triggered more memories and is starting to get real scary, Allison. I'm afraid there is a lot more to Trevor than I ever thought. I knew there were secrets with him, but I'm beginning to believe this could be some serious shit. I just haven't figured it out, and maybe I don't want to or shouldn't. Someone is following me again."

"Oh no, Wendy. When did that happen and are you sure?"

"Yes, I'm sure and it scares the hell out of me. I think somehow Trevor has traced my car to the purchase when I traded cars. I don't know how he did it, but if there's a will there's a way." Then I told her about the incident in the parking lot and being followed.

We talked for about an hour and I told her the owners were coming in a week and I was thinking of going to Florida. Allison tried to convince me to go out West with them and tried to convince me I needed to keep Spook. I told her Josh was coming for a visit for a couple days and that just opened up a very long inquisitive drill about my relationship with Josh. I tried to minimize it and assure her there wasn't a relationship nor would there be, but she just laughed at me.

We hung up and I started picking up and cleaning house. It didn't take very long. Then I went to work on *'My Story'*.

Days had gone by since I had written anything so I had to go back and refresh where I left off. I made a few changes and additions and continued. **The wedding plans were really becoming very simple but very disappointing. I had a very strong feeling that Trevor was controlling in all phases of my life, let alone his children who had become used to his mannerisms. It was so hard to blend into the family and get acquainted with Sheila and Billy, because everything seemed to be an interruption to the children's schedule and that upset Trevor to a rage. But then he would immediately turn on the charm, just like always. I was beginning to have second thoughts about the marriage.**

As recommended by most psychiatrists, I made a list of the 'good, bad and the ugly' characteristics of Trevor. I crossed off and moved characters around until I thought I had a satisfied list. Then I studied it. Like always, Trevor's charm and sweetness won out and I decided this was all as new to him as it was to me and the kids. Time was all we needed for all of us.

Two weeks before the wedding went by pretty fast with packing and sorting and fixing the 'loft' (attic) office. I went shopping for a simple wedding dress and accessories as well as a negligee set. I bought a couple new outfits to take, thinking we would probably go to a dinner show or maybe two.

As the days grew closer things were getting more hectic by the minute. My apartment was a total disaster. I could hardly get around for all of the boxes and I couldn't find anything I was looking for. Trevor was way too busy to help me due to business meetings and social events that I, of course, was neither invited to nor interested in. This seemed to be part of Trevor's life that I wasn't a part of.

I finally got everything moved in that was going to Trevor's with the exception of my absolute necessities and computer before we left for Las Vegas. The last couple days before leaving for Las Vegas were nice and peaceful. Trevor only called because he was too busy winding up business deals before we left. That was okay with me. I was really enjoying the quiet and knew it would never be the same. Even though Trevor was so sweet and loving on the phone, I was beginning to question if I was making the right decision with this marriage. But I convinced myself it was just pre-wedding jitters and most brides and grooms got 'cold feet' at some point before their big day.

The day we left for Las Vegas was horrible. Trevor had a deal that was not going well, he was afraid he was going to lose it. He changed our flight plans from noon until 8:45 p.m. That meant our arrival was going to be 1:00 a.m., with the time change and flight delay. Trevor ended up taking the client out to dinner and wined and dined him and eventually got the deal, case or whatever it was. Needless to say, the flight was a lot more pleasant than it would have been if Trevor had lost his deal. Trevor was very tired and after a couple cocktails he was out like a light.

We checked into our room and I put clothes away while Trevor poured a drink. I started getting ready for bed and Trevor said, "I think we ought to go downstairs to the casino and see what's goin on."

"Don't you think it is a little late? We have lots to do tomorrow or today, as it is. I'm really tired and thought we'd go to bed. It's after 2:00."

"Well, I don't. Come on, we'll go down for just a little while." He grabbed my arm and out the door we went.

In the casino we walked around from the gaming machines to the blackjack tables, then crap tables, to the roulette wheel and then the bar. Trevor ordered a double scotch on the rocks, belted it down and ordered another. He looked at me and asked, "Are you going to order something or just sit there like a bump on a log?"

"Thank you, but I don't believe I was asked if I wanted a drink. I'll have a Baily's on the rocks."

"My, my, are we getting a little cranky?" He said with a smirk of a smile.

"I guess it has just been a very long day and I'm tired."

"Let's just take our drinks and go find you a machine to play and I'm going to play a little blackjack."

"I really don't want to play tonight, Trevor. I think I'll go back up to the room."

"Nah, come on, I'll find you a good machine." We got up and walked around the machines until Trevor found the one he wanted me to play. He gave me a hundred dollars, said good luck and headed for blackjack.

Checking the time I saw it was 2:30. I decided I would play for a half an hour and then go to the room and go to bed. I liked playing the machines and playing the animated games. Allison and I occasionally met in Reno for a long week end in past years. It had been a number of years since we had done that, and sitting at this machine brought back the old times with her. I was wishing she was here.

I got up from the machine Trevor had found and started looking for one of my fun machines to play. I sat down and put a twenty in and got the *bonus room first crack out of the barrel, I had just won $112 and cashed out. With another twenty I continued to play and was about to change machines when I hit the bonus room again. This time, because I had increased my bet I hit it for $500. I cashed out and put a twenty in the machine one seat over. I made three pulls and all of a sudden the bells started ringing, lights started flashing and there was a crowd behind me. I had just hit the machine for $7,500. I was shocked. I had to wait for an attendant to come over to cash me out and then go to the cashiers counter for the money. When I cashed in all three tickets I had over $8,200.*

The cashier suggested I put the money in the safe at the front desk of the hotel. After I made the deposit in the safe, I started looking for Trevor. I was beside myself I was so excited. I walked around all the blackjack tables and the dice tables and I didn't see him anywhere. Maybe he went up to the room, which is where I was headed.

Trevor was not in the room. I went to bed and immediately fell asleep.

Awakened the next morning by a knock on the door, "Maid Service", I groaned, rolled over and glanced at the clock, 10:15. Trevor still hadn't come back. I hollered back, "Not now, later please, thank you." The response was, "Okay Ma'am," and then silence.

Room Service delivered breakfast I had ordered. It was noon and Trevor still had not come back to the room. I couldn't believe he was still out there gambling. Another trait of Trevor's I had discovered.

I looked at the clock and it was after nine o'clock. I closed the computer.

CHAPTER 20

Spook and I went out on the deck. It was a clear night. Stars were out, frogs croaking and the crickets chirping or whatever crickets do. Spook took off for his potty run and I sat down and just listened to all the sounds. I observed some lights out in the swamp; there was going to be crawdad feeds for several people from the looks of the number of lights.

It was a nice evening, slightly cool but pleasant. My mind started working overtime, and bouncing around from one topic to another. Why had I told Allison I was going to Florida? I had never been there and didn't have the slightest idea of where to go. Maybe I should head for Mexico, that idea scared me. The thought of me being alone in Mexico and not knowing that country or the language at all, was a really stupid idea. I still hadn't looked at my map. Maybe someplace would jump out at me if I'd look at the map, what a novel idea.

I knew one thing for sure that Josh would try and convince me to go back to the ranch and I knew that was not even a consideration. Josh had this idea he could take care and protect me. I had become very fond of Josh, he was an honest and sweet man. I just couldn't let myself get seriously involved with him right now; any other time we might be the perfect couple. I wasn't ready for a relationship. There was too much hurt and still too many questions regarding Trevor and his vindictiveness to overcome. I wasn't safe and

I couldn't let Josh get in the mix of it all. I should've never let our sexual encounter happen and I couldn't blame it on my alcohol consumption, just plain old weakness and desire for someone to really love me.

How was I going to handle Josh, I didn't have a clue. Another sign of my weakness and desire for comfort and human connection, plus a confirmation that solitary confinement was not what I really wanted. Another conclusion - I make some real dumb decisions when I do my own thinking.

Spook and I went in the house. I turned on the TV and surfed the channels, but didn't see anything I was really interested in so I turned it off and turned on the music.

I decided this time I was going to plan my move rather than flying by the seat of my pants and just driving. So I grabbed the map and looked at several options. I couldn't go any further south since I was there. East or west was my choice and going north certainly was NOT an option. My finger took me east into Florida and along the gulf coast. This was all unfamiliar territory to me, Mississippi, Alabama and Florida. My next step would be to Google each state and see what was most appealing. The end results were Pensacola and Panama City Beach areas in Florida. Further inquiries would be necessary.

Pensacola was my first task. I got on VRBO (vacation rentals by owner) and what a variety, everything from $70 to $500 a night. Almost all of the rentals stipulated absolutely 'no pets', and if pets were okay, then it was small dogs, 20 lbs. or less, Spook did not fall into that category.

Continuing my search, I found a few that might work. I wrote some phone numbers down and site numbers to check out later. I was getting anxious to move. This house on the river, alone, was really getting to me. Plus the fact that Trevor had apparently found me. At least he thought he had or I thought he had. Didn't matter who thought what, I just needed to go. `

I was hoping while Josh was here he would help me find a car and maybe we could take a drive to Florida and look around for places. Now I was starting to feel guilty about having Josh help me with all this because I knew he wanted me to go to the ranch. I planned to have a serious talk with Josh and get all our cards out on the table. I had to keep 'us' as friends and no more.

It was getting late so I turned off the lights and headed for the bedroom and Spook made a bee line for the door and beat me. "Okay buddy, we are not going to become bed partners. It ain't gonna happen." I went back in the living room and grabbed the bundle of blankets and put them on the floor beside the bed. He seemed to be content with that and laid down.

Waking the next morning, I found Spook had made his place very comfy on the other side of the bed. Head on the pillow, eyes wide open and staring at me, I had to laugh at how sneaky he was. "Okay, let's have some breakfast." Spook jumped off the bed on a run for the kitchen. There was absolutely no question that Spook had now become my dog and was going nowhere.

CHAPTER 21

Josh was flying in this afternoon and should be here about four. I was getting anxious and nervous all at the same time. It is what it is and that is just the way life goes and my life has certainly followed that trend.

I busied myself with last minute tidying up and cooking a big pot roast and that helped the time fly. My plan was to have the roast left over for sandwiches in case Josh and I decided to take a day trip to look around for a place for me to move. I was taking a lot for granted that Josh would want to help me trade cars and look for a new place for me to hide. I thought the car deal would be okay, but I knew I was in for a battle with a relocating conversation.

The day went fairly fast and I even took time to take Spook for a short walk that included stopping by Cecil's to let him know Betty and Bob would be back the following week end. He was almost ready to leave for the week end to go home.

"I guess this means you will be moving on yourself? Do you know where you will be going?" Cecil asked.

"No, not really, I have some ideas but nothing specific. Any suggestions or favorite places you and your wife like to go?"

"Nah. The wife and I are stay at home kind of people. Until the flood we rarely went anywhere. Ordinarily the weather is pretty good around here, most of the year, a little warm in the summer but you get used to it."

"You have another place in town?"

"We do now. We just barely got out with a few things and lost everything else. So my wife went back to work while I keep plugging at repairing the house to move back into. Didn't have flood insurance so she is trying to replace our furnishings. She is damn lucky she got a good job, not many people did. She hasn't been back out here and won't until it is finished and then I'm not sure I will ever get her to move back out here. So it was either fix it or walk away and I couldn't walk away."

"Wow, I am so sorry for you guys."

"Hey, we are one of the luckier ones. Good luck to you, I gotta get goin. Take care and be careful."

"Thank you, Cecil, and good luck to you two as well."

I walked back to the house and was standing out on the deck just looking around at the area. I don't think it actually had sunken in to the devastating disaster these people, here in New Orleans and surrounding areas, had really suffered. Even though I had seen it on television, read about it in the newspapers and Bob's river tour, it didn't register the severity of it all. I had been so consumed in my own little world, not much else phased me anymore. To be planted here and live around the disaster made me think how lucky I have been all of my life.

Looking at my watch for the umpteenth time, I started getting anxious about Josh coming. He should be here in less than an hour. I checked the roast again and it was just fine, not quite done.

I picked up my phone and called Allison again and when she answered I blurted out, "Talk to me. Tell me why I let Josh come here and now why am I so nervous. I think I'm losing my mind."

All I could hear from her was laughter. "Wendy, settle down. Just take a deep breath and put your mind in the mode that he is a friend coming for a visit. What happens after that is up to you. Have a great time and enjoy his company and take your mind off all the other crap that has been going on, okay?"

"I think I'm having an anxiety attack, Allison. Okay, I'm breathing." And I laughed.

"Hey, I keep forgetting to ask you. Matt wants to know how you are doing with your investment accounts. He said he has a new avenue he thinks will work better for you and yield more income. He's not here right now or he could tell you all about it. Just think about it. He's really good at what he does, you know."

"Yes, I know he is. I just don't want to have to learn anything new and so far I think I'm okay. But I'm willing to listen to what he has to say sometime. Uh oh, a car just drove in. It's Josh, I gotta go, I'll talk to you soon. I'm still breathing so don't worry. Love ya." And I hung up.

As soon as I was sure it was Josh, I ran outside with Spook hot on my trail with his hackles up. Down the deck stairs we went and I almost missed the last three steps. When I got to the car Josh grabbed me in a big hug and twirled me around. We were both laughing and all of sudden Josh put me down and looked down at his leg. Spook had hold of Josh's pant leg and a very low growl. I got hold of Spook's collar, "It's okay, Spook, let go. Josh is our friend. Spook? Let go now."

Spook let go and I kneeled down and started talking to him rubbing his head and back. Josh kneeled as well and held his hand out to Spook and talking at the same time. When Spook licked Josh's hand we knew it was going to be okay.

"Wow! That really surprises me. Are you okay? Guess he's a better protector than I thought. I'm thinkin Spook is my new best friend and partner forever." And I laughed.

"Yah, I'm alright. I'm sorta thinkin you're right. Good thing I had on my cowboy boots or I could've lost a hunk of meat." And Josh laughed.

We unloaded the car and went in the house. Josh grabbed me again and gave me a hug and a big kiss. "It's really good to be here, I've missed you a lot."

"I've missed you too." And I meant it and hugged him back.

I checked the roast and it was done so I turned the oven off. I gave Josh a beer and poured myself a drink. We sat and talked for a couple hours, just catching up. It felt good having Josh there and I no longer felt nervous.

Dinner turned out great, along with the bottle of Pinot Noir we polished off. Josh helped clean up the dishes, then, we took Spook for a walk and little tour of the area. We sat out on the deck until well after dark, still talking about anything and everything.

When we got back in the house, Josh spotted my computer on the bar counter. "How'd you do when you searched for files other than what was yours, remember, we talked about that?"

"There's nothing on any of the programs on this computer. I searched everywhere. I don't think Trevor would've ever used my computer, he had three or maybe more that he had access to."

"Did you open up any of the Guest files?" Josh asked.

"No, I never go into that because I have no need to."

"Let's try it, there may not be anything but let's check it out."

I closed everything out and re-booted. When it came back up Josh clicked on Guest and started going through programs and nothing was coming up. When he opened Microsoft Excel, Josh calmly said, "Well, there it is."

"There is what?"

"I think some coded files that are only of value to Trevor. Let me dive into these a little bit more."

"Why would Trevor put stuff on my computer? He has so many other computers at his disposal, why mine? Unless he is hiding something."

"That is exactly what he's doing, Alicia. And that is why he's having you followed. He wants this computer, I'll bet you anything."

"Are these financial reports?"

"Looks like it to me, they are all coded with letters and numbers. We need to see if we can figure out the codes."

"Ya know, Josh, this could be a very lengthy project. Why don't we wait until tomorrow when we are fresh? I'm sure you must be tired after a long day, it's almost midnight. Let's call it a night, okay?"

"I think you're right, sounds good to me." And he shut down the computer.

"Let's have a nightcap and turn in." I suggested.

We sat on the sofa with our drinks and discussed some options. Josh thought the files should be put on a CD for safe keeping or USB stick, or both. I laughed and told him my computer was so old it didn't have those capabilities. I knew I couldn't burn a CD and I'd never used a USB stick.

"Alicia, I wish you'd give serious consideration to coming back to the ranch. You would be safe there."

"Josh, I can't put this burden on you or Jim and Cecelia. I can't become a resident of their guest house, it was enough they let me rent it for a month as it was."

"I'm not talking about staying in the guest house. My house is plenty big, you can stay there and you will be totally out of sight from everyone. You can have your own room and space. I promise I will give you all the space you need."

"I wish I could explain to you and make you understand exactly how I feel. But I'm not even sure I know myself. I care a lot about you. I am trapped in a situation I have to get resolved before I'm free to make any other decisions. I have to get Trevor off my back and out of my life forever, and that is my first priority. What process I have to go through to get there, I have no idea, I just have to get there first. I value your friendship and sincerely appreciate your caring and concern and wanting to protect me." I reached over and grabbed both of his hands, "Josh, I truly do, but can we please keep us as friends doing whatever friends do to fulfill a friendship without pressure, questions or commitment? I can't have it any other way, I hope you understand."

"I know what you are saying and I believe every word of it, I just wish you would let me in and help you. I'll help with whatever you want and I won't pressure you in any way. Do you want me to get my sleeping bag out of the car?"

I put my arms around his neck, "Thank you, Josh. You do what you want to do, but it is late and I'm going to bed." When I pulled away, I smiled, gave him a peck on the cheek and turned to go into the bedroom. Spook followed and got on his bed.

CHAPTER 22

I lay in bed and my head was swimming with first one thought and then the other. I was restless, turning and flopping all over the place and couldn't go to sleep. I hated myself for decisions I was making, but I hated Trevor more.

I heard the bedroom door open and felt Josh slide into bed beside me. "Alicia?" he whispered. "I just want to hold you and be close." And he put his arm under my head and held me.

The warmth and comfort of Josh being next to me was exactly what I needed and wanted. I turned over and cuddled into him and we held each other in silence.

Feeling so safe and comfortable, I wanted to stay there forever. It wasn't long until I felt the desire of Josh rise, causing my desire to rise as well. Josh kissed me ever so gently and passionately as he rubbed my back up and down. I felt a tingle and sudden rush of warmth run through my body. Josh continued to hold me and stroke my back, down my legs and back up again with softness and control. As he found each of my sensual areas I was losing control at a rapid pace. I was already moist and Josh slipped in with ease. It took only a few thrusts and we climaxed at the same time. Still holding me, he gave a sigh and kissed me again and again. Josh looked down at me and whispered, "I'm sorry, I tried to hold back. You are amazing, not because of the sex, but because of who you are. You are one cool chick."

Even though I wanted to say more, all I could do was touch his cheek, smile and give him a gentle kiss and say, "Thank you."

Still wrapped in each other's arms we fell asleep. I assume we slept that way all night, but when I woke the next morning, Josh was already up. I could smell the coffee and Spook was gone as well. I got up and put on my robe, ran a brush through hair, brushed my teeth and went out to the kitchen.

Josh was already working on the computer. He looked up with his cute dimpled smile and said, "Good morning, Sunshine. Did you sleep well?"

"I sure did. How long have you been up?"

"Long enough for a cup of coffee and take Spook for a short walk and work on some of these files."

"Wow, I didn't hear a thing. What time is it anyway?"

"It's only 7:45, and it doesn't matter as long as you slept well. We were up rather late last night. Not to worry."

"What have you found on the computer?"

"Well, it has been very interesting. Either Trevor is very stupid and never thought you would find the files and never counted on you leaving, or he is in way deeper then he intended, or all of the above. But, this code was very easy to figure out."

"I'm sure you are right on all counts. So, how did you figure out the codes?"

"The spreadsheet is set up by first date, then the letters counted out in numerical order indicate the file number, third column combinations spell a name. The fourth column, I believe are initials of investment companies and then dollar amounts and percentages. This really isn't rocket science. Pretty damn simple, if I'm right. I still think we ought to transfer all of this to a USB stick and take it to a computer shop and have all of this information put on a CD and then secure it someplace."

"How are we going to do this?"

"It won't be hard to do, just time consuming because there are several pages."

"I wonder what this means and how long it has been going on."

"Well, the first entry on this computer is January 10th and the last one is December 3rd, but there aren't any years listed. So it's hard to say."

While I was fixing breakfast, Josh continued to work on the computer. This whole thing was terrifying me. I had information Trevor wanted and I knew he would do anything to get it at all costs. I was now positive I would never be safe or free from him.

Josh interrupted my thoughts and asked, "Where is your printer? I think the best way is to print all of this, decipher and then re-enter it in the same format."

"I do have a printer, but I'm almost out of paper and I know my ink is low. After breakfast, why don't we go to town and get the paper, ink, CD and USB stick. That way, when we are done, we can take it all someplace to burn copies."

"That sounds good to me."

We spent the afternoon sightseeing around New Orleans. Josh had never been there and I hadn't ventured out at all, so this would be interesting for us both.

Josh drove his car so there was no chance of us being followed. I still hadn't brought up the idea of trading my car. But then I'd also thought it best to do it in Florida and then again I could be followed to Florida. Another dilemma I had to resolve.

Time flew by having walked the streets of New Orleans, riding the trolley cars, walked Bourbon Street, wandered the market place and listened to music along the way. We were ready to head back to the house after all the walking. I gave the best tour I could with the limited information I had, but it was good enough for Josh. For a guy, he had about all of the touring he wanted.

We stopped off and grabbed a quick bite to eat and then hurried home to let Spook out. He was thrilled to see us and ready to go outside.

We printed almost ten pages of files and spent the evening deciphering the Excel files. We were both flabbergasted at the dollar amount that was adding up.

Turning in for the night, we had a much more relaxed and fulfilling repeat performance of the night before. Josh once again proved what a gentle and caring man he was. I knew he was falling in love with me and I couldn't stop it. Like watching a train wreck and knowing it was going to happen. I responded to Josh in every sensual path he led me and knew I was falling in love with him and fighting it with everything I could.

The next morning, Josh was up again before me, had the coffee on and had already taken Spook out for a walk.

I became more shocked the longer we worked on the files. I kept wondering what it all meant, and the one thing that kept popping into my head was 'Bernie Madoff'. Suddenly, I got violently ill. I made a mad dash for the bathroom and threw up until I had the dry heaves.

Josh came in and handed me a cold wash cloth. I sat on the floor and started sobbing and shaking and was almost in a hysterical state. He took me by the arms and stood me up, held me tight and whispered, "Everything is going to be alright, we're going to get through this."

"You don't understand, Josh. I think Trevor is running the same kind of business as Bernie Madoff. At least that's the way it feels. Some thoughts just popped into my head of incidences that happened that makes this all perfectly good sense and it is scaring the hell out of me."

"I'm sure it does. That's all the more reason to get these files in a safe place and you too. Let's take a break and take Spook for a walk and clear your head."

"I have to figure out where I'm going, remember, I have to be out of here by the end of the week. I know I can't go back to the ranch with you. Josh, that is not an option right now, so let's please not make it a big deal."

"I understand, I don't like it, but I hear ya. So, where are you going? Do you have a plan or direction in mind?"

"Well, I was talking to Allison and I told her I thought about going to Florida, around Pensacola or Panama City Beach area. I've never been there, but I want to take a look. It is a lot more populated than where I've been staying. Maybe I can find a nice gated community, out of the way and safe."

"So you're gonna get in your car and just drive up and down streets without a plan or particular destination?"

"Pretty much. That's what I've been doing so far. Trade cars, change my hair, again, and with Spook in the front seat, I should be incognito and flying by the seat of my pants. This time I have a map and am going to research some areas."

"I wish I had more time to help you with all of this. I have to get back tomorrow and help Jim get ready for the race next week end. I don't know when I can get away next."

"I know. You have a very demanding job and I appreciate all your help and have certainly enjoyed the time we've had. But I have to get through all of this without jeopardizing anyone else."

"You are one stubborn lady."

Josh insisted on finishing the files. Once we had made a chart numbering the letters, it seemed to go fairly fast. I couldn't believe how easy this code was to decipher. How stupid did Trevor really think I was? Actually, I guess he was pretty confident I wouldn't find the file and if it hadn't been for Josh, I wouldn't have. It never occurred to me to look in Guest of my computer. And it never occurred to me that Trevor would do anything illegal, let alone try and hide information on my computer.

We worked the rest of the afternoon on the files. Josh was deciphering as I re-entered the information and saved it. It was a tedious job but we got it done.

"Why don't we go to town with your laptop and get this saved to CDs and the stick? You can run copies of the files and then put all of these in different places for safe keeping? I'll take you out to dinner, how's that sound?"

"That sounds great."

CHAPTER 23

On the way to town, I said, "I can hardly wait to tell Allison about this, she is going to crap her pants." And I laughed.

Josh looked at me with a very serious and almost scary look, "Alicia, I wouldn't do that if I were you. I wouldn't tell anyone about these files."

"Why? I would trust Allison with my life. Why would you say that?"

"I just think the least number of people that know about these files, the safer you are. What do you know about Matt? Isn't he in the same business as Trevor?"

"Not exactly the same business, but Matt wouldn't betray me anyway. He only knows Trevor because of some conference where they had met several years ago. They live on opposite sides of the country, so their paths never cross. Matt would never be a concern for me."

"It just seems strange to me that every time after you talk with Allison, the guy in the black car appears out of nowhere. How many times has he tailed you?"

"Three, I'm not for sure about one of the times."

"The fact that anyone is tailing you and followed you anywhere, no matter how many times, is too many."

"Well, I've ditched him so far. I'm curious why you would be suspicious of Matt and think I should be?"

Josh frowned and started giving me all the reasons why he was suspicious of Matt and it was based on bits and pieces of information I had provided through conversations. Mainly his gut feeling. The number of times Matt asked to let him take over my investment accounts, the number of times Trevor called supposedly checking to see if I was at their house, but only talks to Matt never Allison.

"That's assuming you're right and I think you are way off base. I can't imagine Matt is involved with Trevor. I just can't."

"Okay! Let's find a computer store of some sort, get the copies made and get something to eat. I'm getting hungry." Josh reached over and patted my leg and gave me his dimpled smile. That smile that melted my heart, but also stiffened my neck and shoulder muscles, telling me not to get involved. What an oxymoron that is.

While we were driving, I happened to glance over and saw a Classic Cadillac that looked to be in great condition with a for sale sign on it. Behind the Cadillac appeared to be a computer shop called The Geek and had an open sign in the window.

"Josh, pull in here and let's see if this guy can make copies. See that Geek Shop, let's see what kind of Geek he is."

Even though it was an old building outside, it was neat and tidy inside with computers everywhere. A hippy appearing sort of middle aged man came out of the back room smiling, "Can I help ya?"

"I hope so. I have an old laptop that I need some files transferred onto a USB stick and on two different CDs. Can you do that?"

"Of course I can. I could have them ready for you by the end of the week. By the way, my name is Phil, my mother calls me Phillip, my friends call me Philly and my enemies call me Packin Phil."

"Well, Phil, I was really hoping you could do it now. You see I'm not from this area and I need to have this information back to my company. There is a deadline for this project, so I need to have it ready for pickup tomorrow first thing." I said smiling at Phil, hoping he would relent. It couldn't take that long and it didn't appear he was very busy. But, what did I know.

Josh reached in his back pocket for his wallet and pulled out a bill and said, "Would this be a little extra incentive to put a rush on this? We really do need this ASAP."

Phil smiled ever so pleasantly, "I think I can have this ready in about fifteen minutes. Would you like to come back?"

"No thanks, I think we'll just wait." Josh replied.

We stepped outside to wait and I asked Josh, "How much did you give that guy?"

"Not much, just a little extra persuasion, it was no big deal. Don't worry about it."

"Thank you, but let me pay you. You've helped enough with this project and I do appreciate it."

I started to reach in my purse and Josh put his hand on my arm and said, "Just wait and see how much the bill is."

While we waited for Phil to make the CD copies, I commented, "I have no idea where I'm going to hide these copies. I'm going to ask you to take one of the CDs because no one knows about you."

"Why don't you put one in a safe deposit box in a bank?"

"I can't. I can't open a bank account because my name and social security won't match. And I can't get a box without a bank account. I pretty well screwed myself in that department."

"What about one of your friends?"

"I didn't keep in real close contact with most of my friends after I married Trevor."

"Then, what about a relative, there has got to be someone you can trust? Maybe someone Trevor doesn't even know."

"Okay, I'm going to have to think about this. So, I have these CDs and USB stick hidden all over with different people, for what reason? What do I do with this information and where do I start? Maybe these files are all legitimate and this was just a backup source."

"Alicia, you know this was not a backup source or these files wouldn't have been set up with some kind of a weird code. I would think there should be an investigative audit and maybe the first person to start with is the State's Attorney General. Write a letter explaining you have these files, give as little information as necessary, but still enough to stir up some interest."

"That sounds logical to me and that would be the Attorney General of Massachusetts, I get that. But, I don't have an address to respond to. I'll have to wait until I get settled somewhere and get a private mail box. God, I hope I don't ever have to go back to Boston."

"If this all turns out to be what we think it is, you can count on a trip to Boston. I don't see any way out of it."

Phil came out and told us the CDs were ready. I followed him back in the store to pay and he said, "Oh no, you don't owe me anything, your husband already took care of it."

I decided not to bother with an explanation that Josh was not my husband, but I wanted to inquire about the 1990 Cadillac parked out front. "Phil, what can you tell me about the Cadillac?"

"Well, my buddy actually owns it. The story he told me is he bought it from a guy in Coos Bay, Oregon. It is the original miles of eighty five thousand. He is the third owner and both previous owners kept it garaged. Everything is original, engine, upholstery, paint and has only one little shopping cart ding. Other than that it's in perfect condition."

"What about the engine? How do I know it is in perfect condition?"

"You can take it on a test drive and to any mechanic shop you want. My buddy guarantees perfect operation."

"How long are you here? We were going to dinner and we could talk it over and let you know."

"I am closing in fifteen minutes, but I'll call my buddy and have him meet you here in say an hour. How's that? Let me give him a quick call and see if that will work for him."

"Sounds good to me."

I went back outside and told Josh what I was doing. He looked at me with this confused looked. "Why would you want to do that? The car you have is perfectly good."

"I know, but I need to change vehicles so I don't get tailed again. It has Oregon plates on it now and I won't have to change them for a while, as long as I'm on the move anyway. The guy is only asking thirty five hundred dollars and I can take it to any mechanic to have it checked out. We can talk it over during dinner."

Phil came out of the store and said, "My buddy can be here in a little over an hour. If you change your mind, here's his number and his name is Sylvester. So I think you're all set."

"Thank you, Phil, for your help."

We found a quaint little café that advertised home style cooking that really appealed to Josh. We were talking about the car and Josh, putting his elbows on the table, and said, "I don't think you have really thought this car deal through." I started to say something and Josh held up his hand and continued, "Let me give you a couple scenarios and reasons why I think this is a real bad idea. First, that Cadillac is going to stand out like a red flag. It is a flashy car and going to catch the eye of everyone that passes by you. You need to get a car that is like most other cars on the highway, one that's not going to draw attention to you, like a silver SUV or sedan. A car that has been on the coast is subject to rust. Plus the age of this car and being from the coast, there's no question there will be rust. But it's up to you."

"You're absolutely right, Josh. I just got caught up in ………..I don't even know what I was caught up in. Not thinking, as usual."

Josh didn't offer any argument to where I was moving, he knew it was definitely not back to the ranch. He suggested I might consider going West instead of Florida. I knew his reasoning was because I had told Allison I was going to Pensacola or Panama City Beach. Josh had a gut feeling that Matt could be involved in this financial scam with Trevor and could easily be responsible for knowing where I was and having me tailed. I didn't want to get into a discussion with him over my destination or Allison right then.

Dinner was great and we had talked nonstop until we both realized an hour had past. Josh picked up the check and I called Sylvester that I'd changed my mind about the car.

We drove back to the house each in our own thoughts. Josh broke the silence, "Have you given anymore thoughts to where you are going and what kind of car you want?"

"Some. I'll look around and something will jump out at me, it's really not that big a deal. I'm not sure which direction I'm heading on Friday."

"I would like you to give serious thoughts about not going to Florida. There's got to be some nice areas around the gulf of Texas."

I still couldn't get my head around what Josh had said about Matt and was trying to make sense of it. I trusted Allison with my life; we had been friends way too long and been through so much together I couldn't imagine it being any different. But I didn't know much about Matt either, except they seemed to get along real well and he had always treated Allison's two daughters better than his three boys. Allison never mentioned Matt's work other than he was in the financial business much like Trevor and they didn't talk about it after he got home. Matt provided a great income for the family and that is all Allison cared about even though she had a great job herself.

Josh didn't know either Allison or Matt so his opinions were purely speculation and suspicion, and I had to put that out of my mind and consider it for what it was.

"I need to think about this for a few days. I don't know anything about the Southern states. I don't want to live like this. I want to find a place and get all of my stuff out of storage and get settled. Living like this is bullshit."

"You don't have that much time, my dear. If I can offer a suggestion, since going back to the ranch with me is out. My sister, Tonya, and her husband live in Dallas. She would be more than happy to help you find a place."

"I won't do that. I won't infringe on your family. You have already done way more than I ever thought anyone would do. I'll get it figured out. I have to do this on my own."

"Okay, let's just drop the subject. I can see I will not win and it'll only put a strain between us."

"Good idea."

The rest of the ride home was silent. I was dreading the evening, knowing Josh would be leaving the next day. I knew his thoughts were going in the same direction.

Spook was thrilled to see us and very anxious to get outside. I mixed a couple drinks and joined Josh and Spook for a walk.

CHAPTER 24

My cell phone was ringing as we walked in the door from our walk with Spook. Considering Allison and Josh were the only two that had my cell number, I should've taken time to check caller ID, but I answered the phone to hear, "Wendy?"

"Who is this?"

"Wendy, is that you? This is Sheila. Billy and I miss you so much."

"Oh, My God, Sheila. I miss you both terribly. How did you get my telephone number?"

"I got it off the note pad by the telephone. Where are you? When are you coming home?"

Off the note pad by the telephone? How the hell did Trevor get this number? Somehow he had to have gotten it from Allison and Matt. They wouldn't have given my number to Trevor, they just wouldn't.

"Sheila? Who told you I was coming back home?"

"Daddy said he loves you very much and he says he's doing everything he can to find you and bring you back home and then everything will be just like before. Are you mad at Daddy?"

"Honey, I'm so sorry, but I'm not coming back home. Your dad and I won't be living together anymore. I'm sorry he made you believe it was going to be different. Where is your dad now? Does he know you're calling me? Did he ask you to call me?"

"No. Daddy is still at work and Fran went to pick up Billy from practice."

"Sheila, listen to me. You can't tell anyone you called me. If Daddy finds out, he's going to be really mad at you. Do you understand what I am telling you? Please don't tell anyone, not even Billy. This has got to be our secret, okay?"

"Okay, but I miss you, I wish you would come back home, it was better when you were here."

"Sheila, I love you and Billy, always remember that. You better get off the phone before someone comes back. I don't want you to get in trouble. You have to hang up now."

"Can I call you again?"

I had to think about it, I sure didn't want Trevor to know that she had called. I wanted to tell her no because it was not safe for her, but at the last second, "Yes, but you have to be very careful. You can't call me from the home phone, so no one can ever know you called. Do you understand what I'm telling you, don't call from home?"

"Yes, I understand."

"You have to promise me, just our secret, okay?"

"I promise. Bye Wendy, I love you."

"I love you too, honey. Bye Bye."

"Oh, my God, Trevor has my new cell number. How the hell did he get that? The only ones that have it are you and Allison. I don't call anyone else that even knows or cares where I am or what I'm doing."

Josh turned me towards him and said, "Alicia, listen to me very carefully. You may trust Allison with your life, but all the signs lead to Matt not being so trustworthy."

Starting to offer argument, Josh put his fingers to my lips and continued, "Think about this. He has on more than one occasion asked you to reinvest your inheritance, Trevor has called many times to their house, but talks to Matt. I'm not sure I believe it was quite by chance that Matt just happened to run into Trevor in Boston and introduced you two. I think they are sleeping in the same bed and have for a very long time."

"I just don't want to believe this. This will kill Allison. It can't be right, Josh, you have to be wrong."

"And I could be, Alicia. But, you have to proceed as if this were true. Get rid of that number and only use your prepaid phone, or even get rid of the phone."

"Then I lose contact with Sheila and Billy, if they ever need me."

"You are out of their lives and have to stay that way. There is nothing you can do for them. For all you know, Trevor put her up to that call. Think about your safety and not the kids. You will only jeopardize your own hiding places if you keep in touch with them."

"I hate that man. He has two of the most precious kids and he doesn't even know it. I would take them in a heartbeat if I could."

"Let it go, Alicia, you have to let it go."

Standing out on the deck, I was watching the river rush by and listening to the sounds of the swamp in the background. A flash or bright light caught my eye up on the bridge. I gasped as I realized it was coming from a man with binoculars standing beside a black car.

Shaking as I went back in I blurted out, "He's here, he's on the bridge watching the house with binoculars. He knows I'm here at this house. I've got to get out of here now."

"Alicia, who's here? Trevor? Where is he?"

"On the bridge in the black car. No, I don't think it is Trevor. It's one of his goons."

Josh turned and walked out on the deck. He immediately turned and came back in, "I don't see any car on the bridge."

"Well, then he must've driven off. He was parked right in the middle of that bridge. I saw him and he was watching me. I need to start packing and load my car. I can't stay here."

"And where do you think you are going at this hour? You don't have anything packed, none of your stuff is together. What are you doing about Spook? Think about this for a minute."

"Josh, do you understand I don't have a minute? Spook's going with me and I'll just have to deal with him."

I ran into the bedroom and started throwing clothes in suitcases, then the bathroom, into the kitchen and acting like a maniac. Josh was following me from room to room talking and I didn't hear a word he was saying. I was in a panicked, crazy zone.

"Alright, alright. Let me help you with this. Alicia, come to your senses and get a hold of yourself. You can't run for ever. Let me go talk to this guy and see what he wants. If it's your computer, then give it to him."

"I have all my books on that computer, my records and my life is on that computer. I can't give it up." I screamed.

"Alicia, your life or the computer?"

"I don't want you to go after him, he could kill you. I just want to get out of here. Let's go."

Josh and I loaded the car and emptied the refrigerator best I could. I sort of cleaned as I went. Considering I had cleaned before Josh came it didn't need much. I scribbled a quick note to Betty and Bob and we were out of there in less than an hour.

Spook jumped in the front seat of my car and Josh followed us in his rental car. I didn't know where I was going and neither did Josh, he just followed. Turning onto a side street following an arrow to a motel, we pulled into the parking lot.

"Okay, I need your help Josh. I feel bad because I feel like I am using you and I don't want to do that."

"Look, I know the situation and I understand the rules, I don't have to like it, and I do have a choice. So, having said that, what do you need?"

"I'm so sorry. I never wanted us to ever get into this position. But it has because I didn't stop it a long time ago. Please don't hate me."

"I know, just tell me what you need." Josh's tone was cold, to the point and cut me to the core.

"Oh, Josh." I said sympathetically.

"Just tell me what you want."

"I want to stay the night here, trade cars in the morning, take you to the airport and then take off."

"Fine, I'll get a room." With that, Josh turned and walked towards the office.

"Josh, wait. Please don't be like this."

"Alicia, what the hell do you want from me? I love you, I want to help you and all you do is keep pushing me away *'because you need to do this on your own'*. Well, guess what? You are getting what you asked for. We'll get the cars dealt with, but I can take myself to the airport and then I'm done." And Josh walked to the motel office.

Spook jumped out of the car and run across the street to a small park where children were playing and Spook wanted to play. I sat on a bench next to a big tree so I could watch the street to be sure I wasn't being followed. I started sobbing for what I was doing and had already done to Josh. I had broken his heart and that was breaking mine as well.

When I walked back to the motel, Josh's car was gone. The motel room key was on the car hood with a note, 'See you in the morning'. I had really screwed up.

CHAPTER 25

It seemed like morning took forever. I slept like crap, tossing and turning and couldn't get Josh out of my head.

Spook and I went over to the park and when we came back, Josh was standing by my car. As I was approaching him, my eyes welled up and I started to cry.

Josh put his hand up, "Don't, let's just get this done. I have a plane to catch."

"Josh, can we go have breakfast and talk?"

"I've already eaten and I changed my plane ticket to earlier, so we don't have much time. How do you plan to pay for this car?"

"I have cash."

"What the hell are you doing running around with that kind of cash on you? Never mind, it's none of my business."

"Because I don't want to use credit cards and I don't have a bank account, Josh."

Josh turned and started for his car, "Please, will you just sit here and talk to me for a minute. I need you to talk to me, please."

"Alicia, I can't do this anymore. I'm beating my head against a rock wall. If you are going to be so damned stubborn with your idea that you can do this all on your own, then do it. I lost the love of my life once and I'm not going to let myself fall in love with you anymore than I already have, and then have you still walk away. I'm not going to do it. Let's get your car and I'll help you transfer your stuff, then I have a plane to catch." And he walked away.

I didn't know what to say to Josh because he was right. I am stubborn, I felt like I had to do this on my own and not drag anyone else into this mess. But I already had. Josh was about as deep into my life as one could get and I had allowed it to happen. Now, we were both paying the price.

I went into the motel room to get my keys and purse. I left Spook in the room with fresh water and some food, and hoped he wouldn't bark while I was gone.

We rode to the car lot in silence. Each time I tried to say something Josh would just put his hand up and shake his head. He was angry with me and even more, he was terribly hurt.

I was beside myself in grief with what was happening to Josh and I couldn't stop it. I was torn between my emotions and heart and my head that kept telling me to move on. Deal with your own demons.

Josh pulled into a car dealership and got out of the car and headed to the office.

"Josh, can we please talk about this?"

"Alicia, there is nothing to talk about. Don't make it any harder than it already is. Let's just get this done."

Josh talked with the salesman after I finally decided on a silver SUV. It had enough room for all my stuff and Spook, too. Josh dickered over the price until he felt he had the best price. It took about an hour to close the deal and fifteen minutes to transfer my stuff to the new car.

When we were done, we drove back to the motel so Josh could get his car. He gave me a peck on the cheek and said in a real cool tone, "Good luck," and he turned and walked to his car.

"Josh, stop! Please don't leave like this."

Josh turned around and I could see tears in his eyes. He immediately got in his car and drove off.

Sobbing, all I could do was watch him drive away.

I spent another night in the same motel and all I did was stay in bed and cry. I turned on the TV to watch the news if for no other reason than a distraction. It appeared the entire east coast and southern states were inundated with one devastating storm after another, tornados, hurricanes, rain and big fires in Texas. Now I didn't know where to go.

Josh had not called and I didn't expect him to, it was just wishful thinking on my part. I hadn't tried to call him, either. I couldn't stand the thought of Josh either not answering the phone, or hanging up on me. I only hoped he would come around and we could be friends again. But I knew, once you step beyond the friendship boundaries, it's nearly impossible to go back. For now, it is what it is.

Calling Allison, I had no idea what to say or what not to tell her, but I had a need to hear her voice and pull from her strength.

"Hey you. This is Wendy, how are you guys?"

"We are fine, but you sound like hell. What's going on? Everything okay?"

"No, nothing's okay. I spotted another tail, so I packed and got out of the river house. Josh got mad at me and left in a huff and Spook and I are holed up in a motel."

"Wendy, why won't you come out here? With the girls gone we have plenty of room. You know we can keep you safe. Even if Trevor were to show up here, there is no way Matt would let him get close enough to the property to harm you. I'd feel so much better if you were right here with me."

"I can't, besides now I have this dog that adopted me. I'm going to find a place and settle in and if Trevor finds me, he finds me. I'll deal with him when it happens. I can't run anymore."

"Where are you going this time?"

"Not sure. I had thought about going to Florida, but the east coast is ripping apart with storms. I thought about going somewhere on the gulf on Texas. Still haven't made up my mind. May make my way towards Arizona, I want to stop running, Allison, this is not fun."

"Hey Wendy, you are always welcome here," Matt cut in.

"Matt were you eavesdropping on our conversation?" Allison scolded and laughed.

"Not really, just picked up the same time you did. So how ya doin, my friend?" Matt asked.

"Shitty. I'm just tired of running. Other than that, everything is just peachy," I said to Matt. I didn't want to get into a conversation with Matt, Josh had made me suspicious of him and I didn't know what to say or how to be cautious with him.

Matt volunteered that Trevor hadn't called for several weeks and Allison contradicted him which he replied he had forgotten. Another suspicious remark from Matt. Then he asked again if I was ready to transfer my investments to a great opportunity he was working on?

"Matt that is the last thing I'm thinking about right now." I said.

"Matt, will you leave Wendy alone about her inheritance? She's got far more important things to worry about right now. Wendy, I'm getting off here now and will call you in a couple days. I have something I need to deal with myself right now. Love you." And she hung up.

Allison's hanging up so abruptly put me in a tailspin. I had never heard her talk to Matt in a firm or cranky way. Suddenly, everything Josh had said to me about Matt was making sense. I tried to think what I'd said on the phone while Matt was listening that could be of help to Trevor. With my being so indecisive about which direction I was going and talking about heading west to Arizona maybe would throw them off.

CHAPTER 26

I made my decision to go to Florida and stick to my original plan and so the next morning we headed east. Spook was the best traveler and companion. He listened to me blubber while driving, cry myself to sleep at night and yell at everything that got in my way. He was a trooper. I was a brat.

I decided it was time to do something with my hair again. Several miles down the road, as I started driving east, I found a salon. The hair stylist helped me pick out a new style and different color. When I walked out of the salon, I felt so uplifted and refreshed. I almost forgot what I was facing. It felt good, if it only lasted for a short while.

After we settled into a motel in Pensacola, I wanted to find a park for Spook. Stopping at a small market to ask about a park, I picked up a rental magazine. There was an amazing number of rental options up and down the coast in both Pensacola and Panama City Beach.

Spook and I went to the park someone had recommended. He gobbled down the food and water I had put down for him and then he was off running around, playing with any dog that would play.

Although it was late in the afternoon, I started making calls to rental listings that would accept pets, an eighty pound moose. I set up appointments for the next day.

Three of the rentals were okay, but I really had my heart set on being right on the beach. I took rental applications, but I still wanted to look more and I started driving.

Leaving Pensacola, I followed the scenic route along the shoreline and an hour later, I was in Panama City Beach. There were a lot of cottages, duplexes and condos and a whole bunch of 'For Rent' signs.

We stopped at a public beach access and Spook took off running and playing in the water. Oh good! I was going to have to get him dried off before putting him back in the car. I grabbed a hotdog and water from a beach vendor and watched Spook play.

I started knocking on doors, and towards late afternoon I was getting tired of looking. There were features I didn't want, and an upstairs resident was definitely one of them. I didn't want the apartment complex atmosphere, I didn't want the one room cottage, but I did want to be on the beach. By narrowing my options, I was losing ground and getting disillusioned.

Finally, I spotted what appeared to be the perfect spot, a duplex. The owner was not there, but the other tenant had the key to let me in and look around. I was right. This was the perfect place for Spook and me.

Fully furnished, including the kitchen wares, deck furniture and a carport. Upstairs were three bedrooms, (I only needed one), one and a half bathrooms, (I only needed one), and open living room and kitchen downstairs. It couldn't get any better than this. I asked for the application and wanted to fill it out right then and there and pay the fee. I wanted this place and Mr. and Mrs. Fuller fell in love with Spook immediately.

Mrs. Fuller said, "I need to call Mr. Roberts and be sure he doesn't have any other applicants. I'll be right back."

When she came back she said, "Mr. Roberts was just leaving the office and said he'd come here before going home. He should be here in twenty minutes. Would you like to come in?"

"Thank you, but I think I will go out to the beach and let Spook run for a while, the exercise is good for him. We'll be right out front." I smiled and started for the beach.

Spook took off on a wild chase after some birds, up and down the beach and in and out of the water. It was fun watching him play. I knew I had made the right choice for our new home, for however long it lasted. At least, at this point, I didn't have to worry about leaving in a month.

It had now been over three months since I had left Boston. In some ways it seemed like an eternity, but in most ways it felt like it was only yesterday.

Mr. Roberts showed up within thirty minutes and walked out on the beach to greet Spook and me. Remembering the first encounter Spook had with Josh, I made a quick grab for his collar. This would not be a good beginning for Spook to latch on to the landlord's pant leg.

We shook hands, made our introductions and headed back up to the deck of the duplex. I was already nervous about filling out an application knowing my name and social security number were not going to match. I didn't have a rental history and I was unemployed. How much worse could it get?

Well, it did. The first thing Mr. Roberts did was hand me his business card – Dwayne Alan Roberts – Attorney at Law. My heart sank and I was sure I had turned white as a ghost.

"Are you okay, Ms. Browning?" He asked obviously seeing my facial color change and my surprised expression.

"Yes, I'm okay. I guess I need to know first if my dog is going to be an issue. I should have asked if pets were accepted before you made the trip out here."

"Yes, we are an animal family, however, we do prefer no cats. We have three doxies of our own and our children all have doxies. In fact, we often dog sit for one or the other and occasionally we get'em all."

"Well, this is Spook. I actually acquired him about a month ago when he appeared on the porch where I was staying. He's turned out to be a real good companion. So far he's not a barker, completely housebroken and has a huge appetite." I patted Spook on the head and smiled at Mr. Roberts.

"Great. Then let's go in and look around and see if this will work for you, and if so, we'll go through the application process."

I took a deep breath as we went inside the apartment. I still didn't know how I was going to handle the application part.

"Mrs. Fuller has already shown the place to me and I really like it, so I guess all I need to do is the application. How much is the rent and fees and what is your processing time?"

"The application fee is $35.00 and it only takes a couple hours, but considering the time of day it is now, I won't be able to process it until tomorrow. Rent is $950 per month, first and last and $400 pet fee. So, why don't you take the application, take your time filling it out, think about it and if you are still interested, you can drop it off at my office tomorrow. I can have my secretary process it. Then, I'll give you a call. Okay? Where are you staying now?"

"Right now I'm in a motel in Pensacola. I've been housesitting in New Orleans for the past month. So I'm available to move in as soon as I'm approved. What is the length of your lease?"

Mr. Roberts raised an eyebrow of concern to my quick availability. At least that's what I was reading into it. "The lease is six months or one year, obviously I would prefer a year. This is the first time we have rented other than for vacationers. But we would accept a six month lease."

I took the application and as we were walking out of the apartment I asked Mr. Roberts, "What kind of lawyer are you?"

"I am a tax and wealth management attorney, some family practice but not that much. I have a partner that takes most family issues, but I get a few."

Oh, my God! The lights went on in my head. I had stumbled on to a gold mine if I could make it work out.

"Mr. Roberts, it was nice meeting you and I will have the application back to you in the morning. What will be a good time?"

"I will only be in the office in the morning, I take Friday afternoons off to extend the weekend. You can leave it with my secretary and she can handle it. If you have any questions, you can call and speak with Julie."

"Thank you, I'll be by in the morning."

CHAPTER 27

Driving back to Pensacola, my head was swimming. Spook had gotten in the back seat and was immediately asleep. He had run himself to death.

I don't even know how I found the motel again and I certainly didn't remember the drive. My thoughts went from falsifying the rental application to thinking I'd found someone that could help me with the information I had on Trevor. I was scared and excited all at the same time.

I purchased more ice for the ice chests, and when I returned to the motel, drained off the water. Taking the application and some fruit, Spook and I went to the park. He lay in the grass until another dog appeared and he was off and running.

The application was staring back at me and I was dreading to start filling it out. "Okay, Wendy get with it and fill the damned thing out and face the music." I said to myself, but then realized I had said it out loud.

Precisely as I suspected, the questions were going to be impossible to answer. I put N/A, not applicable, in the spaces for former address, social security number, bank account and previous landlords. Most of the questions I could answer accurately, but the current and important ones were certainly going to raise the 'red flag'.

Counting my money, I separated twenty three hundred dollars for the duplex. I could only hope I would be able to talk my way through the application process.

The next morning, I packed everything back into the car and checked out of the motel. Spook and I headed for Panama City Beach and Mr. Roberts' Law office.

Julie, a very attractive middle aged woman, greeted me most pleasantly, "You must be Ms. Browning? Mr. Roberts said you'd be in this morning."

"Seems I have nothing else to do until I can settle into a place. I brought the application for you to process. Is Mr. Roberts in yet?"

"No, he usually doesn't come in until around ten on Fridays. I will give you a call as soon as I have this processed."

Reluctantly, I left the office and just sat in the car for few minutes. As I was pulling out of the office parking, lot I saw Mr. Roberts driving in. I almost went back so I could talk with him, but thought better of it.

Driving around trying to familiarize myself with the area, I found it to be quite compact. It appeared that everything I would need was close and I didn't need much. What I really needed was to get my own place so I could get back to writing again and take care of the Trevor issue. That shouldn't be too much to ask for. After a while, I went back to the office parking lot to wait for Julie's call.

When my phone rang I was surprised to hear Mr. Roberts on the other end. "Ms. Browning? Ms. Alicia Browning?"

"Yes."

"This is Dwayne Roberts. I've gone over your application for the duplex and there are several places you have neglected to fill out. I'm afraid I can't process this app with the information you have provided. I'm sorry, but I'm going to have to refuse tenancy."

"Mr. Roberts, may I come in and talk with you and explain? There is most definitely a legitimate reason for the voids. I would really appreciate the chance to explain. I promise I won't take up much of your time. Please?"

"Ms. Downing I have thirty minutes before my next appointment. If you can be here in a couple minutes I'll see you."

"I'm in the parking lot in front of your office, I'll be right in."

"Thank you so much for seeing me, Mr. Roberts. I'll try and explain this as quickly as I can."

Mr. Roberts leaned back in his chair and said, "Okay, what's going on?"

I took a deep breath and started in. "Four months ago, I ended a four year abusive marriage and left two adorable stepchildren. Trevor, my ex, made several threats on my life and concluded as we left the courtroom, saying, 'we were not done and he would see me dead'. With police guarding the house, I was able to get my belongings out and put them in storage. I packed the car with clothes and personal items, computer and writing materials and immediately left Boston. I cut and colored my hair. I traded in the car, forging Trevor's name and titled the new car in my new assumed name and acquired insurance at the same time. I was able to find a place in Kentucky and I stayed there for a month. At a dinner party, one of the guests was sure she recognized me as Wendy Nobel, the author of several published novels. I panicked and left in the middle of the night."

"You are actually Wendy Nobel? My wife has a couple of your books." He smiled and leaned forward in his chair. "Go on."

"I thought I was being tailed by a black car with dark tinted windows, but I wasn't sure. I finally made it to New Orleans. After a couple days, by chance I found a couple looking for a house sitter for a month or more while they were on vacation. I was tailed a couple times there and was able to ditch whoever the follower was and just holed up in this house on the Pearl River. During that time I acquired Spook, the dog you met. Then the person tailing me found me at the house and I panicked again and ran.

"I traded my car in again. I got a motel for a couple nights then headed for Pensacola and Panama City Beach. I couldn't figure out why Trevor was so hateful, vindictive and obsessed with trying to find me. Then, I discovered some files on my computer and with the help of a friend; we figured out some coded files that I believe are records of a financial scam Trevor is involved with. I have made three different copies of these files to CDs.

"So therein lies why I couldn't give you former addresses, a social security number or a bank account, I don't have one. There you have it, the short version of my life in the last four plus months."

Mr. Roberts sat back in his chair again and smiled. "That's quite a story. And as crazy as it is, I almost believe you."

"I can assure you every bit of it is the truth. There is only one person that I can give you to verify it. If you want I will give you his name and phone number. Please, you've got to believe me, I really need this apartment. I would like to hire you to help me with these files and advise me which direction I need to go. I know today is not the time to start on that. But I'm not going to get a rental based on the information I can provide. I'll stay in a motel until you have a chance to follow up on what I have told you."

"Okay, this is what I'm going to do. I'm not going to process this app right now. Instead, we'll just enter into a month to month for the time being." Mr. Roberts continued, "Before I decide to take your case, we need to have an in-depth conversation and I need to see what you have. Let's take a look at my schedule for next week and go from there."

"Thank you, Mr. Roberts, I promise you I won't let you down and you won't be sorry."

Before I left the office, we had scheduled an appointment for the following Tuesday and Julie gave me all the information for the duplex.

When I got in the car, I was so excited I didn't know whether to laugh or cry, so I did both. Poor Spook sat in the passenger seat and stared at me and then laid his head in my lap.

CHAPTER 28

I unloaded the car in record time by putting everything in the living room. A very neat living room immediately turned into a dump. I was thrilled to have my own place for more than a few days or month. Spook seemed to sense the same thrill as he ran out front chasing birds and found other dogs to play with.

After unpacking and cleaning out my ice chest, I started making a list of things I needed to purchase. The first thing I observed was there were no bed linens, bedding and pillows or bathroom linens. All of that sort of stuff was in my storage in Boston, but wasn't doing me any good there.

I mixed a drink and went out on the patio and continued with my list and watched Spook. He was having the time of his life.

"Yoo-hoo, I see you got the place." Mrs. Fuller hollered as she appeared around the corner of the partition that separated the two patios.

Startled, I replied, "Yes I did. I was just sitting here making a list of things I need like bed sheets and towels and a few grocery staples. I've been traveling pretty light."

"I won't bother you, but if you need anything at all, please don't hesitate to ask. Curly and I are retired and just hang around and enjoy the view. We bought our unit almost fifteen years ago and love it here."

"Thank you Mrs. Fuller, that is really sweet of you, but I think I will be fine. I will certainly keep that in mind, though."

"Please call me Rachel, Mrs. Fuller is my mother-in-law. She doesn't like me any better today than she did when Curly and I got married forty five years ago." She smiled and turned to walk to their patio, "See ya later."

"Thank you. See ya."

Finished with my list, I called Spook in and dried him off best I could and put him inside on his blanket. Now I was off shopping.

After three hours going from store to store, including a pet shop to get a fluffy bed and some toys for Spook, I headed back to the duplex. We were set for a while.

That evening I called to see if Betty and Bob had gotten home from Hawaii okay. Betty answered cheerfully and made me chuckle, "Hi Betty, this is Alicia. How was the vacation?"

"Hey there, Alicia, our vacation was okay, I'm sure I had a better time than Bob. For some reason, he just wasn't into Hawaii this year. I think he got homesick for that damned boat." She laughed. "How are you and how was your stay here? By the way, thank you for leaving everything so nice and clean, I sure didn't expect that."

"I'm just fine. I need to confess and tell you, while I was at your house a stray dog came by and never left. I tried to locate the owner and made several calls but no one ever claimed him and he is still with me. There was an old blanket in the garage I used for his bed and some rags I used to be sure he was clean when he came in the house, I brought them with me so I will send you some money for them."

"Don't be silly, those were old blankets we had for our dog that we just never got rid of. It's no big deal."

"Spook is a German Short Hair, a great companion, for sure. Thank you for allowing me to stay at your place. It was nice and quiet and I enjoyed the visits I had with your neighbor." I had suddenly forgotten his name.

"You are welcome and it was our pleasure to have someone staying here and to come back to it so clean. Thank you."

"Well, I need to get going, I just wanted to touch base and say thank you. You two take care and say 'hi' to Bob."

"You too and thanks again." And we hung up.

Out on the patio, Spook and I were having dinner, Spook dog food and me a sandwich and chips. My phone rang, it was Allison.

"Hi, how ya doin?" She said.

"Doin great. I found a duplex and Spook and I just got moved in today. It is perfect for us. How bout you guys?"

"Well, I'm not sure. I just ran down to the store to pick up a few things and wanted to call you. Something's going on with Matt and I can't put my finger on it. We've had several heated discussions about a number of different things that never were issues before. I don't think things are going well at work but I can't get him to talk about it and he just takes his frustrations out at home. No big deal, this too will pass, just not a place we've ever been during our marriage. But I do want to ask you not to call on the land line, call me on my cell. If I can't talk, I'll say 'sorry, wrong number' and I'll call you back."

"Allison, I'm so sorry. What do you think is going on?"

"I don't know, but I'm pretty sure it's work related and that's an off limits conversation and always has been."

"That was the same with Trevor, but you've never said anything before about Matt being like that. Do you think he's gotten into something he shouldn't be in?"

"Oh no, it's nothing like that. I think he's under more pressure and with the economy the way it is, it's getting to him. Anyway, enough about that. I wanted to check and see how things are going with you. Are you going to get back to writing again and how is the new beau? Did you kiss and make up?"

"Allison, he never was a beau, just a friend that went a little further than friendship, and no we didn't kiss and make up. I probably won't be hearing from Josh anymore. He was really upset with me when he left. And no, I haven't been writing, but I will. I don't plan to be moving for quite a while."

"Wendy, I need to get back home and start dinner. I just wanted to touch base with you and be sure you're okay. Maybe you and Josh will patch it up with time, that would be nice for you. And don't worry about me and Matt, just a little bump in the road. Gotta run. Love ya. Talk to ya soon."

"Love ya, too, and you take care." I was shocked to hear Allison say something was going on with Matt. I had this gut feeling that Josh was right. I couldn't say anything to Allison about our suspicions about Matt, I knew I should, but I couldn't bring myself to be the one to tell her. Maybe in time, but not right now. I wasn't positively sure I was right about Trevor. Bullshit! I knew I was right about Trevor, I just didn't know how deep he was involved and in what.

After a very busy day and stressful meeting with Mr. Roberts, I was exhausted. Shopping wears me out since I'm not one that enjoys just looking around for the fun of it. I got everything I needed and hopefully that was the end of it for a while.

CHAPTER 29

Morning came very fast and I had slept like a baby. The sun was shining through the drapes and when I opened them, there didn't appear to be any wind. It was going to be a gorgeous day.

Waiting for the coffee to brew, I let Spook out and watched from the patio. Today was going to be a great writing day. I filled Spook's food dish, got my computer and coffee and situated myself on the patio, still in my P Js.

I wanted to call Josh, but I was sure he wouldn't answer his phone and he had every right not to. Then I remembered he and Jim were off on a racing trip with the horses. Perfect, I could call and leave a message on his home phone.

Procrastinating whether or not to call Josh, I finally called. The answering machine message came on and I listened intently to his voice. I missed that voice and it had only been five days.

"Josh, this is Alicia. I know you were going to be off with Jim racing horses or maybe you are just screening your calls. Just kidding. Anyway, I wanted to let you know what's going on with me and Spook. I found a three bedroom townhouse duplex right on the beach. There is a patio off the living room and a deck off the master upstairs. It is perfect for us and Spook loves it. He spent most of the afternoon yesterday chasing birds or other dogs. Ironically, the landlord is an attorney and I told him very briefly about the CD's and asked if he would be interested in taking the case. We have an appointment on Tuesday to go over everything more thoroughly, I'm really excited. Well, I guess I better get off here. I just wanted to bring you up to date and say hi. I hope you are having good luck and fun at the races."

Several thoughts were going on in my head, all at the same time and I couldn't get them sorted out. I felt horrible about what I had done to Josh but I knew I had to let it go, for now anyway. I was terribly upset about Allison and Matt and there was nothing I could do about it. I didn't know what would happen to Sheila and Billy when this all came down on Trevor. It broke my heart to think the kids could go into foster care.

Trevor had been an only child and his parents had been killed in an auto accident. Ironically a similar automobile mechanical failure caused an accident, that also took his wife's life. Briefly, my thoughts went back to a newspaper I'd found in the attic that had questioned an auto mechanic and then Trevor about his parent's accident. I wondered if I had stayed if that accident would've happened to me. Trevor never spoke of any other family members, another subject that was off limits.

Spook had finally had enough running for a while and was sleeping on his blanket I'd put on the patio.

Back in the house I poured more coffee, went upstairs and jumped in the shower, threw on some clothes, made the bed and went downstairs, fixed a fried egg sandwich and went back outside.

It had been a couple of weeks since I had done any writing. I had to go back and refresh my mind.

I had left off with the horrible trip to Las Vegas when Trevor and I were to be married. He had stayed out all night. I assumed gambling, and still had not returned to the room by noon. So, I picked up from there.

In the casino, I walked around searching for Trevor. Today was to be our wedding and it was not starting out well. This should have been one of several red flags thrown up. After an hour of looking, I knew this was not the relationship I thought I was getting into and I went up to the room to pack and go back to Boston.

After packing my suitcase, I called the front desk for a cab and send a bellman up for my bag. I was standing in front of the hotel waiting for my taxi when Trevor pulled up in another cab. He was a total mess, looking as though he had slept in his clothes for a week and appeared to be very inebriated.

"Oh, my God, Trevor! Where the hell have you been, you son-of-a-bitch?"

Trevor looked at me and said, "Please, don't start, just help me to our room and I will explain everything."

"Trevor, this is supposed to be our wedding day. This is not what I want in our marriage. I am calling this whole thing off and going back to Boston."

"Please……………." and with that he stumbled and passed out, at least, that is what I thought. The bellman called for the house doctor and they got him inside on a sofa. The doctor examined Trevor and said he thought he was having a heart attack. The doctor wanted to send him to the hospital, but when Trevor rallied enough to hear 'hospital', he immediately went into a refusal mode and insisted he was just fine. All he wanted was to sleep. Refusing medical attention, there was no choice but to take him up to our room and, of course, I followed.

Trevor slept the rest of the afternoon. I ordered soup, toast, juice and coffee from room service but he barely ate any of it.

When he woke, he was extremely apologetic and had every excuse in the world to explain how this had happened. He had run into a couple business colleagues and time just got away. They had left the hotel and gone to another bar and met up with some other colleagues and he didn't know where he was. His friends had insisted they would bring him back to the hotel, but they were having way too much fun playing cards and drinking to leave when he wanted.

Trevor finally got up, showered and we went downstairs for dinner. The conversation was light and Trevor refused to talk about his old friends, claiming it was just business and it would be more than boring for me. He repeatedly apologized for his behavior and how bad he felt for having left me. He knew he'd been rude but he'd been so uptight before we left Boston that he'd considered no one other than himself. He assured me this had never happened before and promised it would never happen again. He loved me more than anything in the world and the wedding would go on as planned, only a day later. Of course, I fell for it, hook, line and sinker.

The wedding ceremony was beautiful and Trevor kept telling me how beautiful I looked, and he would cherish and take care of me forever.

Our honeymoon night was exquisite. Trevor made love to me like he had never done before. He was passionate and gentle yet bringing me to an exited high with every touch. It was a perfect honeymoon night.

I'd had enough writing and reminiscing, I closed the computer.

CHAPTER 30

I knew it was going to be a long week end until my appointment with Mr. Roberts on Tuesday. Spook and I went for several walks on the beach and it felt good to get out. Exercise had not been important to me since I had left Boston. But Spook was good for me to at least get some fresh air. This was the most relaxed I had felt since I had left the ranch.

My thoughts went to Josh and I was curious as to how successful the races had been. I wondered if he was still really mad at me or extremely hurt, and I suspected it was both. He had every right to be both. I needed to move on and not think about Josh because I knew I couldn't do anything about it. He's in Kentucky and I'm in Florida and that is the way it has to be.

I went back to my writing.

When we got home from Las Vegas, Sheila and Billy were thrilled to see us. They both chattered like little magpies and both trying to talk and ask questions at the same until Trevor lost it and ordered them back to their rooms.

Once again, I tried to talk to Trevor about being so harsh with the kids, they are only excited to see us and hear all about the wedding. We needed to spend some time with them and share our happiness and we shouldn't shut them out.

But Trevor's response was if I wanted to fill them in on that crap, then go ahead, he was too tired and going to bed. That was pretty much Trevor's attitude with his children during our marriage, so I played referee most of the time. The kids and I would spend time together when Trevor was either at work or asleep. We had a very close, trusting relationship and as time went on, Trevor became more resentful of my time with his children. I could never understand his resentment. But there were a number of things I never understood about Trevor and the numbers continued to grow.

After Thanksgiving, that first year Trevor and I were married, he was to attend a conference in Las Vegas and would be gone for a week, Sunday through Saturday. Sheila and Billy told me they had not had Christmas decorations up since their mom died. So we decided it would be fun to surprise Daddy when he got home to find the house all lit up.

As soon as Trevor left on Sunday we got boxes of decorations out from under the stairwell. We checked all the bulbs for the outside strings of lights. We started decorating the house inside and having a great time. By that evening the inside was a knockout and the kids were thrilled, even putting some decorations in their rooms.

On Monday, I called the high school and asked for their director of fund raising for the students. The Honor Society boys would put Christmas lights up on the outside of the house as their project. I could also purchase a Christmas tree from the Athletic Club and they would deliver. We were set and excited.

When the kids got home from school, we went out a couple evenings for Christmas shopping. I had given Sheila and Billy money so they could purchase gifts for each other and their dad and they sneaked in a couple things for me. They had so much fun wrapping and hiding their presents from each other, it was equally as thrilling for me.

While I was rearranging the boxes in the stairwell to put the empty decoration boxes away, I found a box that was full of pictures of the kids' mother. I thought it strange that there were no pictures of her in the house and certainly none in Sheila or Billy's rooms. I asked them about it and they both said their dad wouldn't let them have any pictures. She was dead and out of their life and they didn't need to be reminded of the painful ordeal. How sad they were not allowed to remember their mother.

By Friday evening, the night before Trevor was coming home, the house was decorated inside and out, the tree had lots of packages under it and looked fabulous. The kids were anxious for their dad to get home and see what they had done.

The three of us were standing in the hall smiling and waiting for our praise and admiration of all our work when Trevor came home.

None of us were prepared for Trevor's explosive tantrum that erupted the moment he walked in the door. What we encountered had me speechless. "What the hell is all of this? I want it taken down and out of my sight." Trevor glared at me, "You had no right to put this shit up in my house. Get it out!" The kids started crying, turned and ran to their rooms.

"You have got to be kidding. What is the matter with you? This is what Christmas is all about and we are not taking it down. Get used to it." And I stormed out.

Trevor and I had a serious fight about that holiday season, but in the end we did leave the decorations up. It was understood that as long as I was in that house, and the kids were still home, it would be a Holiday tradition like all other American Christian families. And we did.

I had spent most of the weekend writing and taking walks with Spook on the beach. But every time I sat down to write '*My Story*' I would get depressed all over again. I had to limit my writing time even though it felt good to have the space and time to write.

My thoughts wandered to my appointment with Mr. Roberts and whether or not he was going to take my case. I was thinking about Allison and Matt and curious how things were going in their home. I wanted to call her but knew I shouldn't. End result, I did call Allison.

When I called Allison's cell phone, I was not surprised that she answered me with, "I'm sorry, you have the wrong number." Then she hung up.

CHAPTER 31

Tuesday morning, I was up early, gathered papers, my computer and all the notes Josh and I'd made. I was nervous, yet excited at the same time.

"Come in, Ms. Browning, have a seat." Mr. Roberts said and motioned to the chair in front of his desk.

"Thank you and thank you for looking at these files."

"Let's see what you have."

I had brought a folder with the files Josh and I'd put together, one of the CDs and my computer. Explaining all of the steps Josh and I'd gone through and watching Mr. Roberts's expression, I could hardly keep focused. Mr. Roberts had no expression one way or the other and I was getting nervous not knowing what to think.

Sitting back in my chair, I waited for him to ask some questions or give me some indication of interest, or just give me an indication of something.

Mr. Roberts finally leaned back in his chair, putting his folded hands behind his head, and said, "I think Mr. Aston has gotten himself into more trouble than he ever bargained for. But, before I make any kind of commitment to you, I'd like to have my partner go over this information with me. Do you have a problem leaving all of this with me for a few days?"

Smiling I said, "Do you mean my computer too? I made copies of the original files found in my 'Guest' files. I have copies of the revised version that

I'll leave with you. I would really prefer not to leave my computer. I'm in the process of writing a book and I would be lost without it."

"Let us study this and I will get back to you. In the meantime, don't worry any more than you already have.

"Will I have to go back to Boston?"

"If my findings warrant a grand jury hearing, then yes, you will have to go to Boston to testify. It is out of your hands now."

Leaving Mr. Roberts' office, I was excited and scared all at the same time. Going back to Boston was the last thing I ever wanted to do.

By the time I got back to the duplex, my head was swimming, going from one thought to another. It was going to be a long few days waiting for Mr. Roberts to go over all the information I'd taken to him.

Spook and I went for a long walk on the beach. I walked, he ran as fast as he could, chasing everything in sight. I threw sticks and he retrieved. It was good for both of us, got my mind off stuff and gave Spook the exercise he needed.

Settling in for the evening, I tried to get interested in television and nothing appealed to me. I hadn't heard from Allison since she'd hung up and that made me nervous that something was seriously wrong. I needed to talk to someone and I knew I couldn't talk to Allison about the files. Josh hadn't called back either, but I guess I didn't really expect that he would. I had hurt the best friend I'd had in a very long time. I didn't know how much I missed Josh until he was really out of my life. I couldn't call him, not now. Another bad decision for which I would pay the consequences.

∽

The next few days, I tried to keep occupied to prevent myself from fretting about having to go to Boston to testify.

Back at the computer, I continued on with *'My Story'*. **Things seemed to go along fairly smoothly for the most part. We certainly had our ups and** *downs and I quickly learned the areas of which I dared not enter and lines I dared not cross. However, I felt I had established my own lines of family standards and moral issues. Most of our arguments were about the children and Trevor's strictness and the lack of affection he showed Sheila and Billy, and me, for showing too much.*

I did the best I could to be congenial and keep everything running smoothly and I devoted as much time as I could to the kids. We'd get homework done right after school and then play games until time to start dinner. Sheila and Billy were always in their room when Trevor got home from work. Sometimes Trevor met clients after work and didn't make it home for dinner, but I had learned not to ask where he'd been, why he was late or who he was with.

My friends soon stopped coming to the house for dinner or cocktails. I had either not noticed the subtleties of Trevor's rudeness and sarcasm towards my friends, or chose to ignore them until one day it was very obvious and I could no longer ignore it. Trevor had been so condescending and sarcastic towards a girlfriend and her husband and then laughed. It finally sunk in that Trevor's humor was sarcasm at everyone else's expense.

I thought I was strong and assertive, but soon realized I wasn't. I also learned to pick my battles. Making my point on most issues in our marriage became an ongoing effort to change a man that could care less about anyone other than himself. I gave up trying and chose to meet my friends elsewhere.

One day, I was rearranging my office in the loft and putting some stuff in boxes in the storage area of the attic. The storage was rather unorganized and I decided to straighten it up and mark some boxes for identification.

I needed an empty box so I was trying to consolidate and label as I went. My project was going along very nicely as I emptied boxes, refilled and labeled. The last box clear back in the corner was stuck and hard to get out and heavy. I thought about just leaving it but I wanted to get it labeled and start putting them all back and keep my stuff separate.

Finally, getting that last box out so I could see what was in it, I discovered newspaper articles about Trevor's parents who had been killed in an automobile accident. The accident had been almost twelve years prior.

There had been a police investigation and Trevor had been questioned extensively as a person of interest. His parents' car had been tampered with, the brakes had failed and the car plunged over an embankment and burst into a fiery inferno. The car had been destroyed by the fire, consequently, leaving no tangible evidence.

Trevor had filed a civil suit against the shop owner where he had taken his parents' car for an engine checkup prior to their taking a trip. I scanned through the article and read that the mechanic shop owner had not been charged with wrongful death or product liability for failed brakes.

The kids were coming in from school and I hurriedly put boxes back in the attic. I hollered to the kids that I'd be right there and to hang up coats. I quickly put some old tax files in a box and some manuscripts I planned to get at someday and put them in the storage part of the attic and shut the door.

When I stood up and started for the stairs I was startled to see Trevor standing there, smiling I walked towards him to give him a kiss. He turned his head to avoid the kiss and accused me of snooping in the attic.

I tried to assure him I wasn't snooping, I was cleaning out some old taxes and manuscripts of mine, put them in a couple boxes and put them in the attic to get them out of the way. I was merely tidying up my office. Then I made the mistake of asking what the hell he was hiding that was such a big secret. That of course started a big fight.

There were so many fights with Trevor. I was constantly walking on egg shells, trying not to provoke him.

My vodka was about gone and after writing I wanted a drink. So off to the liquor store we went, Spook in the front seat as usual.

When we got back and I pulled into the driveway of the condo, starting to open the back door, I could see through to the patio some guy looking in the window. I picked up a stick of drift wood, and walked around to the edge of the patio. Just as I was getting ready to swing at this guy, he turned startled to see me, I connected with the stick to the side of his head and he went down with a groan.

He started muttering, "I'm sorry, I'm sorry, I'm so sorry don't hit me again."

Yelling at him, "Who are you? What are you doing here?" He cringed further away and Spook was in an attack mode on top of the man.

I had the stick in upward position when Curly came around to my patio. "I heard some yelling, are you okay?"

"Call 9-1-1!" I yelled.

Then Curly leaned down to take a closer look at the person on the patio, "Carl, what the hell are you doing here?" Turning towards me Curly said, "This is my twin brother, we don't need to call 9-1-1."

"Curly, I'm sorry, I thought I was looking in your window. I knocked on the door and could hear the television, but you didn't come to the door."

After talking about the incident and understanding it was an accident and confusion. Carl was at the wrong place and wrong time and definitely had picked the wrong person to window peek.

Curly and Rachel were so apologetic and more than embarrassed as was Carl. In the end, it could've been funny for everyone other than me.

Now, I really needed a drink.

CHAPTER 32

Calling Allison, it immediately went to her voicemail, so I left a brief message. I wanted to call Josh so badly, but I knew I shouldn't. He had made his position very clear when he walked away.

Spook and I went for a run on the beach and as usual, Spook would run way ahead of me and then run back, turn and run ahead again. I picked up a stick, threw it as hard as I could, quickly realizing how out of shape I was. One of these days I will get back to exercising like I used to.

Watching Spook chase anything that moved, I wondered what his previous owners must be thinking. Do they miss him, did they ever look for him? They had to love him because he was so well trained and gentle. But, I was the lucky one, Spook found me.

Fascinated by the variety of structures and landscaping of the beach homes, I watched Spook chasing birds. I was laughing as he come running back to me, straight at me, suddenly jumped on me and pushed me out of the way of a vehicle racing down the beach. I had not heard that vehicle coming up from behind. My only vision was the back end of a pickup as it raced down the beach. I was in shock and just sat there in the sand.

Residents from the houses along the beach started running towards me. "Are you alright?" Everything was such a blur, so confusing and noisy, that I couldn't focus. The next thing I remember was Spook licking me on my face.

Everyone was so concerned, talking all at once, wanting to help me. All I wanted to do was take Spook and go back to the condo. "I'm alright, thank you so much, I need to go." Then I heard a siren, it was the beach patrol. Minutes later, I heard more sirens and saw an ambulance and two police cars racing down the beach. Crap, I didn't want this, not the police.

Three Panama City Officers drilled and questioned the witnesses while one of the officers questioned me about the incident.

"Officer, I didn't see or hear the car coming. If it hadn't been for my dog, the car would have run me down."

"Do you have any idea who would want to run you down?" The officer asked.

I didn't want to get into the whole story so I said, "He must have thought I was someone else or wasn't paying attention. I have no idea who it could be. I'm afraid I can't give you any information. Can I go, I just want to take my dog and go home."

"I need information from you so we can contact you later. Here is my card in case you remember anything else."

After I gave the officer information, my false identification, assuring him I was unharmed, Spook and I walked down the beach towards the condo. Obviously, I was terribly shaken and just wanted to get behind closed doors and hide.

Inside the house, after checking all the locks and closing the drapes, I poured myself a stiff drink. I had to sort through all this. The vehicle that tried to run me down was not the black sedan with blackened windows, but a silver or gray pickup.

The person in the black car had always stayed his distance, only keeping track of my location. So, who was this person that was determined to run me down? And, how had he found me? Obviously, I was under closer surveillance than I'd thought and that terrified me.

My mind was racing from one thought to another. Was the person in the pickup actually Trevor? It couldn't have been because he would want my computer. But then, if he knew where I lived, he could kill me and then break in and take the computer. Maybe things were closing in on him and he needed to get those files to clean them up. No, I don't think he could clean up those files. He was too far into that scam.

Matt came into my thoughts and I wondered how involved they were together in this, or if they were at all. I needed to talk to Allison, but she had not returned my call.

This really sucked. I couldn't talk to Allison like I always had. I wanted to talk to Josh, but he was too far away to be of any help and I didn't know if he even cared anymore. I hadn't talked with him since we were in New Orleans.

Checking the time and knowing it was two hours earlier, Pacific Time, I figured Allison would be home from work by now. I was surprised when she answered as I had expected her voice mail greeting.

"Allison, how are you? When you didn't return my call I got worried. Everything okay?"

"I'm sorry I didn't call you back. It has been a little crazy around here. But we're fine." She didn't sound too convincing, not her usual cheery tone.

"Good, so what have you been up to?"

"Not much, just trying to stay neutral. Work is about the same, always busy. Matt had to make a trip to Las Vegas and a spur of the moment trip to Atlanta. He's still cranky with his work and bringing that attitude home. I just stay out of his way."

"When did he go to Atlanta? I wish you'd gone with him, I could've met you there."

"He's still there. He left in such a hurry I couldn't get off from work. That would have been fun, but I didn't think of it at the time. I was just looking forward to the time alone and not having to deal with his attitude."

I stopped breathing. Oh, My God! Could that have been Matt in that truck? Stop this! You're being paranoid. You've known Matt way too long and there is no way he would do something like this to his wife's best friend.

"Hello? Wendy, are you still there?"

"Yes, I'm still here, I was pouring some coffee."

"That would've been fun if I could've flown out with Matt. It has been too long since we've been together. How bout you and I plan a trip to Las Vegas in the next month or so? I could sure swing a few days off from work. What'd ya think?"

"I think that is a great idea, let's work on it. Allison, I need to go, I have to check on Spook. I'll call you soon. Call me anytime. Bye." And I abruptly hung up.

Wow! What did I just hear? Should I call the police officer who gave me his card and tell him of this possibility? NO! Of course I can't. It is totally ridiculous to give one second thought to the idea that Matt could be after me.

What would I tell the police? I didn't have one bit of evidence that there was any kind of connection between Trevor and Matt. Besides, I would have to tell the officer everything and I wasn't prepared to do that. It took everything I had to put my trust in Mr. Roberts and I still didn't have any answers from him. I needed to sit on this and hope whoever this truck driver was didn't come back.

Of course, of all evenings, the wind came up and by night it had kicked up quite a gale. Trees brushing up against the condo, wind and rain blowing so strong it rattled the windows at times and I was sure someone was trying to break in. I got very little sleep and felt like I had a hangover the next morning. But it was another day and I would deal with it.

I couldn't get Matt out of my mind. I needed to talk to someone and I only had two choices, Josh and Mr. Roberts. Josh still had not called me and

I didn't want to be hung up on if I called him. Mr. Roberts had not called for another appointment and Spook didn't get any of this, he just hung out.

Back at the computer, I decided I would write and see if I could get all this crap off my mind, instead, I was taking on another set of crap. My life was one big pile of crap and I was sinking deeper into it.

There was a light knock at the door and it startled me and Spook's hackles went up as he raced to the door.

"Hi, Mrs. Fuller, please come in."

"I can't stay. I wanted to bring you some fresh cinnamon rolls, right out of the oven. I haven't seen much of you, you are a busy one."

Smiling I replied, "I try to keep occupied."

"Did you see what happened on the beach yesterday? A lady was almost run down by a big pickup. We saw the truck driving fast right here in front of our condo. She was lucky."

"Sounds like it." At that moment my phone rang. Mrs. Fuller excused herself and left.

CHAPTER 33

"Ms. Browning? This is Dwayne Roberts. Is there a possibility you could come to the office this afternoon, say about 1:30? My partner and I have gone over your files and have a few questions."

"Absolutely, I will be there at 1:30. Thank you so much."

"You're welcome, see you this afternoon."

Oh, my God, shit is going to fly real soon. Then what? When Trevor finds out he is being investigated there is no telling what measures he is going to take and that thought terrified me even more.

As I was getting ready, my phone rang. "Hey, Alicia, this is Josh. I got your message, how ya doin?"

"Hi Josh, good to hear from you. How am I doing? I don't know if we have enough time to cover all that. Just more drama."

He laughed, "I'm sure, are you alright?"

"I am now. Yesterday I was running with Spook on the beach when a pickup tried to run me down. If Spook hadn't jumped on me I would've been hit. I had no idea who it could've been for a while. You're going to love this, I found an attorney that is looking over the files. In fact, I have an appointment with him this afternoon to answer questions. How were the races?"

"The races were good. So, what did you mean by 'you had no idea who was trying to run you down for a while'? You think you know who it is?"

"Josh, I'm not sure. It is merely a gut feeling and coincidence at this point. I hate to even say it out loud."

"Okay. Well, I guess I better get back to work. You take care."

"Josh, please don't hang up."

"Alicia, what do you want from me? You lead me along so far and then cut me off."

"I'm sorry, Josh. I need you, I need to have someone to talk to and you are the only one I can trust. I know you want more and I can't give that to you right now. I'm not saying it won't ever happen, just not now. I do care about you, Josh, more than you know. Please be my friend and confidante. You have become the only one I can trust and you keep me on track."

"Alicia, I don't know if I can be just a friend. I'm already too emotionally involved and want more for us and you don't. I've had the best and I want that again. I had hoped to have that with you."

"Josh. I'm so preoccupied with all this shit from Trevor I can't think straight most of the time. I do know I have missed you terribly, and I'm truly sorry I've hurt you. I never wanted to hurt you, I hope you know that."

"I'm sure you didn't Alicia." Josh's silence was deafening.

"Josh, can I call you back this evening? I need to get ready for my appointment with the attorney. Then, I can fill you in with what he has to say."

"I won't be home this evening. I'll call you in a couple days." Josh hung up. He sounded so cool and matter of fact and I guess I couldn't blame him.

I let Spook out to run for a little bit and I sat in the sand just beyond the patio. When my phone rang, I answered and all I heard was a muffled disguised voice, "You won't be so lucky next time. Better watch your back side." And my phone went dead. Immediately I checked the number and it had been blocked.

At that moment, I made up my mind I was not going to run again. It didn't matter where I was, this person seemed to find me. The only place I'd been safe was at the ranch. I probably should've stayed there and the rest of this shit wouldn't have happened. Maybe!

The office wasn't open when I arrived at 1:15, so I waited in the parking lot. Julie was the first to return from lunch and I followed her into the office.

"Hello, Ms. Browning. Have a seat, Mr. Roberts and Mr. Rockfield should be here in just a few minutes."

Seated and thumbing through a magazine, I didn't even see one page or its contents. I was too nervous to concentrate.

The two men came in a few minutes later and Mr. Roberts nodded to me, "We'll be right with you."

It wasn't long until Julie's phone rang and she told me I could go into Mr. Roberts' office.

"Ms. Browning, this is Harry Rockfield, he is my partner and a private investigator. We have several questions to ask about these files. First and foremost, how did you discover these files and what made you look for them on your computer?"

"Like I told you, Trevor threatened me after the divorce and I believe he has had me followed. I couldn't figure out why, because people get divorces every day. A friend of mine suggested maybe it was my computer Trevor wanted. So he went into 'guest' files and found all these files in excel."

"You told me Trevor was an attorney and worked for a firm that deals in financial investments among other aspects of the law. But financing was his expertise."

"Yes, that is correct."

"Mr. Rockfield and I've gone over everything you have given me, and we agree these files are some sort of a 'Ponzi scheme', meaning a scam to manipulate money out of people. If you remember the trial of Bernie Madoff, it is the same sort of thing. Did you know Trevor was involved in this scam during the time you were married?"

"Absolutely not! Trevor made it very clear that he left work at the office and didn't want to discuss it when he got home."

"When did Trevor put these files on your computer?"

"I didn't know they were there until Josh found them. It was Josh's idea to look in the guest files." I was so nervous I was really wishing Josh was sitting beside me.

"We just need to know you were not involved in any way and had no knowledge of these files."

"I swear to you I didn't know anything about these files."

"Do you know anyone else that was involved, co-workers or associates?"

"Not for sure. I didn't know Trevor's co-workers, only socially, cocktail parties or dinners and that's it."

"What do you mean by 'not for sure?"

Suddenly I felt chilled and shaky. "I hate to say anything because I don't know for sure, but a couple days ago, I was running with my dog on the beach and a pickup tried to run me down. And just before I was coming here today, I got a muffled call on my cell, 'You were lucky this time. Better watch your back'."

"Do you know who it was?"

"Not really, and it makes me sick to even think about it. The voice was muffled"

"Alicia, you have to tell us everything, even if you don't think it is important, if we are going to get to the bottom of all this."

So far Mr. Rockfield hadn't said anything, he just sat in his chair listening intently and taking notes.

"It is so complicated." I tried to summarize my friendship with Allison, the repeated questions from Matt regarding my investments, Allison telling me Matt was in Atlanta at the same time I was almost run down– too coincidental- Allison catching Matt in lies and Matt's sudden change of disposition with his job.

"Did Matt and Trevor work together?"

"I don't know. Matt and Allison live on the west coast. I knew Matt was in the financial investment business, but as far as I ever knew they never worked together."

"Did you call the police after the pickup tried to run you down?"

"No, I didn't have to, the people on the beach did."

"What makes you think the driver was after you?"

"I don't know, but it was no accident, it was intentional."

"Did any of the witnesses identify the driver as male or female?"

"I don't know. I have not had any more conversations with the police."

"We need information on Matt, last name, address, phone numbers and anything you can think of about him. How long have you known him? Could his wife be involved?"

Lowering my head, tears started flowing as I took my address book out of my purse. "I am positive Allison knows nothing about all this. I've known Matt about eleven years since they married, but from afar since they live in Seattle, but I've known Allison most of my life. Allison is not involved."

"I know this is hard for you, but you know we have to do this. Let's call it good for today. Give us a week to look this all over and if we have any questions we'll give you a call. You can schedule an appointment with Julie."

CHAPTER 34

One week later I was sitting in Mr. Roberts' office again and didn't like what he had to say.

"Ms. Browning, we've been in touch with the authorities in Boston and there has been a definite investigation going on with this Ponzi scheme. However, the information you provided is information they didn't have. There have been some arrests made in the last several weeks. Unfortunately, Trevor Aston wasn't one of them. They will be looking for him as well."

"What about Sheila and Billy? What will happen to them?"

"Who are Sheila and Billy?"

"They are Trevor's children."

"I don't have any idea about them, but I'm sure the children will be cared for when they pick up Mr. Aston. There's nothing you can or should do about his children. In the meantime, we have to keep you safe."

Mr. Roberts continued, "The information I'm about to tell you is going to be very upsetting. We checked all the car rentals and traced the pickup to having been leased by your friend, Matt Harper from Seattle, WA. Mr. Harper will be picked up and charged with attempted murder, but he hasn't been found yet."

Even though I suspected Matt, my heart sank into the pit of my stomach. He was right, this was very upsetting to me even though I suspected Matt, and I still didn't want to hear it. "Oh, my, God! Has anyone talked to Allison? What am I going to say to her?"

"I assume they have talked to her. Ms. Browning, you aren't going to say anything to her. You can't talk to her right now. I know this is going to be difficult, but you can't talk to anyone. We are giving you police protection and Julie is arranging that now. It is imperative that we move you to a safe house, away from the condo. Do you understand what I am telling you?"

"Mr. Roberts, I am so tired of running and hiding. This has been going on now for over six months, I can't do this anymore. I just want to go home and let the cards fall where they may."

"Alicia, you don't have a choice in this decision. This has now become an FBI case and you are a prime witness and they want you protected."

"What about my dog, he has to come with me. I need to pick up some personal stuff and Spook." I put my head in my hands and tried to think this through, it just kept getting bigger and bigger. When was this ever going to end? It can't get any worse than it is.

"You will have a female officer go with you to get your dog and whatever you need. In the meantime, you can wait out front in the waiting room. Would you like some coffee? This shouldn't take too long."

"No, thank you, I'm fine."

What seemed like hours, as I waited, was actually less than an hour when two officers walked into the office.

Julie spoke with them and gave them a piece of paper, I assume to be the address of my new home. Mr. Roberts came out and the two officers went in his office.

"What's going on?" I exclaimed.

Julie replied, "Mr. Roberts is explaining the situation to Officers Ort and Ford. They'll be out in just a few minutes. Please sit down and try to relax. I can't imagine what you are going through, hopefully, this will be over soon for you."

"You have no idea what it is like to have your life threatened and then actually have someone you once trusted and loved try to kill you."

Mr. Roberts came out and introduced me to the two officers as Wanda Ort and Jack Ford. Instructions were that they would take me to the condo, get my stuff and Spook and then on to an undisclosed location.

As we were leaving the office the phone rang and Julie answered, excitedly she handed the phone to Mr. Roberts, "It's Mrs. Fuller."

Mr. Roberts put up his hand indicating for us to wait as he stepped back into his office. He came out and put his hands on my shoulders and said to me, "Please sit down."

My heart sank, what now? Mechanically I sat and waited for the next blow.

"Someone has broken into your condo and apparently your dog has been shot. The police said no one is in there now and they have taken the dog to the vet. He is still alive, but I don't know any more than that. Officer Ort is going to take you to the vet right now, while Mr. Rockfield, Officer Ford and I go to the condo. We'll be in touch, but you need to go see your dog right now. Alicia, I am so sorry."

When I stood up, I immediately went to the floor, passed out cold. Julie was wiping my face down with a cold paper towel and Officer Ort was trying to get me sitting upright. I slowly realized what had happened and felt like my whole world was spinning out of control. I was on the fastest merry-go-round in the world and couldn't get off. Everyone was hovering over me trying to bring me around.

"Where is your computer Alicia?" Mr. Roberts asked.

"Under the front seat in my car. I need to go see Spook, please." I said pleading.

"We'll go in just a minute Alicia. Let's get some juice in you first." Juice was a sprite and they had cookies in the office. "When was the last time you ate?"

"I haven't eaten yet today. I want to go see Spook now, I can eat later."

On the way to the clinic Ms. Ort tried to console and comfort me, but it wasn't working. This was becoming too overwhelming for me and I was about to go over the edge. I was totally alone in this ordeal now and possibly losing my dog. I didn't know how much more I could take. I needed Josh here.

Arriving at the clinic the receptionist informed me Spook was in surgery. I filled out the papers with as much information as I had, which was slim to none, considering I had only had him a couple months.

The vet finally came out and introduced himself as Dr. Fred Cutter. "Spook, is it?" I nodded. "He's going to be just fine, he was shot in the right shoulder. I was able to remove the bullet without any difficulty, he should recover one hundred percent. He's going to be sleeping for a while and I would like to keep him overnight and maybe even through tomorrow night. We'll see how he's doing tomorrow. You may as well go home; he's in good hands here. We'll call if there is any change you should know about. We do have a phone number for you?"

Officer Ort stepped up and said, "I'll give you mine; Ms. Browning's is temporarily out of order." I didn't know why she made that statement; my phone was working perfectly. I would address it with her later.

"May I go in and see Spook?" I said, barely holding back a bucket of tears.

"Sure, follow me. He is one lucky guy, that bullet could've only gone a fraction either direction and could've done some serious if not fatal damage."

Spook had a huge bandage wrapped around his torso, a cone type apparatuses over his head and an IV in his front leg. So pathetic looking, but I was glad he was alive and going to be okay.

Instead of being emotional and crying at the sight of Spook, I just got angry with a vengeance towards Trevor. All I could think of now was to hang his ass and everyone he was involved with. This had gone on way too long and now, it was my turn to want Trevor dead.

CHAPTER 35

Once Officer Ort and I were in the car, I said, "Where are we going now?"

"We need to go by your place and get a few personal things and then we're going to the safe house."

"What about my car?"

"It will be taken to the storage lot at the police station. It will be safe there."

"I need to get my computer and cell phone out of it. Can we stop by and get them first?"

"Remember, you can't call anyone." Officer Ort said.

"I know what I can and can't do, don't start treating me like a damn child. I just want to have them with me, okay?" I retorted back to her.

"Yes, of course. Sorry, I didn't mean anything by it."

I got my computer and cell phone out of the car. I had twelve messages on my phone.

When we got to the condo, there were more police cars than I'd ever seen in one place in my life. Yellow tape strung across the front, and officers everywhere.

They let us in and I was flabbergasted at the mess. Furniture turned over, book case pushed over and books scattered, kitchen drawers pulled out and cupboards emptied with dishes and glasses broken all over the floor. I didn't even want to go upstairs because I knew it was more of the same, and I wasn't disappointed.

I stumbled through the rubble and gathered a few bits of clothing, and the bathroom wasn't in any better condition but I found the necessities. I grabbed one of the small coolers and took some of the food out of the refrigerator and some of the snacks.

Officer Ort said, "That won't be necessary, everything is furnished."

"That's fine. I'll take this stuff anyway, if you don't mind, it'll just spoil so we may as well eat it." I was in shock over the mess and didn't think what I needed or wanted and kicked my way through it all.

By the time we left it was dark and I had no idea which direction we were going. I didn't think I would get a straight answer so I didn't even bother to ask.

I dozed off and on and dropped off to sleep and woke as the car stopped at my new residence. Officer Ort tapped me on the shoulder and said, "We're here." Officer Ford was already there and walked towards the car and opened the door for me. Between the three of us we were able to take my valuable belongings inside with one trip.

It was a small cabin set in amongst some trees, but that was about all I could tell in the dark. I glanced at my watch and it was 4:17 in the morning. Inside, it truly was a small, two bedrooms and one tiny bathroom cabin. The kitchen, if that's what you wanted to call it, was open into the tiny living room and small eating table for four, barely.

I put the refrigerator stuff away and looked in the cupboards to see how well equipped it was, and it was sparse. The refrigerator and cupboards were supplied with only the essentials. Two things I assumed, at this point: there probably wasn't a big shopping mall nearby, which, hopefully, the other assumption meant we wouldn't be here long.

Neither of the officers were in the cabin and I couldn't see them outside. I sat in the only overstuffed chair and cuddled up with a blanket. Officer Ort came in and sat on the sofa saying, "You may as well settle in for the rest of the night and try to get some rest. You've had a rather stressful day. Jack and I will be on watch and you are safe here. No need to worry."

"How long are we going to be here, Officer Ort?"

"It's hard to say. Can we be on a first name basis? May I call you Alicia? You can call me Wanda and the guy outside is Jack."

"That's fine. So what happens now?"

"We wait for instructions and information as it becomes available. There are no calls out of here, only calls coming in as needed. May I have your cell phone? It's not that I don't trust you, I just want to remove any temptation."

That pissed me off, "I have twelve messages, may I listen to them?" I said sarcastically.

"Look, Alicia, let's make things easy for all of us. There's no need for you to listen to those right now. You can't return calls and they will only upset you more. We are here to keep you safe and try and relieve your stress as much as can be possible. Just give me your phone and we'll retrieve messages later." Wanda reached over and held my hands, "I'm so sorry you are going through all this, I can only imagine how betrayed you must feel and how scared you are. We'll get through this."

"Thank you." I said sarcastically and handed Wanda my phone. "I may as well just go to bed." And I stormed out.

There was one little lamp and no windows in the bedroom with only a double bed. I crawled in clothes and all. I don't know what Wanda and Jack did the rest of the night but I never heard a thing. They were quiet as 'church mice'.

When I finally woke sometime that day, I just stayed in bed and tried to digest everything that was happening. I wanted to get Spook and bring him here, but that was out of the question. Spook would remain at the clinic or foster care until I was out of this 'safe house'.

In the kitchen, Jack had made fresh coffee and heated some cinnamon rolls. "It smells good in here."

"Thank you." Jack poured a cup of coffee and took a cinnamon roll and went outside.

Well, he was certainly friendly. This is going to be a real fun time, full of conversation and games. I was completely alone with two other people in a tiny cabin.

I went outside and found this tiny cabin was in the middle of a grove of trees. As I was walking around the cabin I ran into Jack, "You can't be out here. You have to stay inside. Sorry."

"If this place is supposed to be so safe, then why can't I just get a little fresh air?"

"That's the rule. Please, go back inside."

Slamming the door as I went back inside the cabin, apparently it woke Wanda. She came out of the other bedroom with her weapon drawn. "What's going on?"

"Nothing!" I yelled. "I am just a prisoner now in someone else's place and not mine."

⁓๏

Prisoner? Yes, now I had become the prisoner. I was the one being punished and under a twenty-four hour watch. No phone, no computer or internet and a television that had an antenna with three very fuzzy channels. This was what it had all came down to, and I had no say or choice in the matter. The only calls came into Wanda or Jack and they wouldn't tell me what they were about.

My patience had disappeared, my nerves were shot and my disposition sucked. Wanda and Jack stayed away from me and our communication was nonexistent. I was at my wits' end. Days and nights seemed to blend together. I couldn't sleep at night and one or the other of the two was taking turns sleeping day and night. The silence was deafening.

When the cell phone rang and Wanda answered, she immediately went outside. I followed her and stood within hearing distance. As she moved further away, I moved closer. Wanda turned to me, "Alicia, would you please wait inside? I'll be right in."

"Actually, no I won't. I believe all these calls are related to me and I have a right to hear them. So, if you will just give me the damn phone I'd like to hear what whoever is on there has to say." I held out my hand for the phone.

"Call me back in a few minutes I have a situation I need to deal with." Wanda was saying as I grabbed the phone out of her hand.

"Hello, who is this? Hello, Hello!" The phone was dead. "Okay, what's going on here? You need to tell me and you need to tell me now!" I was screaming at Wanda.

"Alicia, settle down. Nothing is going on. We are waiting for instructions as to when you can go back home. That hasn't happened yet, but it will very soon." Wanda spoke gently and matter of fact. I wasn't buying it.

"I'm not waiting! I am out of here! Either you take me to town so I can get my car, my dog and go home or I am walking out. Do you understand I'm done with all of this? I'm on the brink of hysteria, make it happen." I was still in a screaming mode which brought Jack out of the house.

"Hey, what's going on out here?"

"Alicia's having a little meltdown, that's all." Wanda replied.

"A little meltdown? Is that what you call it? Well, let me show you what a little meltdown really is." I turned away and started running down the road.

Jack came after me and grabbed my arm, "Wait, lets' talk this over."

"Take your goddamn hands off of me. I'm done talking and I'm leaving." I was still screaming.

"Alicia, you can't walk out of here. You need to give this a little more time. We'll get you back as soon as we hear it is safe for you."

"Don't you hear me at all? I am done with safe and this nothing life. I want to go home and now."

I heard the phone ringing and turned to see Wanda answer it. I started walking towards her and Jack said "Let's see what this is about." He put his hand on my arm to stop me. I turned and glared at him. He knew exactly what I meant by that look. He threw his hands up, "Sorry."

As Wanda talked she occasionally looked back at me then turned away. She was pissing me off. Wanda got off the phone and walked over to where Jack and I were in a standoff position.

"Okay, here's the deal. I just got off the phone with Dwayne Roberts. They still have not picked up Matt Harper, however, there is a Grand Jury Trial date set. Mr. Roberts wants us to leave here in the morning and be at his office at one thirty. At that time, he'll give you all the details of what is happening next. So, let's go back inside and get ready for an early departure tomorrow."

We'd only been in this remote, Godforsaken cabin for five days and it seemed like an eternity.

CHAPTER 36

We arrived at Mr. Roberts' office a few minutes early and Julie had me go right in, he was ready.

"I'm sorry you have had to go through all of this, Alicia, I really am. I thought we would've picked up Matt Harper by now, but that didn't happen. So, here's what we know and what's up next." Mr. Roberts leaned back in his chair, cleared his throat and continued. "There will be a Grand Jury hearing in Boston at the Federal Courthouse this coming Monday. You have to be there. You will be questioned about the files and the relationship between you and Mr. Aston. Because of all the threats you have encountered, you will have a bodyguard present at all times. We have booked you in a hotel room not too far from the courthouse. During your stay in Boston, you must not make contact with anyone. We don't want Mr. Aston tipped off in any way. I will not be there. However, I've contacted an associate that will be representing you, Leo Steele, I think you'll like him. I don't know for sure how long this'll take, but I can't imagine it being more than a day or two at the most. After the indictment, and I assume there will be one, you'll get on a plane back here. Hopefully, Trevor and Matt are picked up real soon, then it'll all be over for you. Do you have any questions?"

I had so many questions I didn't even know where to start.

"You're sure Trevor won't be in court?"

"Yes, I'm sure. The only people in the court room will be the prosecuting attorney, Mr. Steele, the jury members and you. There won't be any spectators, so it's pretty simple and straight to the point. This is a hearing to see if there is enough evidence to indict Trevor. There is already an investigation going on with this Ponzi scheme and your files have already been given to the Feds. Trevor Aston is a name they didn't have and that pretty much sealed the deal."

"Will he be picked up immediately?"

"A warrant for his arrest will be immediate, finding him is another issue. Now, why don't you go on home and try and get some rest. If you think of any other questions, give me a call. Oh, and by the way, we had the cleaning lady go in and clean up the mess and we replaced all the broken dishes. There was hardly any damage or anything broken other than dishes, all of your stuff was just thrown around. Anyway, it is all put back together."

"Thank you. I need to get my car, wherever it is, pick up Spook and get my cell phone back from Wanda. She took it and wouldn't even let me pick up messages. I wasn't happy."

"I understand that. I'm going to ask you not to discuss this hearing at all, with anyone. If you talk to Mrs. Harper, you can't let on about this at all. I discourage you from even talking to her."

"I got it, but if I don't either answer her calls or respond to a message, she will be very suspicious. I think I can handle it."

As we walked into the waiting room, Wanda and Jack stood up; I held my hand out to Wanda and said, "Phone please." She looked at Mr. Roberts, he nodded and she reached in her duffle bag and gave it to me.

"By the way Mr. Roberts, who is paying for all of this, the damage to the condo, Spook's vet bill, my little vacation away from home and the trip to Boston?"

"There will be a settlement and cost recovery, so don't worry about it."

When we got in the car, Wanda said, "Please don't be angry with me. I was only following instructions and doing my job. Jack and I both were."

"I'm sorry. I had no right to take it out on either of you. My nerves are just plain shot."

Wanda told me I would have to leave my car in lock up, so she took me to pick up Spook. Mr. Roberts felt my car was safer left at the police station.

Spook was thrilled to see me and was in much better shape than I thought he would be. It was just going to take time for everything to heal from the inside out and keep the wound clean from infection. I didn't have enough cash with me and promised I would be back to pay the rest.

I was surprised to see how nice the condo looked, just like when I first rented it. Mr. Roberts had put up venetian blinds over the windows on the ground floor, the kitchen window and small window by the dining table and replaced the front door with only a peek hole. All the other windows had drapes.

Wanda made her rounds to be sure the place was secure, inside and out. Once she was satisfied she settled into a bedroom upstairs. I had gone about my business and got Spook situated on his bed. He was still a little groggy from medication and I was supposed to continue the pain pills to keep him comfortable.

I put away what little stuff I had taken to the 'safe house', mixed a drink and went out on the patio to listen to the twelve messages on my cell.

The first one was from Alison, "Just touching base, Matt is supposed to be home tonight. He got delayed for some important meeting. Give me a call."

The second was Sheila, "Wendy, I know you told me not to call unless it was important. But Daddy hasn't been home for seven days. Fran is taking care of us, but Billy and I are scared. Have you talked to him? Please call me."

Josh was the third call, "Hey there, I told you I would call in a couple days, sorry it took longer. How ya doin? Give me a call."

Fourth, fifth and sixth calls were from Allison with various degrees of stress that Matt was not back home. He had not called and she was afraid something had happened and didn't know where to start.

The seventh call was blocked, but I recognized the attempt to disguise the voice as Trevor. "You can run, but you can't hide, this ain't over, Bitch." I saved the message as I had the other threatening message.

Number eight was from Fran, "Wendy, this is Fran, the nanny for Billy and Sheila. The children are really scared because they haven't heard from their Dad. They wanted me to call and see if you could come see them." That broke my heart because I knew I couldn't do that, and I was suspicious enough of Trevor that he could've put her up to the call.

Allison called again, and again hysterical, "Matt called and said he has been detained in Atlanta. He didn't give me a reason why or where he is. I'm scared. Please call me!"

The last message was from Josh, "Hope everything is okay. Give me a call."

I called Josh. I knew I wasn't supposed to, but I had to talk to him. He needed to know what was going on since he had helped me start this whole ordeal.

Josh answered on the first ring, "Hey Josh. Sorry I didn't get back to you right away, I have been rather busy."

"You okay? Anything new going on with the case?"

"Oh, wow! If you only knew what has been going on. I can't go into it right now other than to tell you I'm going to Boston on Monday. It has been a rough couple weeks. One of these days I can tell you all about it, but not right now."

"Do you need me to go to Boston with you?"

"I don't think so. Mr. Roberts said it wouldn't be necessary. The copies of those files speak for themselves. This is just a hearing to see if there is enough evidence for an indictment. I don't know what will happen after that."

"You know, if you need me to go, I will."

"I know that and thank you Josh, I really appreciate it. So how have you been? Keeping busy?"

"Oh, yah. We're about to take off with the horses for more racing. This is the fun part."

Wanda walked out on the patio and glared at the sight of me on my phone. "What are you doing?" She said.

"Josh, I need to get going, I'll talk to you later."

"Okay, take care."

Wanda still glaring at me asked again, "What are you doing?"

"I was talking to a friend, do you have a problem with that? If so, get over it. I am not a child, I know what I can say and not say, so back off." This relationship between Wanda and me was not getting any better. She acted like a drill sergeant and was treating me like a new recruit. I picked up my drink and went upstairs and slammed the door shut.

This woman was getting under my skin big time. We were clashing like a bull in the ring with a red flag. No way was she going to Boston with me, I'd kill her before we got back.

I called Mr. Roberts office. He was with a client so I left a message on his voice mail, "This is Alicia and I want to request a new bodyguard, this is not working between Wanda and me."

CHAPTER 37

Walking on the beach with Spook I knew was risky, but I just had to get out of the house.

I placed a call to Allison. "Wendy, where the hell have you been? I am frantic with worry. I haven't heard from Matt and you aren't returning my calls. What the hell is going on?"

"Allison, settle down. I'm just fine. I took a road trip for a few days and didn't have my phone with me. I forgot it." That was partially true, the road trip part anyway. "So, what's going on with Matt?"

"I don't know what's going on with Matt. He has called twice since he went to Atlanta. Once that he was delayed for a special meeting, and then delayed again for a special project. He was supposed to be gone for two nights and it has now been seven days. The police were here looking for him and asked me questions about his business in Atlanta. I am terrified something has happened."

"Did the police say why they were looking for him?"

"No, just that they needed to talk to him. I have no idea what they want. I know Matt has been upset with work, but I just thought it was co-worker issues or pressure from clients. I don't know, only speculation on my part. Matt never talks about work."

"Allison, let's plan that trip to Las Vegas, get you away from all that and have some fun? I know it will take some time for you to arrange it from work, but let's put a date on the calendar and make it happen. We have talked about it for too long." I needed to change the subject about Matt in Atlanta.

"Right now, I can't plan anything until Matt is home and I know what is going on."

"I'm not talking about right now, in the next month or so. We'll talk about this later, after everything settles."

"Okay. Wendy, I really need to get back to work, you caught me at work. Please keep in touch. I am really scared."

"I know, Allison. I'll talk with you soon."

I sat on the beach for a few minutes after hanging up with Allison to reflect on what she must be going through. I can't even imagine how betrayed she is going to feel when this all comes down around her. I wanted so badly to give her some warning of what could be a possibility, but I couldn't.

Spook and I went back inside and got the usual glare from Wanda, which I ignored and went straight upstairs.

Mr. Roberts called that I had a new bodyguard and she would be on duty at six. Jody had the plane tickets and schedule for the next three or four days.

I went through my closet to lay out clothes to take on this dreaded trip. We were leaving the next day for the trial on Monday. I had no idea what to expect.

Promptly at six Jody came on duty and Wanda left with no more than a cold cordial "Good Luck." I wasn't sure if she was saying good luck to me or Jody.

Tall, slender and blonde, Jody appeared to be thirtyish with a bubbly personality, certainly refreshing from Wanda. It didn't take her long to get familiar with the condo and the beach.

"How bout we get acquainted and go over this schedule? I've read all the information given to me regarding your case, but I don't know what makes Alicia tick. Tell me about yourself."

Wow, Jody was right to the point in a pleasant sort of way. I gave her a very brief summary of my life up to the current date.

"Fascinating life you've had and very scary as well. You are one tough survivor, I'd say. What're your plans for the future when this ordeal is all over? Any plans to further the relationship with Josh? He sounds pretty cool to me."

Smiling at her, "I don't know if there is a future for Josh and me. I think I pretty much squelched any possibility there. What about you? Tell me what makes you tick."

"We'll talk about me later. I want to go over the next couple days and what you can expect. We fly out at 12:45 tomorrow, check into the hotel not far from the courthouse. Monday morning we meet with Mr. Leo Steele to brief you on the trial. That's the short version and the rest just happens."

∽

The plane ride was uneventful, leaving on time and arriving on time, but I was as nervous as a 'long tailed cat in a room full of rocking chairs'. Jodi was chattering like a magpie trying to keep conversation light. She was the only one talking and I wasn't listening.

Josh had called the night before and again offered to go with me to court. Assuring Josh at this point, it wouldn't be necessary, he inquired what I was doing with Spook. Rachel and Curly, next door, were delighted to take care of him. Spook and Curly had become pretty good pals and walked the beach often. Rachel on the other hand had an abundance of treats and occasionally had a nice roast bone for Spook and they were becoming as attached to Spook as I had.

We had taken only carry-on luggage so departing from the airport was easy. In front was an unmarked police car to take us to the hotel. The driver gave Jodi our room key and we entered through the back of the hotel. All of this was making me even more nervous.

When we got in the room, which was a very nice suite and exquisitely furnished, I said to Jodi, "Tell me, why all the pickup service, prearranged room key and back door entry into the hotel? Something tells me this is bigger than I thought."

"Alicia, sit down." She patted the edge of the bed. "I don't think you have any idea the magnitude of this whole thing, it's big. This financial law firm has offices all over the United States, mostly major cities. There are a few guys out of the firm that thought they saw a way to make a ton of money, and of course, not get caught. Someone within the organization smelled a rat and started an inquiry about two years ago. All I know is that Aston and Harper are two, thanks to you, of six others that are in this together. It will only be a matter of time before they're all caught. But, you coming forward with this information, has given the authorities the keys they needed. Considering there have been life threats on you, as well as an attempted murder, you are a prime witness."

"Oh, my God! I had no idea. I thought I was only turning in Trevor and not until recently did I know Matt was involved, at least, I guess he is. So, now what does this mean for me? Am I going to live the rest of my life afraid someone will come after me and I have to continue to run?"

"No, I don't believe your life will be threatened any longer and you won't have to run. Eventually, these guys will be put away for a very long time. You will be safe when this is all said and done. So, don't worry. Okay? Hey, let's figure out what we want for dinner and call room service. This is high class living, so let's take advantage of it."

We dined on steak and lobster with all the trimmings, red wine and followed with cheese cake. I hadn't had a meal like that in so long I was sure I would be sick before the night was through. We watched a movie and turned in.

I had a fitful, restless sleep and got up early. We ordered breakfast in and then got ready to leave for the courthouse. Leo Steele, the attorney, would meet us and go over the proceedings. I had no idea what to expect. The only court I had ever been in was when Trevor and I divorced and that was a nightmare. This was going to be a different kind of nightmare.

I was beginning to wonder if my nightmares were ever going to end.

CHAPTER 38

Jodi and I exited the hotel the same we had entered, by way of the service area, and arrived at the courthouse promptly at ten.

Mr. Steele met us in the front foyer. "Ms. Browning, I'm Leo Steele, and you must be Officer Jodi Dillon?"

"Yes, I am, nice meeting you Mr. Steele." Jodi replied and showed her badge.

"I will be representing you in this trial Ms. Browning. Let's go to one of the conference rooms and go over what you might expect. We have to go through security first. Turn your cell phone off, lay your purse down flat, remove your jacket and shoes."

Jodi handed her weapon and badge through to an officer and walked through the metal detector and then holstered her weapon.

In the conference room, the first question Mr. Steele asked me was, "I'm a bit confused. You seem to have three names, Alicia Browning, Wendy Aston and Wendy Noble. It has been explained to me, but I need clarification from you." I gave him the short version.

"You've had quite the run, haven't you? So this is what you can expect. The court will address you as Wendy Noble and you will have to explain the reason for the other two names. The Prosecutor, George Goldstein, will drill you about your relationship with Mr. Aston. He will question you about your knowledge of these files, how you found them, why it took you so long to find them, if you knew about these all along. He will question your integrity. He's going to ask about your relationship with the Harpers. He will ask you time and time again in every different angle he can come up with. He will try to trip you up. He will accuse you of being involved and knowing about the files. If you need a break, just ask and we can regroup. Do you have any questions?"

"Who is going to be in the court room?"

"There are no judges in a grand jury trial, the prosecutor, me, you and the jury, are the only ones allowed for this procedure. Jodi will sit behind you."

"How long will this take?"

"I don't know for sure. I hope we can wind this up this afternoon, we could go into tomorrow. It's hard to know for sure."

"I am so scared, I just want this to be over and be able to lead a normal life, whatever that is."

We had been in that conference room for a couple hours when Mr. Steele suggested we should break for lunch. He had ordered sandwiches and soft drinks, showed us where the restrooms were and said he would be back before court convened.

My hands were clammy and I didn't think I could eat. I was sweating and nauseated. Jodi was trying to cheer me up and change the subject. Small talk wasn't working. I was in my own world anticipating the afternoon.

Twenty minutes after one, Mr. Steele knocked on the door, "It's time to go." He put his hand on my shoulder and said, "You are going to do fine. Remember to answer the questions directly and don't add anything that you are not asked. Take a deep breath and try to relax."

We were the first to enter the courtroom and took the table on the left side. It wasn't long when the prosecutor came in and sat at the table on the right. The men exchanged smiles and a nod.

From the side door at the front of the court room the court recorder walked in and took her place at the recording machine.

George Goldstein, the prosecutor, asked, "Mr. Steele, are you and the witness ready to proceed?"

"Yes, we are."

"Bailiff, please bring in the jury."

I was called to the stand, sworn in and questioned all afternoon. I was doing well with all of the answers until the prosecutor, George Goldstein, started insinuating Allison and Matt were in this scheme together as well as suggesting Allison and I both knew about the scheme. He asked the same questions over and over again in different wording.

Frustrated, I turned to Mr. Steele, "May I have a break?"

Mr. Goldstein nodded, "We will recess for fifteen minutes."

In the foyer Mr. Steele reassured me, "You are doing great. Don't worry about the questions, all you can do is tell the truth."

"Will we finish this today? I can't do another day of this."

"I can't answer that. Everything is moving along very well. It will be up to the prosecutor if he is satisfied with all the information to get an indictment."

Back on the stand, the prosecutor started in again, "Ms. Noble, you stated you and Mrs. Harper grew up together and graduated from high school the same year, is that correct?"

"Yes."

"When did you meet Mr. Harper?"

"A few months before they married."

"And you never met Mr. Harper prior to their marriage?"

"Yes."

"So you had met Mr. Harper prior to the marriage."

"NO!" I exclaimed. "I had met Matt only a few months before he and Allison were married."

"How well did Mr. Harper and Mr. Aston know each other?"

"I don't know. I didn't think they knew each other hardly at all."

"What do you mean by that?"

"All I know is what Matt said, that he had run into an old associate at a bar."

"That could mean most anything."

I didn't reply and there was a long silence.

"Ms. Noble, what did you think Mr. Harper meant by an old associate?"

"That he hadn't seen Trevor in many years. They could have met at conferences, meetings or someplace else. I didn't think about it."

"When did you discover the men were more than old associates?"

"I never ever thought there was anything more than Trevor and Matt being old acquaintants."

"My question was, when did you discover the men were more than old associates?"

"I guess when my friend suspected there was more to it, but I didn't believe him, and then I found out Matt had tried to run me down on the beach."

"Who is your friend?"

"Josh Townsend."

"Does Mr. Townsend know these men?"

"No, he has never met either one of them."

"Are you sure?"

"Yes, I'm sure."

"What made you think it was Matt Harper that tried to run you down?"

"Because witnesses described the pickup and the police traced the truck as a rental and Matt's name was on the contract."

"Do you know where Mr. Harper is now?"

"No."

"How long were you married to Trevor Aston?"

"About four years."

"What happened, why did you divorce?"

"Because he became very abusive."

"Did he ever hit you?"

"No."

"Then explain why would you say Mr. Aston was abusive?"

"He was controlling, condescending and rude. He made threatening remarks and towards the end of our marriage I was terrified of him and feared for my life."

The prosecutor, put his hands on the railing, stared me in the eye and said, "Ms. Noble, if Mr. Aston never hit you, would it be safe to say you just wanted out of the marriage and made all of this up?"

"Objection, Mr. Goldstein, the conditions of the marriage were stipulated in the Divorce Decree. This is irrelevant."

"I think I've heard enough." Mr. Goldstein returned to his table and sat down.

"I only have a few questions of Ms. Noble, purely for clarification." Mr. Steele said.

"Go on." Mr. Goldstein replied as he glanced at his watch.

∽

"Ms. Noble, you have made it very clear that Mr. Aston had threatened you but he never hit you. Is that correct?"

"Yes."

"What did he say to you?"

"Many times he made remarks about how easy it would be to kill me, then he would laugh and say he was joking. But when we were leaving the court room the final day of the divorce, Trevor whispered in my ear, 'We are not done, I will see you dead' as he walked out."

"The court placed a restraining order on Mr. Aston long enough for you to get all of your personal belongings out of the house, is that correct?"

"Yes."

"What made you look for the files on your computer?"

"I didn't. It was Josh that suggested there could be information on my computer."

"What made Mr. Townsend so suspicious of Mr. Aston and Matt Harper? You said they had never met?"

"Just from what I had told Josh. It all made sense."

"When did you finally get into the files?"

"Josh had come down to New Orleans and stayed a couple days and we started looking. He went into my Guest file and found it. It didn't really take a rocket scientist to decipher those files. I don't think Trevor ever thought I would look there. It was my computer he wanted."

"What did you do with the files?"

"We made copies. I gave Josh one to keep in case anything ever happened to me. I hid one in a pocket of a suitcase, I carry the USB stick in my purse and Mr. Roberts has one."

"How did you come to hire Dwayne Roberts?"

"I was looking for another place to live and he happened to be the owner of the duplex I wanted to move into."

"How long were you living in the duplex before someone tried to run you down?"

"A little over two weeks, I think."

"I think this pretty much covers everything, I have nothing more."

"Then we will recess until tomorrow morning at nine o'clock. Mr. Goldstein stood and addressed the jury, "Jurors, remember you are not to discuss any testimony you have heard in this court today or watch the news. You are excused until nine a.m. Thank you."

"Does this mean I won't have to go on the stand tomorrow?" I asked hopefully.

"Yes, it does." Mr. Steele said smiling. "It means you have done all you can do. I believe you did a great job."

"Do you think Trevor will be indicted?"

"It's up to the jury, but I have a good feeling about it. The prosecutor appeared confident or he would have requested more questioning. So, let's call it a night and I'll see you back here in the morning at nine."

"Thank you and good night."

Jodi walked out with me to the hall. "Whew, am I ever glad that's over." I said to her.

"I think you did great. What an ordeal for you to have gone through, and I'm sure there is a lot more to your story."

"Mr. Steele seems to think it went alright. At least I don't have to go back on the stand in the morning."

"Well, let's go to the hotel and order a bottle of wine or champagne and celebrate." Jodi gave me a quick pat on the back and said, "Let's get out of here."

Standing on the front steps of the courthouse I took in a deep breath. "This is all over. Trevor will be picked up. Matt will be picked up and both sent away for a long time. All I have to deal with now is Allison and getting my life back in order."

"I'm glad it is over for you. There's our driver."

We started down the steps and the last thing I heard was when Jodi yelled, "GUN!"

Jodi jumped in front of me as I felt a sting above my right ear and I was down and the whole world went black.

I was gone.

CHAPTER 39

"This is Dwayne Roberts, may I help you?"

"Hi Dwayne. This is Leo Steele and I have some terrible news. At the closing of the hearing today as Wendy Noble and Jodi Dillon were leaving the courthouse, they were both shot. At this time, I can't tell you of their condition, but, Dwayne, I'm afraid it isn't good. They have been rushed to the hospital."

"Oh, My God! How did this happen?"

"I don't know. Apparently it was either a drive by shooter or someone from a building across the street. I don't have any details yet."

"Which hospital were they taken?"

"Massachusetts General. I wanted to let you know right away. I haven't had a chance to follow up on any details."

"No one has been picked up?"

"Not that I'm aware of, this incident happened less than an hour ago. I'll call you as soon as I have anything new to report."

"Let me give you my cell number so you can call me any time." Dwayne gave Leo the number and continued, "I need to contact the police department for Jodi Dillon so they can call her family. Wendy doesn't have family, but there are a couple close friends that need to be called. We'll be in touch."

"Okay. Dwayne, I am so sorry. This sort of thing rarely happens. These two guys must really be desperate and nuts."

"Yah, I'm thinkin. I'll get back to you. Thanks for the call, I guess."

The call to the police department that employed Jodi was not pleasant. They would handle the details regarding her family.

Dwayne had no idea where to start for Wendy. He needed her cell phone to get phone numbers. Did she take the phone with her or was it at the duplex? Then there is the dog. First call he made was to his wife.

"Hey there. I just got a call from Leo in Boston. Wendy Noble and her bodyguard were shot in front of the courthouse this afternoon. I don't have any details on their condition. Leo is supposed to call me when he gets more information."

"Oh, my God, Dwayne. What can I do?"

"Right now, I don't think anything. I need to go over to the duplex and look for Wendy's cell phone. I don't know if she took it with her or left it home. Rachel and Curly have her dog for right now. I don't know what to do about that. I'm gonna be late getting home, just wanted to let you know."

"Do you want me to go with you to the duplex?"

"Not now, I'll call you later. Love you."

"Love you too."

At the duplex, Dwayne first knocked on Rachel and Curly's door. Once inside, he explained the situation as he knew it. Rachel and Curly were both shocked and sympathetic, and then assured Dwayne that Spook would be just fine until Alicia got back. Dwayne thanked them and then went next door to Alicia's place.

Inside, he looked around briefly and her computer was on the table, no phone. Dwayne went upstairs and found the phone on the night stand. Opening it up he found there were five messages. Feeling like he was invading Alicia's privacy he felt the need to listen to each message anyway.

First was from a Josh, "Hey, I meant to call last night and wish you good luck in court on Monday. Give me a call and let me know how it went."

The next two calls were from Allison, "Wendy, I need for you to call me a.s.a.p. Something is wrong. Matt is still in Atlanta and I can't get a hold of him. I am scared shitless. Call me."

"Wendy, call me!"

"Wendy, this is Sheila, please call us."

And the last one was a blocked number, "You are the same as dead. You should have tended to your own business."

Dwayne sat down on the edge of the bed thinking out loud said, "That poor girl has gone through hell and back and carrying one hellava load and for what purpose? I just hope she can live to tell about it."

He wasn't sure who to call first. Probably Josh would be the easiest one to deal with for now.

Josh listened to Mr. Roberts intently and responded with the natural panic, caring concern and the need to go to Boston to be with Alicia. Dwayne assured Josh he'd keep him up to date.

Allison answered her phone with a panicked tone, "Wendy, where have you been? I left you two messages. What is going on?"

"This is Dwayne Roberts in Panama City, Florida. Is this Allison Harper?"

"Who? Who are you?"

"I am the attorney representing Alicia, I believe she is a friend of yours. Are you Allison Harper?"

"Yes, I'm Allison."

"I am calling about Alicia Browning or Wendy Noble as you know her. There has been a tragedy and Alicia has been shot. This happened a couple hours ago and I can't give you any more information. I know it is very serious."

"Oh, no............Trevor got to her didn't he? Where is she?"

"She's in Massachusetts General in Boston, that's all I know."

"Boston!" Allison exclaimed, "What the hell was she doing in Boston?"

"Mrs. Harper, I can't tell you that. All I can do is inform you of Alicia's condition and tell you where she is. I promise I will get back to you as soon as I have an update."

"Mr. Roberts. Wendy is my best friend and I need to know what is going on. Is this about Trevor? Did he shoot her? You can't keep this information from me. I am theoretically the only family she has."

"I understand that, but at this time this is the only information I can give you. I will get back to you soon. I need to go."

"This is total bullshit."

"I'm sorry. I'll talk with you soon." And Dwayne hung up.

Leaving the duplex, he took the computer and cell phone to keep at his office. Dwayne's cell phone rang. "Dwayne, this is Leo. I don't have any good news for you. Jodi Dillon didn't make it through surgery. She died about a half hour ago. Ms. Noble is still in surgery and it isn't looking too good. The surgical nurse just came out and said the bullet had gone through the right side of her head. At this point, they have not determined the extent of damage. Dwayne you've got to know any time there is injury involving the brain, it is a crapshoot."

"Yah, I know."

"This is a tough one, she wins and then she loses. Not right. I'll let you go, talk with you soon."

CHAPTER 40

"Mr. Steele, I have been informed of the tragedy of yesterday. I am so sorry. Do you have an update of your client's condition and her body guard?"

"I called the hospital last evening and this morning and unfortunately, Officer Dillon died during surgery. Ms. Noble is in very critical condition and not expected to survive. She is in a medically induced coma. That's all I know."

"Considering the circumstances, I would agree to a postponement if you request it."

"It would be my preference to continue. I believe we have revealed enough information for the jury to agree if an indictment is in order." Mr. Steele replied.

"Then please bring in the jury." Mr. Goldstein requested of the bailiff.

The stoic jury single filed in and quietly sat down.

"Jurors, you have been instructed not to discuss any information regarding this hearing or watch any news that might have been available. I assume you have honored those instructions." There were nods from the jury members. "Good. We will proceed with the closing summations by myself and followed by Mr. Steele."

"Ladies and Gentlemen, you have heard the testimony from Ms. Noble, the former wife of Trevor Aston, the accused. You also heard testimony regarding a Matt Harper. However, as strong as some of those accusations were, you must disregard all of that testimony. Mr. Harper is not the person of interest in this hearing. Only information regarding Trevor Aston is admissible."

Mr. Goldstein continued, "We have established there is a Ponzi scheme in effect. I believe we also proved Trevor Aston is one of several involved in this scheme. Ms. Noble testified to the abusive characteristics of Mr. Aston and his many threats towards her. Ms. Noble was followed, someone tried to run her down, her apartment was vandalized and it is believed that it was in search of her computer. Ms. Noble and a friend discovered the files in the 'guest' portion of her computer. They were able to decipher those files and come up with names and addresses of clients, dollar amounts and investment companies. There are in excess of ten pages to these files. Ms. Noble consulted an attorney to verify the seriousness of these files to find out that this Ponzi scheme was already under investigation by the FBI. I believe we have proven that Trevor Aston is among a group that is involved in the scam of deceiving clients for the sole purpose of his personal financial gain. It is my belief you will come to a unanimous decision with a verdict to indict. Thank you."

"Mr. Steele, do you have anything to add?"

"Yes, I do." Approaching the jury box, Mr. Steele, with hands in his pockets, stood silent for a moment. "Ladies and Gentlemen, thank you. Thank you for your time in doing your civic duty. I know how valuable time is and how fragile life can be, so I will try to make this brief."

"I believe Mr. Goldstein confirmed during his questioning of Ms. Noble that she is an innocent bystander in this scam with Trevor Aston. We have proven from testimony that it is probable Mr. Aston acted alone and it did not include Mrs. Harper, Mr. Townsend or Ms. Noble. Mr. Aston had Ms. Noble followed in the attempt to get her computer where he had hidden the more than ten pages of a scrambled bunch of files. These files have been turned over to the FBI and will complete an already in progress investigation. I can't imagine that Mr. Goldstein or I left any stones unturned or questions left unanswered. I am confident that given the information you currently have, you will come to the agreement of a verdict to indict. Thank you." With Mr. Steele's conclusion, he sat down.

Prosecutor Goldstein addressed the jury, "Members of the jury, you are excused to deliberate at this time. Upon reaching your decision, you will report to Officer John standing outside the deliberation room. If, at any time, you feel the need to have testimony repeated, you may ask Officer John for the court recording of your questions. You are excused."

"Court is recessed."

Both Mr. Goldstein and Mr. Steele left the court room and paused briefly in the hall.

"Leo, I am so sorry about your client's attempted murder. Have you viewed any of the surveillance cameras? Any news at all regarding the shooting?"

"Thank you. George. I haven't had a chance to check into anything with the police. In all my thirty two years as an attorney, I have never encountered such a horrific ordeal. I'm going to hang around here for a little while and make a few phone calls. I think we both did one hell of a job and I can't imagine the jury is going to take very long. I expect we should hear something real soon. Although, I imagine the jury will want to at least get lunch out of this." He gave a light chuckle.

"I think you're right, so I'll plan to see you after lunch if not sooner." With that, George gave Leo a soft pat on the shoulder and walked away.

Leo went downstairs to the security office to check on the surveillance cameras. The head of security took him into the room where they had been going over every film available. Considering Leo had no idea who they were looking for, none of the people in the films made any sense to him. Besides the images were so fuzzy, considering the distance to the vehicle and that the vehicle was moving rather fast.

"It appears that two men were in that white SUV and the one on the passenger side is the one doing the shooting. It is believed that several shots were fired. Jodi Dillon, I believe, was the body guard, and Wendy Noble was your client. Is that correct?"

"Yes sir, that is correct."

"Ms. Dillon spotted the gun and yelled 'gun', you can see that right there", as he paused the digital camera. Continuing, "That's when she turned in front of Ms. Noble and pushed her down. I believe the first shot missed them both and it is difficult to tell which shot hit first. More shots were fired but both women were down on the steps by then. The area was secured and Ballistics has the shells. No reports have come back. Until we have photos of Mr. Aston and Mr. Harper, we cannot identity these guys. It's early, but we'll be on it as rapidly as possible."

"Thank you. I know there is a warrant for the arrest of Matt Harper, currently in place, on a different criminal charge. I am hopeful an indictment will come through this afternoon, which will call for an arrest warrant on Trevor Aston. Let me know when reports come in, please."

"You got it."

Leo called the hospital next to check on Wendy's condition. There had been no change. Still on a respirator and in a medically induced coma she had not improved. The nurse explained they had removed a small portion of her skull to allow for swelling. He had not expected the news to be any different, but was saddened nonetheless. He decided to wait until the verdict was in to call Dwayne in Florida.

Not far away was a small café, Leo ordered a sandwich and picked up the newspaper from the counter. Front page headlines read: **WITNESS SHOT, BODY GUARD DIES.** It went on to read the suspects were still at large and the details of the article were vague. How the reporter got anything about this was amazing. News reporters seem to be like mice, get in anywhere through any crack in the wall, not quite as bad as the Paparazzi, but close.

Glancing at his watch, it was 1:15. Leo was hoping to get a call anytime that the jury was in. Continuing to scan the paper he looked for the puzzles, this would take his mind off the anticipation.

Promptly at two o'clock Leo's cell phone rang. The jury was in.

CHAPTER 41

"All rise."

Court reporter in place, the jury filed in taking their seats and made no eye contact with either Mr. Goldstein or Mr. Steele.

"In case number 2145, FBI vs. Trevor Aston, has the jury reached a verdict?" The prosecutor asked.

"Yes we have."

"Bailiff, would you hand me the verdict?"

The bailiff took a piece of paper from the jury foreman and handed it to Mr. Goldstein. Reading the verdict, he handed it back to the bailiff, who in turn, handed it back to the foreman.

"Foreman of the jury please read your verdict."

The foreman stood with solemn, expressionless eyes and glanced in neither direction. Clearing his throat the foreman read, "We find in case number 2145, Trevor Aston, guilty of a financial scam for the sole purpose of Trevor Aston's personal financial gain."

"Mr. Foreman, is this a unanimous decision of our jury?"

"Yes it is."

"You may be seated, Bailiff please poll the jurors. Jurors, answer yea or nay in accordance to your vote. Bailiff."

Answering as each juror's number was called, it was yea from the first to the last juror called.

"Thank you, Jurors. It is with great gratitude for your civic duty and giving of your time. It is so ordered that the contents of this hearing are to remain secured information within this court room. Violation of such order is punishable by contempt and charged accordingly. You are excused."

After the jurors had left the court room, "Mr. Steele, this has been a tragic hearing. The loss of a life of one of our own law enforcement officers is never taken lightly. The possible death of the key witness to this hearing will not be taken lightly, as well. I am issuing a warrant for the arrest of Trevor Aston plus making the warrant on both men, Aston and Matt Harper, an APB warrant with all border exits prioritized. Do you have any questions to ask of this court before we adjourn?"

Mr. Steele replied, "Yes, I do have one request, and that is the court order a twenty four hour security for Wendy Noble."

Prosecutor Goldstein replied, "It is so ordered. If there is nothing further?" he paused, "Court is adjourned."

In the hall, both men shook hands and congratulated each other for a job well done. They exchanged a few pleasantries and then went their own directions out of the courthouse.

Leo got to his car and immediately took his cell phone out of his briefcase and called Dwayne Roberts in Florida.

"Dwayne, this is Leo. I thought you'd like to know we got a verdict to indict Trevor Aston about twenty minutes ago."

"That's great news, Leo. Good job. Is there anything new on Ms. Noble's condition?"

"I'm afraid not. I called this morning before court. The nurse told me that during surgery they had removed a portion of Ms. Noble's skull to allow for swelling. It is going to be several days before they will know much. They need to keep her in a medically induced coma and for how long, no one really knows. I wish I could've given you better news."

"Thanks Leo, I really didn't expect anything different. Guess I had better make a couple phone calls, so I'll let you go. Thanks again for everything."

"No problem. If there is anything I can do from this end, just call."

When the men hung up, Dwayne called Josh, "Josh? This is Dwayne Roberts."

"Hey Dwayne, how is Alicia?"

"I wanted to give you an update and it isn't good. I just talked with Leo Steele in Boston. He called the hospital this morning and this is where it stands, Alicia is in an induced coma, they removed a portion of her skull to allow for swelling and it is going to be several days before they know anything for sure, if then. It is not good, Josh, and the doctors are not giving much hope, I'm sorry. However, the grand jury did come in with a verdict to indict Trevor Aston. A warrant for his arrest is in place and an APB and border alert. Josh you can't discuss the trial with Allison"

"Okay, I won't, but what is a border alert?"

"That is when security is watching airports and exits from the United States. Of course, they can't guard them all, but, hopefully the ones that count."

"That makes sense." Josh said. "So, what are the chances of seeing Alicia? I'm not family, but then she doesn't have any. I really want to see her."

"Josh, I can't answer that and I know how you feel. But I would give it a few days before you go to see her. It is too crucial right now."

"How am I going to be able to call and check on Alicia? I'm not family and I know the hospital won't give out information to anyone else."

"I know. So here's what I can do or at least try. I'll call Mr. Steele and see if he can have you and Allison put on Alicia's family list. Josh, we need to refer to Alicia as Wendy Noble from this point forward. You won't get anywhere otherwise."

"Yah, okay. That is going to be really weird. What about Spook?"

"The neighbors have him right now, but I don't know how long they want to keep him."

"That's good. I won't keep you. Call me anytime you have anything new and I will wait for your guidance in all this. Thanks Dwayne."

Dreading the next call, Dwayne dialed Allison's number. He related the same information to her that he had told Josh regarding the updated information on Wendy. Allison's reaction was the same as Josh's as to how she could get in to see Wendy. Dwayne reiterated his attempt to get her name put on Wendy's contact list, being two, she and Josh.

"Mr. Roberts, I have to ask why Wendy was in Boston."

Even though the trial was over and a warrant was out for Trevor's arrest, he couldn't tell Allison anything about the grand jury indictment. He knew there would be more questions and he was right.

"My husband has not been home for over a week now and I have not heard from him. Is Matt involved in something with Trevor?"

"I can't answer that. I don't know."

"The police have been here a number of times looking for Matt, do you know why?"

"Have you asked them? Mrs. Harper, my connection here is between Wendy and me. You'll have to pursue information on your end with the police. I can't answer your questions. I will do the best I can to get your name where you can check on Wendy directly. I think we are pretty much done here. I'm sorry I couldn't be of more help. Good luck to you."

Before Allison had a chance to offer any further arguments Dwayne had hung up. His only hope was that he was done with her.

CHAPTER 42

Phone calls at 5:30 in the morning are never a good sign and this morning was going to be no different for homicide detectives Sam and Brenda Lou Davis.

"Sam, this is Sheriff Crane with King County. We have a partially decomposed body down here at the Duwamish Waterway. We need you to come down."

Still half asleep, Sam muttered, "We'll be right there."

"Bea, you need to wake up. The Sheriff just called, we need to get down to the Duwamish. They have a body."

Sam woke the nanny, "Hey Sylvia, sorry to wake you, but Bea and I just got called out. It's only 5:30 so go back to sleep. Just wanted you to know." Sylvia was used to these calls, but Sam always hated waking her just the same. They absolutely never left the house without telling Sylvia, a 'cardinal rule' for the Davis house.

An hour later Brenda Lou and Sam were on the waterfront where the body had been discovered by a couple of fishermen.

Sheriff Crane greeted the homicide detective team, "It is apparent the body has been in the water a couple weeks or so and is partially devoured by crabs and any other creatures that hung out in the waters."

The medical examiner had arrived shortly before the Davis's. The area had been taped off and the fishermen had been questioned, but they didn't have any information to provide, only that they had discovered the body as they were launching their fishing boat.

It was obvious that the body could only be identified by dental records and the careful study of what appeared to be some kind of company ID badge or a laminated convention badge. It was hardly legible and most of it missing.

Sam questioned the fishermen, the first officers called to the scene, as well as the medical examiner. They had already spent nearly three hours on the waterway and it was cold and damp.

Brenda Lou leaned into Sam and said, "I think we've done all we can here. Let's take the ID badge to the lab and see if we can get any identification from of it. Besides, I'm freezing."

Sam agreed, but couldn't resist a teasing remark to his wife, "You are such a wimp. You'll never get used to this Seattle weather versus San Diego will you?"

Laughing, "Yep, you're right. I do like it warm, so get that car warmed up."

The lab took the ID, but sounded very skeptical that they could get anything out of it. It was determined it had been in the water so long that it was barely legible and only in parts, most of it had disintegrated. However, most ballistic labs could find something out of very little and that was what the Davis' were counting on.

After Sam and Brenda Lou left the lab, Sam suggested they go to breakfast. They didn't get quiet time alone very often with three teenagers, two dogs, one cat and three parakeets at home. So, even though they were called out very early in the morning, they were taking advantage of being alone.

It has been over a year since the Davis' moved to Seattle. Life moved into such a fast pace for the family of five that they all had no choice but to make it a positive venture. With Sam's parents deciding they could no longer take care of their home and yard on Lake Washington, they found a much smaller house in a retirement housing development.

Brenda Lou put her house up for sale after she and Sam had married, but, due to the declining economy, the house wasn't selling so she decided to rent it. Brenda Lou loved Sam's family and they had accepted her without reservation, but she was nervous about how the three kids would react when she moved in. However, Sylvia had prepared the kids so well that everything went without a glitch.

Sam had recovered from the last case he and Brenda Lou had solved. Instead of going back to the San Diego Sheriff's Department, they had started their own homicide investigative business. They were doing real well and keeping as busy as they wanted to.

Then Paul, Sam's dad, called and told them Sam's mother had all the symptoms of the beginning stage of Alzheimer and he was concerned about taking care of the big house, the yard and his wife. Sam went to Seattle and helped his dad find another place and they agreed Sam and his family would move into his parents' home and help his dad. When Sam and Brenda Lou sold their homes they would buy his parents' house.

The Davis' had been in Seattle for a year and went to work for King County Sheriff's Department as homicide investigators. The kids were doing well in school, Sylvia hated the weather and Sam's parents were adjusting to their new home.

Sam and Brenda Lou took advantage of their alone time and talked about the kids and their progress in school. Discussing Sam's mother and her declining health and how this would eventually involve them.

"This is Sam. Yep, we'll be on our way." Sam turned to Brenda Lou, "That was the lab, they have some information for us. Let's go see what they have."

The lab technician told Sam and Brenda Lou. "I think we have enough here at least for a start. It looks to me like this was a work ID badge from one of those financial institutions in the towers downtown. I could make out some of the numbers, but most of them are either smudged or gone."

Sam took the information and was looking it over carefully and said, "Well, I think we can just start knocking on doors at the towers and should be able to come up with a positive ID."

"You know this could be some small business that is off the beaten path and not in the main stream of the big firms. Maybe we're looking for the wrong kind of business, maybe it isn't even in the financial end at all. What about a lending company? Let's try there." Brenda Lou suggested.

An hour had past and they were still looking on the computer and nothing had caught their eye.

Then Brenda Lou blurted out, "Sam, look at this one. I've looked over this one a couple times. I think this is it, NW International Financials, Inc." Brenda showed it to Sam, smiling he agreed it was the closest to a match they had come across so far.

After making a few phone calls, jumping through the hoops of corporate bullshit, they were able to make an appointment to talk with an officer with some special title.

The receptionist smiled and when she stood up to go tell Mr. Mohamed Aliah his appointment was in, she was wearing a skirt that barely covered the cheeks of her butt and stiletto heels we were sure she would fall off of, and a strut that should've thrown both hips out of their sockets.

"Mr. Aliah will see you now, suite 10, straight ahead."

"Thank you." Sam and Brenda Lou said simultaneously, looked at each other and smiled knowing each was thinking the same thing.

After introductions and the Davis' were seated Mr. Aliah asked, "How may I help you? I believe you're inquiring about an employee?" He spoke very good English even with a strong dialect.

Sam was first to speak, "Yes we are, and quite frankly, we're not even sure we are in the right office. We found a body in the Duwamish Waterway early this morning that is pretty much unidentifiable. But the badge this person had on him has a symbol that we've traced to your firm. We need your help to confirm this and possibly come up with a missing employee."

"Well, let's take a look at what you have." Mr. Aliah replied.

He took the copy of the badge and studied it for only a few seconds. "Yes, I do believe that is our logo. Beyond that, I don't know how else I can be of assistance."

"You see, Mr. Aliah, there are at least three legible numbers on this badge, I would assume this is an employee ID number. Wouldn't you have some kind of tracing procedure to locate an employee?"

"Mr. uh, what was your name again?"

"Davis, Sam Davis and my partner Brenda Lou." Sam said with a slight bit of irritation.

"Yes, of course, my apology. Here in lies the problem. We have over 50,000 employees within our offices all over the United States, from the West Coast to the East Coast. With only three numbers legible it will be nearly impossible because the numbers accompanied with letters are the identifying factors, without those, it won't happen." He stood from his desk, hands in his pockets clearly giving the body language – this meeting is over.

Sam and Brenda Lou didn't budge; in fact, they crossed legs and settled back in the chairs. "Mr. Aliah, this will happen. I just hope you're not going to force us to subpoena your over 50,000 employee identification list. Because we can do that, in fact, I can have that order by the end of the day. It will be so much easier if you will cooperate. How bout we start with your list right here out of your office, after all, the body was found here in Seattle. We could assume he was employed here. What do you think, the simple way or the hard way?"

Sam continued, "Mr. Aliah, let me ask you this. Has anyone within this office turned up missing, or has anyone asked about an employee that has been conspicuously absent?"

Shifting positions and slightly fidgeting, he appeared to be carefully selecting his words to answer, "I would not have that information. That would go directly to DHR (Department of Human Resources)."

"Well then, why don't we start with a phone call to your DHR personnel and ask that very question. Would it be fair to ask if your DHR personnel would also have an employee list or would that be found in your payroll department – OR – both?" Sam asked with a bit of sarcasm.

To this point Brenda Lou had not uttered a word, just sat there appearing to be taking notes, but mostly doodling.

"Let me see what I can find out." Mr. Aliah said as he started out of the office.

"Hmmm. Does your phone not work here? I think you can make your calls from your office, okay?"

Irritated, he sat down and called the receptionist to have the DHR come to his office.

When the DHR walked into the office, Mr. Aliah asked, "Has anyone been reported absent from any of our employees, in house or those working out of the office?"

"Mr. Aliah, it would be hard to know that, because as you know, a lot or most of our representatives work out of the office from their homes. Reporting is sporadic. But no one has been reported missing, if that is what you are asking."

"Perfect." Sam addressed her, "then we'd like an employee list so we can confirm the whereabouts of each."

CHAPTER 43

Sam and Brenda Lou left NW International Financials, Inc. with the list in hand. Now all they had to do was call each of these people so they could narrow down their options.

Sam called home and talked to Sylvia, checking in what was happening. Sylvia was so competent that she always had everything under control. "I'll have dinner ready when you two get home. The kids have already eaten and doing their homework, so all is quiet here. Anything I can do for you, Mr. Davis?"

"No, thank you. We're on our way home now, just checking to see if we needed to pick anything up."

"Nope, we're fine. See ya soon."

"That woman is amazing. I don't know how I ever survived without her. She is a godsend to our family."

"She sure is, makes my life much simpler. I adore that woman, she's become a very good friend."

As they drove home, Brenda Lou said, "So, if we don't find any missing persons from this list, I guess we work our way across the United States. We could take another road trip. Remember the one we took from San Diego to Florida and then on to Chicago? That was fun wouldn't you say?" Brenda Lou said smiling.

"Oh yah. We could do that," Sam said as he winked. "But I think we can get this figured out by phone. We'll see what we get out of this office." And their work began.

Spending time with the kids and listening to their trials and tribulations of the day, it was hard to hear when all three were talking at the same time. This evening was no different than any other.

Soon the kids started homework again, while Sam and Brenda Lou went to the office and started making phone calls before it got too late.

They started down the list and marked each name with either a check (talked with the employee), LM (left message) or DA (didn't answer). The list was dwindling at a rapid pace. With only about one hundred and fifty names and both making calls, it didn't seem to take too long.

Calling it a night, they decided they would hit it hard in the morning and get through the rest of the list and then go door to door until all were accounted for.

The next day, Sam and Brenda Lou narrowed the names down to ten they could not account for.

Sam called NW International Financials, Inc.'s DHR and made an appointment with her to go over these last few names.

"Mr. Davis, I'm afraid I can't do that. You see our DHR files are confidential and I am not at liberty to provide any information to you."

"Well then, I suggest you get your liberty from Mr. Aliah and I will be in your office, let's say in about an hour." And Sam hung up. He hated playing games with those who thought they could get away with it.

Promptly one hour later Sam Davis was sitting in the reception area waiting for 'Miss Congenial', or whoever she was, to see him and answer his questions.

It didn't take her long and a few phone calls to determine the only person that couldn't be accounted for was Matt Harper. The last time he had turned in any reports or shown up at the office had been over three weeks. She tried all the contact numbers the company had listed for Mr. Harper, but there were no answers.

Sam called his wife, "Hey, we finally got it figured out, the only one not accounted for is a Matt Harper. I'm going to the ME's office and give him this information, might speed up his work considerably. Then, I'm going to the office and run a background on this guy. I shouldn't be long. Everything good at home?"

"Yes, of course. I actually am trying my luck at cooking dinner. Poor Sylvia had to leave the house and go visit a friend, it was too painful watching me flounder around in this kitchen." Brenda Lou said laughing.

Chuckling back, Sam replied, "Well, don't hurt yourself or burn the house down. See ya in a bit."

When Sam got home he was full of all kinds of information. "How's dinner coming along?"

"It's ready for the oven, about half an hour. What's up?"

"Let's mix a drink and sit and have a chat. I'm full of all kinds of news." They went out on the patio with drinks in hand. "So, this is what I have. I have all Mr. Harper's vital statistics, D.O.B., home address, wife's name and background. It seems our Mr. Harper has an APB out on him for attempted murder. And get this, clear down in Panama City Beach, Florida. Why there, I have no idea, so we have some work to do."

CHAPTER 44

Josh hung up after talking with Dwayne Roberts and pondered going up to the main house to talk with Jim and Cecelia. He had kept his word with Alicia/Wendy and had not discussed this with anyone. It was now time for him to confide in his boss.

When Jim opened the door, he was somewhat surprised, considering he and Josh had spent most of the day working with the horses.

"Is something wrong Josh?"

"No, well yes! Can I come in and talk for a bit?"

"Of course. What's going on? Let me get us a drink, you look like you can use one."

They went into the family room and Jim turned the TV off and sat down. "Cecelia is out for the evening, so what's up?"

Josh told Jim everything, from what he learned about Wendy during her stay at the ranch to his visit to New Orleans (which he had spoken little about) to the phone call he had gotten from Dwayne Roberts less than an hour prior.

Jim listened intently to his friend who had gone through so much with the loss of his wife and two daughters. It was heartbreaking to hear this story and see Josh near tears. He knew something had happened in New Orleans with Alicia – now Wendy, but he never pressed the issue. Josh had always been fairly quiet about his personal life.

"Josh, I am so sorry. What can we do? What do you need? You know Cecelia and I are here for whatever you need."

"I know you are Jim, and I appreciate that. You and Cecelia have always been there for me. At this point, I don't know what I need. I want to see Wendy," he paused, "that is going to be hard getting used to calling her Wendy." He smiled.

"Do you need some time? Maybe take a few days and go to Boston and see her?"

"Mr. Roberts suggested it might be too early since it has only been one day. But I do need to see her."

"Then go. You need to be there. Can you get in to see her, you're not family? How does that work?"

"I know I'm not family and that could be an issue, but Mr. Roberts is going to see if that can be arranged for me and Allison."

"Have you talked with Allison? Does she know what all has happened?"

"No, I haven't. I know Mr. Roberts was going to call her. I don't have Allison's phone number, all I know is they live in the Seattle area."

"Why don't you try to give her a call? Unless they have an unlisted number, you should be able to get it from information. Is that something you want to do?"

"I don't know. I don't know what she knows by now. I don't know if her husband has been picked up or not. Actually, I don't know anything about all that, only what Wendy has told me."

"You might give it a try." At that moment Cecelia walked in.

"Josh, how are you? Is everything alright?"

Glancing at Jim, both men smiled, "Hi Cecelia, I'm going to let Jim fill you in. I better head back to the house. Thanks a lot Jim, see ya in the morning."

"Remember what I said, just let us know if we can do anything. Night."

"Thanks, I will."

On the way back to his house, Josh considered the time difference in Seattle. He didn't know what to expect if he called Allison, but also felt the need to do so.

Josh called Information for Matt Harper or Matt and Allison Harper or any combination, voila, he had a number and he placed the call.

"Hello, Allison Harper? This is Josh Townsend, a friend of Wendy Noble."

"Yes, Josh, I know who you are. Have you heard anything about Wendy?"

"I have and the news isn't good. I assume you've heard from Dwayne Roberts, Wendy's attorney. That's all the information I have right now."

"Mr. Roberts did call me about Wendy and I'm terrified she's not going to make it. Is Trevor responsible for shooting Wendy?"

"I don't know and I don't think they know either. I guess they don't really have a clear photo from the surveillance tapes of the shooter."

"Josh, I'm still confused, why was Wendy in Boston? What do you know about all that?"

"Nothing more than what Mr. Roberts told you."

"What has Wendy told you about Matt and me? I'm sure she has told you about us."

"Yes, I know quite a bit. She spoke very highly of you and Matt, long-time friends and trusted you with her life."

"I have to ask you and you need to be honest with me Josh. Is Matt involved with Trevor?"

"I don't know that, why do you ask? Do you think he is?"

There was long silence before she answered, "I don't know, but I'm beginning to wonder. Matt left for a business meeting in Las Vegas for four days, and then he got a call to go to Atlanta for a one day emergency meeting or something. The last time I heard from Matt was when he said he had to stay for a project for another couple days and that has been almost two weeks now. The police have been here several times looking for Matt. He's not answering his cell phone and I have no idea where to turn. Do you know anything?"

Josh knew that question would eventually come up and it may as well be now. Allison needed to know what she was facing.

"I do, and I hate to tell you, Allison, but you need to know. Wendy and her dog were walking on the beach and a pickup tried to run her down. The pickup was leased to Matt, that information came from the car rental and the police. Matt is being charged with attempted murder."

"That can't be, no way would he hurt Wendy. He loves her as much as I do. They are wrong. Josh, this isn't true. Matt was in Atlanta and doesn't even know where Wendy is, neither do I for that matter. Wendy never told me where she was, that was our agreement."

"I'm sorry Allison, but that's what I know and that came from Wendy. She couldn't tell you because she hoped it would be wrong, too. But she also knew it wasn't wrong."

"Oh, my God. I can't believe this. I have to go see Wendy."

"I don't think that is a good idea right now. Wendy is in a coma and she won't know you're there. Besides, I don't think either one of us can get in to see her, we aren't family."

"Josh, she doesn't have any family. I'm the closest to family she has, we are like sisters, grew up together. They can't keep me out."

"Allison, wait a few days. Leo Steele, the attorney in Boston, is trying to get you and me on her visitation list as family. Mr. Roberts is calling me if that is possible. Let me call you when I know. Okay?"

"This is a nightmare. Wendy has been through hell these past few years. The sweetest person in the whole wide world and this has happened to her. I can't believe this. I need to call Missing Persons for Matt. How do I do that?"

"I don't know, probably call the police, I have no idea what to tell you. Maybe you better get an attorney. That would be a start. I'll call you soon."

Josh went in the kitchen and poured another drink and walked out on the front porch. Looking up to the sky, he watched the sparkle of all the bright stars. Taking a slug of his drink, he choked and uncontrollably started crying. Josh couldn't stop thinking about Wendy and all she had gone through and he sobbed all the more. There was nothing he could do.

All this took Josh back to the day of the accident that took his wife and two daughters. He sat in a swing rocker and started talking to the stars that he believed were his wife and girls looking back at him. Josh stayed out on the porch and fell asleep. Waking two hours later, he went inside and went to bed.

CHAPTER 45

The next morning Josh was up early and placed a call to the hospital in Boston. He was taking a chance that arrangements had been made for his name to be on Wendy's visitation list. Mr. Steele had come through.

Josh gave his name and asked for Wendy Noble's nurse in ICU. When she answered, "Nurse's station, may I help you?"

"This is Josh Townsend and I want to check on Wendy Noble's condition."

"Yes, Mr. Townsend. I'm afraid there has been no change. She is in an induced coma and we plan to keep her there for several days. We are turning her every hour and moving her legs so her muscles won't atrophy and she is on a respirator. Ms. Noble is in a restful state which is where we want her to be for healing. That's about all I can tell you right now. It is still a bit early to be expecting much more."

"Do you have any idea how long the doctor intends on keeping her out like that?"

"No, I don't know. That will depend on the swelling. Right now her vitals are pretty unstable. We have her on antibiotics to prevent infection which is always a high risk. So, for now, that's about the best I can tell you."

"Thank you. When can I come see her?"

"I would give it another few days or so. You can call anytime and the nurses will give you an update. Okay?'

"Yes, ma'am, thank you." And he hung up.

Heading down to the horse barn, he decided he would talk to Jim about a day or two off to go to Boston.

"Mornin. How ya doin? Did you get any sleep last night?"

"Mornin. I slept okay. I was thinkin maybe after the races this weekend maybe I'd go to Boston for a day or two then back home. I'll stay and be sure everything is loaded and you're on your way then go on up to Boston. What cha think?"

"That's fine, Josh. But we can take one of the guys from here to help and you can just leave after the last race. We can handle the rest. So plan on that."

"Thanks Jim, I really appreciate it."

Seemed like the next few days dragged on forever. Josh called every day, morning and night, and there had been no change. The doctor had talked about taking Wendy off the respirator to see if she could breathe on her own, but then decided to wait another few days.

Allison had called a couple times just to chat. She had the same information Josh had from the hospital, but just felt the need to talk with Josh.

There was still no information regarding Trevor or Matt being arrested. That was unnerving to Josh. Allison was still in denial that Matt was in any way involved. However, his lack of communication with her was leaning her more to a believable accusation.

Josh told Allison he was planning to see Wendy after the weekend for a couple days. She didn't know what to do and Josh didn't offer any suggestions. Actually, he was hoping she wouldn't decide to go at the same time.

"Have you contacted an attorney yet?"

"Yes and no. I called our family attorney and we have an appointment tomorrow afternoon. He is as shocked as I am with what little information I gave him. He's getting the police report to see what he can find out. So, I can't leave here for a while and I don't know if I want to leave before I hear from Matt. I'm in limbo right now."

"I'm sure you are. I need to go for now. Keep in touch and I will call you from Boston after I've seen Wendy."

"Josh, thank you for being such a caring friend for her. I know she has given you a hard time, but I do know she does care about you. She's just afraid of any commitments right now, and I guess I understand better now why. Hang in there. Talk to you soon."

"Thanks, you too."

Josh worked diligently preparing the horses for the race. What was usually routine was turning out to be a lot of work for Josh. He couldn't concentrate and his mind kept wondering to Wendy.

The horses were all ready for their road trip and they always seemed to sense a race coming up. Running and snorting and kicking up their heels and showing off for those who had to stay home.

Bags packed, including airline tickets and car rental in order, Jim and Josh, along with Manuel, would be leaving in an hour. The day of race departures, Cecelia always made a hearty breakfast for the guys and packed a cooler of drinks and snacks. Jim told her it wasn't necessary, but she insisted she would never send her men off on an empty stomach. He soon gave up and enjoyed her cooking.

Ordinarily, preparation for a racing trip was an exciting time, Jim and Josh were happy joking with each other and whistling while they worked. However, this time, the trip was quiet, very serious and all business. Jim could see how uptight Josh was.

CHAPTER 46

The racing event was another success. Although only two of Jim's racers placed, he was extremely happy because his prize filly came in first and the gelding came in second in a different race. This was the gelding's first race and Jim and Josh were ecstatic. These two horses made Jim some big bucks.

Jim was an extremely fair and generous man. When he won, he always made sure he gave his guys a percentage, and this time it was a healthy one.

They spent the rest of the afternoon taking care of the horses, walking and rubbing them down, feeding and watering and settling in the stalls for the night. Jim never loaded the horses in the trailer for a trip home the same day as a race. They always left early the next morning. He treated his horses with more concern and care than most people did their kids.

When the gear was all loaded and locked in the trailer, the three men went back to the motel, showered and then went out to dinner. Josh's plane left the next morning for Boston. He had tried to get a late afternoon or evening flight out, but nothing was available.

They had a nice evening even though Josh appeared to be preoccupied. Jim was good at keeping the subjects light and off anything that'd be personal. Josh left early and went back to his room so he could make another call to check on Wendy.

The nurse had told him she had stirred a bit and was agitated with the breathing tube down her throat, so they were sedating her more and considering removing it in the morning.

Josh was excited and thought that to be a good sign. He slept restlessly getting up a couple times during the night, and just paced.

He was up early the next morning and called a cab for the airport. Arriving in Boston on schedule, Josh made his way to the car rental shuttle. He only had a carry on duffle bag and made the airport departure rather easy. The map in the car, plus the GPS direction, was a cinch for this country boy and he was feeling real confident about driving straight to the hospital.

Checking in at the front desk, he was instructed where to go and who to check in with. He was surprised there was a security guard in front of Wendy's room, but relieved at the same time.

When he was cleared with Security, Wendy's nurse took Josh to her room. He was not prepared for what he saw.

Wendy was lying on her side in a fetal position with a tennis ball in both hands. She had a tube down her throat, IVs in her hand, heart monitor wires from her chest to a machine, her head wrapped in white gauze and tape, heavy Vaseline on her eyelids and lips. Josh just stood and stared at her with tears streaming down his cheeks and made no sounds.

The nurse walked over to Josh and offered him a chair. She sat down beside him and tried to console him and explain what was going on with all the tubes and monitors. At this point, considering the kind of trauma Wendy had gone through, it was all very normal. What was not normal was that it had now been eight days and there had been no change. Within the next couple of days, someone was going to have to make a decision to remove the breathing tube and see if she could breathe on her own.

Josh sat there not saying a word, listening and tears still streaming. The nurse finally said, "I'm going to step out and let you be alone with Wendy. Just talk to her as if she can hear you. Say anything you want, talk about things that you know she can relate to. I know this is hard Josh, but maybe something you say will spark a reaction from her. You can stay for fifteen minutes then we will be moving positions for her." With that, she walked out of the room.

At the side of Wendy's bed, Josh held her hand. He didn't know what to say. There was so much he wanted to say and had already said, he didn't know where to start. Holding Wendy's hand, he removed the tennis ball and started massaging her fingers. When he removed the tennis ball he felt her fingers tighten into a fist.

Staring at her closed, still eyelids Josh started talking, "Wendy, this is Josh. You are giving me quite a scare here. Can you open your eyes and talk to me? Jim and I had a race this past weekend and two of the horses placed. We're real happy with their performance. Wish you could've been there. You'll have to go with me to one of our races, you'd love it." He paused and continued to stare at her trying to see a reaction and there was none.

Josh sat and massaged her hand, rambling on about anything, everything and nothing until the nurse came back and told him he needed to go for a while. The doctor would be coming in and then he could talk with the doctor.

Waiting out in the lounge area, Josh thumbed through first one magazine then another and didn't see a thing. He was helpless and it took him back to his wife and daughters. Even though they had never made it to the hospital, as they had been killed instantly, Wendy's condition took him back.

Dr. William Boyer came out after over an hour and sat down beside Josh. They made their introductions and Dr. Boyer brought Josh up to date, which was pretty much everything Josh already knew. There had been no change.

"I would like to take the tube out today and see if Wendy can breathe on her own. If that happens, then we can gradually take her off some of the medications and try to bring her around. All of her vitals look good, kidneys are functioning and that is a good sign. The only thing we don't know is the brain damage. When she gradually wakes we can tell more. I can tell you there are brain waves, but what that means, is up to Wendy."

Josh listened intently and wanted to ask so many questions, but he didn't know what to ask. Finally, "Are you giving any speculations to Wendy's recovery? Will she ever be the same as before?"

"No, I'm not speculating. Head injuries, plus all the trauma Wendy has already experienced, is really an unknown. All I can say is that the next several days could give us a better idea. One step at a time and today is removing the ventilator. That will be a start. You can check with the nurses later, how about later this afternoon?"

Considering Josh had gone straight to the hospital and had been up since six a.m., he went to a restaurant to get something to eat, check into the motel and then back to the hospital and wait.

In the motel room, Josh thought about calling Allison, but decided to wait till evening and maybe have a better report after the doctor removed the breathing tube. He hated the waiting and being out of control. But then he had never been in control with Wendy. Just as he was leaving the motel his cell rang. It was Allison.

"Hey, Josh, this is Allison. What's going on? Anything new? Where are you?"

"I'm in Boston and not much is going on right now. I did talk with the doctor this morning. He plans to take the breathing tube out this afternoon to see if she can breathe on her own. I was with Wendy for about fifteen minutes, that's all they'll let me stay each hour."

"How's she look?"

"Not good. She was all curled up and there are tennis balls in each hand. Of course her head is bandaged, tubes everywhere, monitors attached for lord knows what." Josh paused to choke back tears. "It's so hard to see her like this."

"I'm sure it is Josh. I don't know what to say. I still haven't heard from Matt and the police aren't much help. My attorney is only telling me there is nothing I can do. So, I'm thinkin I'll fly out day after tomorrow. What motel are you staying at and I'll book a room. I assume it is close to the hospital? I'll call you when I have my flight schedule, Okay?"

"That'll be great." Josh gave her the name of the motel and phone number.

Josh walked back to the hospital and through Security to ICU. The curtains were pulled around Wendy's bed, so he told the nurse he would be waiting in the lounge area. Nodding, she said she would send someone out.

Josh waited for what seemed like an hour and it could've been even more, he wasn't a clock watcher and never wore a watch. His days and nights were routine and time didn't matter. But now this was different, time was weighing heavy.

Finally, the nurse came out and stood in front of Josh. "Doctor Boyer was in earlier and removed Wendy's breathing tube. She was quite agitated for a while so we increased her medication. Other than that, there are no changes, vitals standing the same. You can go in for fifteen minutes."

Wendy was now lying on her back, pillow under her knees and her bed was in a slight upright position. She no longer had the breathing tube and was laboring to breathe. The nurse explained that was normal and hopefully she would settle into a rhythmic breathing pattern by evening.

"What happens if she continues to breathe so hard?"

"That will be up to the doctor, we need to give it some time. I'm sure she's going to be just fine."

Sitting beside Wendy's bed, he held her hand, talking or just plain rambling about first one thing then the other. Hoping something would bring her around, hoping she would hear him. But nothing was happening. He laid his head down on the edge of the bed and sobbed still rubbing Wendy's hand.

The nurse came back in and told Josh it was time to go. She sat and held his hand trying to comfort him.

CHAPTER 47

When Josh got back to the motel room, he lay down on the bed and stared at the ceiling. He couldn't get his head around why all this was happening to Wendy. Killing Wendy would not have solved Trevor's problems, it would've only enhanced them. Matt still being at large was strange. Allison not getting any questions answered from either the police or her attorney was also weird.

Josh dropped off to sleep, clothes and all on top of the bed. He woke after midnight, took his clothes off and got into bed. He had a fitful sleep with one ugly dream after another, wake up, pace and go back to bed only to wake up to another ugly dream.

Calling the hospital, hopefully for good news, Josh got the same – no change. Since it was only six a.m. he went to breakfast and tried to read the paper for distraction and kill time.

When Josh got back to his motel, he called Mr. Roberts to give him the update on Wendy.

"Thank you so much for the updates, I really do appreciate your calls. I wish I could help in some way, but I know there is nothing I can do. Keep your chin up, I'm sure things will start looking up. At least, she has been holding her own and that is good news. In fact, I'm not sure if you knew someone tried to run Wendy down while she was walking Spook on the beach, then someone broke in to her condo and shot Spook. On top of that, she got a call from an unknown that she was 'lucky' and next time they wouldn't miss. So, at that point, I had her put in protective custody until just before the trial."

"Oh, my God! I didn't know all of this was going on. The only thing Wendy said was someone had tried to run her down on the beach and she had been rather busy for a couple weeks and someday she would tell me all about it. I can't believe what all she has gone through."

"I know, Josh, it is unbelievable. But this brings me to a question I need to ask you. I hate to dump this on you, but I need to know what to do with Spook. He has been with Rachel and Curly, Wendy's neighbors, since she went to Boston. Spook has recovered from being shot and they want to go on vacation to visit their kids and can't take the dog. Is there any chance you can take him? I don't know what else to do with him."

"I don't know, I'll have to check with my boss. He's always been very protective of his race horses. I don't know if this is even an option. I'll have to get back to you on this. Wendy has to know Spook is still around when she wakes up."

"You're right. See what you can do and let me know. Talk with you soon."

"You got it, and thank you for telling me what had happened to Wendy. Later."

Beside Wendy's bed again, Josh massaged her hands and talked and talked. He watched for the slightest movement or twitch of an eye, but nothing happened. He stayed the allowed fifteen minutes and went outside just to walk around. Staying with that routine for the morning, he decided he would go back to the motel and call Jim. May as well bite the bullet and find out Spook's destination.

"Hey Jim. Wanted to let you know there is still no change in Wendy's condition. Just the same. But she is at least breathing on her own since they removed the breathing tube. Guess that's improvement."

"Yah, it sure is. How are you doing buddy? This can't be easy."

"I'm okay. I can only stay fifteen minutes every hour, sure gives a lot of time to think. Jim, I need to ask you a question. Apparently, Wendy's condo got broken into and her dog was shot, so he has been staying with the neighbors recuperating and is going to recover. But, they are going on vacation and can't take Spook with them. Wendy's attorney called and asked if it was possible I could take the dog until they get back or Wendy gets well. I know you've never had a dog because of the horses, but Spook is a German Short Hair and very well trained. This breed, typically, is not a stock chaser. I will keep him down at my place and if it does become an issue, I'll make other arrangements. I just can't get rid of the dog right now. Wendy would be devastated if she wakes up and finds her dog is gone."

"Josh, under the circumstances, I can't say no. I know you will be cautious with this dog and that is all I'll ask of you. I hope when Wendy wakes up she realizes what a great caring friend you are for her."

"She knows that. The only problem is I wanted more. I need to get back to the hospital and I better call Mr. Roberts and tell him I'll take Spook. I'm thinkin I'll come home tomorrow, but I'll let you know for sure."

"No problem, take your time. Keep us posted and take care of yourself, Josh."

"Thanks Jim, I really appreciate this. Later."

Josh called Dwayne, but his receptionist said he was with a client. He told her to leave a message that he would take Spook, just let him know when so he can make arrangements for transport.

Wendy had been moved to a new position when Josh returned to the hospital. He thought her hands seemed to be more relaxed and not clinching the tennis balls as tight as previously. He stayed more than fifteen minutes, talking nonstop, and then left.

CHAPTER 48

The first step Sam and Brenda Lou decided to pursue was to call the Panama Beach City police and get a copy of the APB and details. Next was to pay a visit to Mrs. Harper. The rest they'd play by ear.

When Sam got off the phone, he acted as though he had just found a pot of gold. "The Panama City Beach Police Chief is emailing a copy of the police report of the attempt to run down an Alicia Browning, a list of witnesses and the phone number of the victim. Apparently, they traced the vehicle to Enterprise Auto Rentals in Atlanta that was leased by Matt Harper. This could be looking like you might get your wish for that road trip after all. How's the Florida Gulf sound?' Sam smiled at Brenda Lou.

"Wow, how did Harper end up in the Duwamish from Atlanta or Panama City Beach? Let's see what the report reveals and then call this Alicia Browning."

"While they're putting the report together, let's take a ride to the Harper residence."

Knocking on the door and ringing the doorbell got no response whatsoever. Sam walked to the side of the yard just looking around when a neighbor hollered over the fence.

"Can I help you? Obviously, no one is home."

"Ma'am, we are looking for Mrs. Harper. Have you seen her?" Brenda Lou asked.

"Who are you?"

Sam walked to the fence and handed the neighbor a business card.

"King County Sheriff's Department? What is this all about?"

"I'm afraid I need to speak with Mrs. Harper. Have you seen her?"

"I believe she is out of town and I don't know where. She's been doing a lot of traveling lately, haven't seen her for a couple weeks now."

"Do you know where she works?" Brenda Lou asked.

"I don't think she is working right now."

"Do you know where she used to work?"

"Allison used to work for the State, but I don't know what she did. We aren't friends, just over the fence acquaintances."

"Thank you so much for your help. What is your name?"

"Sally Schmidt."

"Hmm, that was certainly interesting. I wonder how this is going to fit with the Panama City Beach police report."

When they got back to the office there were emails of reports from the Panama City Beach Police. "Let's take these reports home and look them over and attack it all tomorrow."

"Okay, but I really do want to call Alicia Browning and chat with her for a bit."

CHAPTER 49

Dwayne Roberts went to the office early so he could get organized for an afternoon divorce hearing. He hated these kinds of divorces where abuse was involved. No one ever won, because the abuser usually never quits taunting the spouse. Some of these guys never gave up the fact they had lost control and power in the marriage. This guy was scary in that he had a permit to carry a weapon, and was smart and smooth enough to talk his way out of any confrontations with the law. He was on the edge of all aspects of his bad behavior.

Although, Dwayne had never read the three books of *Fifty Shades of Grey,* his wife had told him the gist of the story. This was truly a Domineering vs. the Submissive relationship, the only difference being, the Sub was not a willing participant.

Dwayne had covered his bases by having extra security at the courthouse. He didn't trust the guy by any stretch of the imagination.

His thoughts turned to Wendy Noble. He hadn't talked with Josh for a few days, and made a note to call later. He wished he had had the forethought to have hired more security at the courthouse in Boston. He wished he had gone to the hearing, but then he wasn't licensed in Massachusetts so there would've been no point in going.

In deep thought, and not at all accomplishing any work, he could hear an occasional beep. Ignoring it, he started shuffling papers again, taking notes and trying to prepare for the trial. Dwayne didn't know how long this beep had been going on, but it was starting to get real annoying.

Dwayne went into their lunch room, put on the coffee and tidied up a bit. As efficient as Julie was with her job, the lunchroom seemed to be off limits to her. Must not have been in her job description. When the coffee was half done he grabbed a cup and went back into his office.

Finally, the beep was driving him nuts. He'd already checked to be sure his cell phone was on a full charge, not his phone. He checked the batteries in the smoke detectors, not them. He was standing in the middle of his office when Julie came to work at 8:30.

"Julie, would you come in here for a minute?"

"Of course, let me hang my coat up."

Note pad and pencil in hand, Julie walked into the office, "What can I do for you?" She sat down ready for dictation.

"Listen, do you hear a beep?"

After several seconds, "No, I don't hear anything. Where was it coming from?"

"It's in here somewhere, I don't know exactly where. I've checked my phone and the smoke detectors and it's not them." Just then, it beeped again.

Julie walked over to Dwayne's desk and opened the bottom drawer and pulled out a cell phone. "Isn't this Wendy Noble's cell? You put it there so if anyone called you could return calls. In fact, there's a call."

"Oh yah, that's right. I forgot all about it. So, who's the call from, is there ID?"

Julie responded, "It's from the King County Police. Where's that?"

"I have no idea, give 'em a call, see what they want." With that, Julie went to her desk and Dwayne went back to shuffling papers.

Dwayne's client was coming at 10:30 to go over the court proceedings. He sorted through the papers and got them in order then took out the yellow note pad and started listing topics he wanted to discuss with his client to be sure she understood thoroughly.

Julie came back into Dwayne's office with information from the call on Wendy's cell phone. "Dwayne, this is really weird. That call was from a Brenda Lou Davis, homicide detective with the King County Sheriff's Department in Seattle, Washington. She wants to talk to Alicia Browning regarding the alleged attempt to run her down on the beach. Now, why would someone from Seattle want to talk to her?"

"I don't know other than Matt Harper is from Seattle, Washington. Look, why don't you call them back and tell them I will be in court most of the afternoon and will try to give them a call this evening or in the morning. Thank you Julie."

Mrs. Grant was on time and they went through the process. Dwayne felt confident she completely understood and was ready to get this over and done. "I'll see you at 1:15 in the foyer of the courthouse."

The hearing went as he expected, Mr. Grant was showing his obnoxious, arrogant personality and pissing the judge off to where Mr. Grant was taken from the court room. Mrs. Grant got her divorce, awarded spousal support and child support, plus a restraining order against Mr. Grant. Of course, a restraining order is only worth as much as the paper it is written on. Many stories have been written regarding the violation of such an order. Dwayne could only hope for the best for his client.

It was 4:30 when Dwayne got back to his office, which was 1:30 in the afternoon in Seattle, Washington. He placed the call to Brenda Lou Davis.

CHAPTER 50

As soon as Josh walked out of the hospital his phone rang. "Hi Josh, it's Allison. I just landed in Boston and waiting for a cab. Where are you? I thought I would go directly to the hospital. I can't check into my room till four."

"I just now walked out of Wendy's room. I'll wait for you here."

Surprised, he hadn't expected Allison to get here so soon. Still confused about the whole situation, Josh was leery of meeting with Allison. He felt he would have to be very cautious with what he said to her, so being a good listener was his best approach.

Josh walked around trying to figure out how he was going to react to Allison. He had so many mixed emotions regarding her and Matt. In fact, he knew he didn't like Matt and wasn't so sure he liked Allison any better. There was just something he didn't trust and he couldn't put his finger on it.

Dwayne had told Josh about several incidents that had happened to Wendy before she'd gone to Boston for the trial. Josh couldn't decide if he should share this with Allison or not, playing it by ear was his best idea.

Waiting out front of the hospital, an hour or more had passed when a black limousine type car pulled up. Not a taxi as Josh was expecting. A flashing thought went through Josh's mind that a black limo was constantly following Wendy. Allison got out of the front passenger side, while the driver, not in uniform, took her two big pieces of luggage from the trunk. The two chatted for a very short moment, but Josh noticed Allison did not pay the driver. He assumed this must be Allison.

The woman was dressed to the nines, not at all what one would think to wear when traveling across the United States. But then Josh only dressed up for weddings and funerals and one dark suit fit both occasions. Wendy had made the statement that Allison had always been high maintenance and her appearance certainly proved it.

Approaching Josh, Allison had a big smile and extended her hand, "You must be Josh? I'm Allison. Nice to meet you, sorry it's under these circumstances. How is Wendy doing?"

"Nice meeting you too. There's been no change. She's breathing on her own and all her vitals are good. The nurse told me they were starting to decrease some of the meds that are keeping her comatose. What brain damage there is they won't know until she wakes up. How long this will take, they don't know that either. So right now it's all status quo and a waiting game. How was your flight?"

"Actually, it wasn't bad. I was at a conference in Las Vegas for three days, and I decided last minute to come out here before going home."

That statement stopped Josh dead in his tracks. From all their phone conversations, he was under the impression she was home waiting for Matt to call, or the police to give her some information and meet with their attorney. She didn't appear at all to be the upset wife of a husband that has been missing for the last two weeks or more, plus being a suspect in trying to run down her best friend.

"Sorry, my mistake, I thought you've been in Seattle all this time."

"Well, I was, but I was having no luck with the police, attorney or Matt so I just took a break and went to the conference. Everyone has my cell phone so they can get in touch with me anytime. Let's go in and see Wendy. I'm dying to see her. This has all been so unnerving to me. She doesn't deserve any of this. I hope whoever shot her is caught. Do they have any suspects yet?"

Josh stopped, "I don't know, but Allison, do you understand it is your husband that is a suspect in trying to run her down on the beach? I can only imagine he is right up there at the top of the list as a suspect."

"Yah, I know, that's what you said, but I find this so hard to believe, Matt loves Wendy the same as I do. That's got to be a big mistake."

"Considering the truck was rented under Matt's name, I don't think it is a mistake at all. Let's go in."

Allison gave Josh a rather strange look of which he ignored. Already, he didn't like her. Josh took hold of the large bag while Allison took the smaller one, which he thought to be a lot of suitcases for a three day conference. They went to the reception desk and Allison asked if she could leave her bags there for a little while.

When they walked into ICU, Allison had to be cleared with Security and Josh saw a real irritation with her as she acted very insulted and responded rudely to the security officer. Josh went on into Wendy's bedside and held her hand as he usually did. It wasn't long till Allison came in and suddenly broke into tears.

"Oh, my God, Wendy, I am so sorry this has happened to you. You don't deserve it. You have always been so perfect in everything you do, your goals, your life and you made it happen. I envy you so much and always have. This is totally a bullshit tragedy."

Josh stepped away and walked over to a chair and sat down. He watched Wendy to see if there was any reaction to Allison's presence. Josh thought he saw her fingers grip the tennis ball tighter. He stood up and walked closer, removing the ball from Wendy's hand, he held and massaged her fingers, then relaxed his hold and waited.

After several minutes, Wendy moved her little finger ever so slightly.

Josh's cell was vibrating in his pocket, he recognized the number as Dwayne's. "I need to take this call, I'll be right outside here in the hall." Josh said to Allison and stepped out.

"This is Josh."

"Hi Josh. This is Dwayne. Have you heard from Allison?"

"Yes. As a matter of fact, she just got here a little while ago. We were just walking into see Wendy when you called. What's up?"

"I just got off the phone with a homicide detective from King County Sheriff's Department in Seattle. They found Matt's body in the Duwamish

Waterway a couple days ago. I don't have a lot of details, but they want to talk with Allison."

"Wow! How long do they think he's been dead?"

"That I don't know, but it sounded like for a little while. But here's what is going to happen. I'll call them back and tell them Allison is in Boston. Do not let her know about this call and don't give her any indication anything is up. She may be innocent as hell, but if not, we don't want to give her a chance to run. Can you do this?"

"Absolutely! If she had any part of this whole ordeal with Wendy, I want her prosecuted. You can count on me for whatever you need."

"Thanks, I'm going to call Seattle right now. So just keep her there, okay?"

"Got it. Call me if anything changes, my cell is on vibrate and in my pocket."

Oh, my God! Josh thought to himself. What the hell is going on? He knew he didn't like Allison from his first impression, but he sure never thought it would come down like this. That is 'if' what he is thinking right now is correct. How will Wendy ever recover from this?

As Josh stood inside the door of Wendy's room, Allison was leaning over Wendy talking in a very low voice. She had a pillow from under Wendy's head in her hands and appeared to be lowering the pillow and Josh said, "Allison?"

Allison turned towards Josh, "Oh hi, I didn't hear you, have you been standing there long? I was just fluffing Wendy's pillow." Then she gently lifted Wendy's head and put the pillow back. "Everything okay? That was a pretty long conversation."

Josh simply stared at her in disbelief with what he thought he had just witnessed. Calmly, he replied, "Everything is fine, it was my boss asking how Wendy's doin."

"I thought I would fluff her pillow and talk about the past and see if she would respond, but she didn't. I wonder how long she will be in this state.

I would think the longer she is in this semi-coma, as they call it, the more damage there is apt to be. Don't you agree?"

"Maybe, but I also know they are saying she is healing while she is out. Guess it could be one of those double edged swords."

"How long are you planning to stay here?"

"I'm not sure, just depends on what the doctor says when he comes by this afternoon or evening. Guess I'll make my decision then." No way was Josh telling Allison he was planning on leaving in the morning. In fact he had no plans of letting Allison out of his sight. "How bout you?"

"Well, I want to get checked into my room, come back and see Wendy, then go have some dinner. Want to join me for dinner? Would be a good chance for us to get better acquainted."

"I really want to hang out here and wait for the doctor. I'd like to hear what he has to say. We can decide later, if that's alright with you? Are you booked at the same motel as me?"

"No, I don't think so. I couldn't remember your motel name so I booked one that I thought was close to the hospital."

Josh was thinking everything that came out of her mouth was bullshit. Allison specifically had him repeat the name twice and took the phone number. There should've been no question where he was staying.

"You are acting awfully restless, is something wrong?" Allison asked.

"No, I'm not used to just sitting around, besides, I hate hospitals."

"I'm not particularly fond of them either. So, I think I'll go check in and then come back."

"Why don't you wait here until the doctor comes in to see Wendy? That way, you'll get the first hand information." Josh hoped that was a good enough reason for her to stay for a while longer.

"I'll wait for little bit, but my feet are killing me. I would love to change into something more comfortable."

When Josh's phone vibrated in his pocket, it startled him and he jumped. He answered it and listened as Dwayne told him there would be two police officers coming to the hospital to escort Allison back to Seattle. So, just play it cool was his advice.

"You got it." And Josh hung up.

"What was that all about?" Allison asked.

"It's personal."

CHAPTER 51

Staring out the window several floors down, Josh was wishing the police would hurry up and get there. But then, he wasn't sure he was looking at the same front area where he came in. There was more than one entrance to the hospital and he could get turned around very easily. He could manage forward, backwards and left and right, but don't give directions to north or south and east or west, he'd be lost for sure.

Josh was remembering several times that he had been lost and how funny the outcome had been and how stupid he had felt. He sort of chuckled out loud.

Allison asked, "What's so funny?"

"I was just trying to figure out if I was looking at the front entrance to the hospital or if I'm turned around. Which then reminded me of a few times I got ridiculously lost for no good reason and how humorously funny it turned out. I'm horrible about directions."

Suddenly, a black limousine pulled up and parked. They were too many floors up for him to tell for sure if it was the same one that had delivered Allison earlier. But familiar enough for Josh to look more closely. He wanted to keep Allison away from the window just in case it was the same one.

Matt being dead added another bit of twist to the whole scenario. Josh was curious how long Matt had been dead, which could answer a lot of questions. Was Matt really in Atlanta or someone else with Matt's ID? Has Allison really been in Las Vegas for a three day conference? She sure had a lot of luggage for such a short time. Then Trevor popped into his head, where the hell was he during all this shit? Maybe Trevor was in the black limo downstairs. Being an outsider and not knowing any of these people, all he could do was speculate and he had done plenty of that since having met Wendy.

Deep in his own thoughts, he was startled when the doctor came in and he asked Allison and Josh to step out while he examined Wendy. He said he would come out and talk to them when he was done.

Josh and Allison hadn't been in the waiting area very long when two police officers were walking towards them. Josh looked at Allison to see how she was going to react and she was totally calm as she thumbed through a magazine.

"Are you Mrs. Harper?" One of the officers asked.

"Yes, I am. Why do you ask?"

Allison sat up straight in her chair.

"Is Matt Harper you husband?" he asked.

"Yes, what has happened to Matt? Has he been found?"

"Mrs. Harper we have some bad news. Your husband was found dead in the Duwamish Waterway a couple days ago. According to the King County Sheriff's office, it appears to be a homicide. We don't have any other details. I'm sorry."

Allison sat there and stared at the officer, tears streaming down her cheeks, but she didn't make a sound. She put her head in her hands as she wept in silence and her body shook uncontrollably

Josh moved closer to Allison and put his arm around her, "I'm so sorry Allison, is there anything I can do?" He couldn't read whether this was genuine sadness from Allison or an act. But he still felt sorry for her even if it was only for a minute.

"Mrs. Harper, the Sheriff's office wants you back in Seattle. We have been instructed to escort you to the airport and get you on the plane. The Sheriff will meet you in Seattle."

"Oh, my God, Josh. I don't know what to do?"

"Allison, you have to go with the officers. You probably need to call your daughters and have them meet you at the airport in Seattle. Call some of your friends there to be with you. But we need to get your luggage and you have to go now."

CHAPTER 52

Josh watched as the two officers walked Allison out of the hospital and put her in the back seat of the car along with her luggage. It was a pathetic sight. He wasn't completely sure how he felt at the moment. His emotions seemed to be running hot and cold.

The limo that Josh had spotted earlier was still parked and no driver. As the police car pulled away from the hospital and made its' way to the exit, the driver of the limo popped up, started the car and followed behind. The vehicle was too far away to get the license plate number.

This was too much of a coincidence to just let it go. Josh went back in the hospital and found the lobby pay phone and called 911. He explained the situation as best he could and hoped it was enough to prevent another situation, whatever that might be.

Josh went back up to Wendy's room and seeing the door shut, he went to the waiting area. He hated all this sitting around with time to think. He wished Wendy would wake up so he could talk to her, knowing very well there was a lot he couldn't tell her right now. Some stuff would have to wait for quite a while.

Not knowing what was going to happen with Allison regarding Matt's death, and what the outcome would be, Josh felt he was the only one Wendy had left in her life if things went south with Allison. However, he wouldn't know for sure for a very long time where in Wendy's life he would be, if anywhere.

Leaning his head back against the wall, Josh didn't hear the doctor walk up until he sat down in a chair across from him.

"I've just come from Wendy's room. We changed the bandage and the wound looks good, healing very nicely. Kidney function is good, her liver looks good and all her vitals are strong. I checked her reflexes and she responded normally. I have decreased her medication some more and that should help bring her around more quickly. There are strong brain waves, but that still doesn't tell us what damage was sustained or what she will remember. It is a possibility she could experience amnesia, temporary or permanent. In most cases it's temporary, but there are no guarantees. The brain is a very complex organ and how it recovers from trauma is never the same as the case before. I wish I could be more specific and give some definite answers, but this is the best I can do. I will say we are far more hopeful and encouraged than those first few days. She is a fighter. Do you have any questions?"

"I have lots of questions, but I wouldn't even know where to start." Josh smiled and continued, "You have probably answered most of them. I guess my main question is if you have any idea how long it will take Wendy to wake up as you decrease the medication?"

"Before Wendy is completely coherent and can understand what has happened could take weeks or months. Bearing in mind we won't know for sure till she wakes up completely. It will be a slow wakeup. We don't want her to come out fighting."

"Would you think it safe to say I could go back home and take care of business and come back next weekend?"

"Absolutely, and maybe even two weeks. You can call any time and if things start happening faster than I expect, then you can come back. Am I correct in that Wendy doesn't have any family? You and her best friend is all she has? Where is her friend? I thought she was here earlier."

"That was Allison and they found her husband dead near Seattle. They believe it was a homicide so she got a police escort back to Seattle. And you're right, Wendy doesn't have any family. Her parents were killed in an automobile accident after she got out of college. So, she has seen a lot of tragedy in her life, a lot more than any one person should have to go through."

"Yes, I would agree. If you don't have any other questions I need to get on with my rounds. Like I said, I think you are safe for coming back in a couple weeks. Keep in touch and you'll know." He stood up and shook Josh's hand and went on down the hall.

Back in Wendy's room, Josh took his position beside her bed. Rubbing her hands and talking to her, he intently watched her face. "Allison was here to see you today. She wanted to stay longer but had to go back home unexpectedly. Do you remember her being here? She is really sorry you got hurt and wants you to get better real fast. I do too, I want you well, I want to keep you safe and I love you. The doctor said you could be waking up any time but it will be a slow process. So, I think I will go back to the ranch for a while and get back to work. Besides, I'm going to go get Spook, and take him to the ranch until you are well. I hope that is okay with you. Curly and Rachel can't keep him while they're on vacation."

Still massaging her hands, Josh just stared at her. Wendy was such a pretty woman, but suddenly he realized he didn't know her. He had met her under a different name, different profession, different color of hair and a different story. Some he learned later to be the truth, but then what was the real truth? So, who was he in love with, Alicia or Wendy? He had been in love with Alicia, but she had turned him away. Now, was it sympathy for Wendy that brought him here? Josh, all of a sudden, felt really confused. He had a lot of sorting out to do.

Josh went back to the motel and called the airlines to see what was available the next morning or even later that night to return to Lexington. Then, he called Jim to let him know he would arrive at eleven the next morning.

Curious about what was going on with Allison, Josh wondered if he would ever hear the outcome of the situation.

It's amazing how life can make such a drastic turn in such a short amount of time. Josh's life had been so simple and routine for quite a while even after the death of his wife and two daughters. Although Josh had suffered tremendous heartache and devastation over his loss, he mechanically moved on. It was still painful every time he was reminded of his wife and girls, but he was thankful to have had them in his life, even if it was too short a time. Wendy and Josh's wife were completely different in almost every way possible.

Josh decided his brain was in overload, so he started packing his stuff to get ready for an early departure the next morning. He was looking forward to getting back to the ranch and getting busy. He always did better with busy.

Dwayne still hadn't called back about Spook and Josh hadn't given much thought on how that dilemma was going to be solved or when.

The motel clerk was surprised Josh would be checking out the next day and asked how the lady was doing in the hospital.

Blindsided by the inquiry because Josh had not mentioned anything about a lady in the hospital. "How do you know about the lady in the hospital?"

"Your friend mentioned why she would be here when she called for a reservation. As a matter of fact, she still hasn't picked up her key and a couple calls have come in for her. I'm sorry is something wrong?"

"Uh, no nothing's wrong. The lady in the hospital is about the same. You may as well cancel Mrs. Harper's room, something came up unexpectedly and she had to go back to Seattle. Did whoever called leave a message or a number?"

"No, he just said he would call back."

Outside the office, Josh tried to figure out the information he had just been given. First of all, Allison lied about the motel and where she was staying and for what reason. It sure didn't matter to Josh where she stayed, so why the lie? Then, there were the two calls from a guy who left no message or number. He would've expected a call from her daughters, but with Matt being dead, who was the guy? Could it have been Trevor? Is there something going on between them? Josh thought about going back in the office to see if there was caller ID, but changed his mind. It was none of his business and he wasn't an investigator.

Josh grabbed some dinner and made two more fifteen minute visits to Wendy before he went back to the motel. He felt sad as he left her room, not knowing when he would be back. He left phone numbers with the nurses in case there were any changes. They assured him they would call and he was welcome to call any time.

It seemed like an eternity that Josh had been in Boston, but it would only be four days by the time he left the next morning.

Dwayne was calling as Josh walked back to the motel, "Hi Josh, how's everything going?"

"Just about the same." Josh went on to explain everything the doctor had told him earlier. Before Dwayne had a chance to ask about Allison he told him that the Boston PD had picked her up. Then he explained the event with the limo and motel clerk.

"That's interesting, I wonder what that's all about? I may need to follow that through and make some calls. By the way, I talked to Rachel and they'll be leaving next Wednesday. Rachel said Curly is taking Spook in tomorrow for his last vet visit, she said he is doing great. They're hoping you could come get him Saturday or Sunday?"

"Wow. I'm still in Boston, but I'm leaving in the morning for the ranch. I can't leave again that soon, Dwayne. Here's what I'll do, if you can get him to the airport, I'll buy a ticket and have him flown to Lexington and I'll pick him up there. I just can't take the time to drive down and then back again with the time I have already taken off. Can you do that?"

"Yah, I guess I can do that. Do you know if Wendy had a crate for him?"

"No, I'm sure she didn't. Get one and I'll pay for it."

"That won't be necessary, I'll take care of it. So, I'll let you know when to pick him up and the details of the flight. Thanks Josh"

CHAPTER 53

Landing at SeaTac International Airport, Allison was greeted by both of her daughters, Tara and Pam, and two police officers.

Hysterical, the girls clung to Allison crying and asking at the same time, "What happened to Matt? What is going on? Why are the police here Mom?"

"It's okay, everything is going to be okay. I don't know what happened to Matt. He was found dead near the Duwamish Waterway." Sobbing, Allison replied to the girls.

One of the officers touched Allison's arm and said, "We need to go Mrs. Harper."

"Oh, for God sake! I just learned my husband was found dead and you won't allow me to console my girls. What kind of animals are you?"

"Please, Mrs. Harper, let's not make this difficult."

At the King County Sheriff's Precinct, Allison was taken into one of the interrogation rooms after they took her purse and put it in a locker and gave her the key.

With only a table and three chairs, Allison snidely commented, "Wow, this is lovely, just like on TV. May I have some water or do I have to wait a minimum of thirty hours like in the movies?"

"I'll get you some water, Ma'am."

It was well after midnight when they arrived at the precinct. Allison was exhausted from all she had encountered that day and just wanted to go home and be with Tara and Pam. Allison was losing her patience very rapidly.

Finally, two detectives came in and introduced themselves as homicide detectives Brenda Lou and Sam Davis.

Brenda Lou was first to address Allison, "Mrs. Harper, I am so sorry for your loss. We need to ask a few questions and hopefully, this will be quick so you can get home to your family. I understand it has been a very rough day for you. Okay?"

"Thank you, it has been a devastating few weeks, but who's counting? I would like to be home with my girls. So let's get this over with."

"When was the last time you talked with your husband?"

"It has been a couple of weeks."

"Where was he and why so long?"

"He had been in Las Vegas for a work related conference and then had to go to Atlanta for some emergency meeting. He called me from there and that was the last time I ever spoke to him."

"What kind of work did your husband do?"

"He worked for a financial investments firm."

"What did he do there?"

"He was in sales, I don't know much about his work at all. That is a subject that was never discussed at home. He always said he wanted to leave his work at the office and he did."

"Did you call his work to try and find out where he was?"

"No."

"Why not?"

"First of all, I've never known the name of his company and secondly, Matt told me to only call him on his cell phone."

"Didn't you find that rather strange?"

"In the beginning I did, but I got used to it and it wasn't a problem."

"Did you call the police and file a missing persons report?"

"Yes, I called the police but they wouldn't let me file a missing persons report."

"Really, and why was that?"

"I'm not sure. They said too many times guys go off to a convention and are having too much fun and forget to go home, but eventually they do."

"Wow. I find that hard to believe. So, where were you during the time Matt was gone?"

"I was home and working most of the time."

"Most of the time? Where were you the rest of the time?"

"I went to a four day conference and then to Boston to visit a girlfriend who is in the hospital. Why all the questions? Am I a suspect?"

"Everyone is a person of interest at this point, Mrs. Harper. Where do you work?"

"I work for the State Family Services."

"Why, if your husband has been missing for two weeks, would you take off for a four day conference and then go clear across the United States to visit a girlfriend in the hospital?"

"Wendy, my friend, had been shot and was in serious condition and I needed to see her. The conference was pre-scheduled so I went. Everyone has my cell number, so I can be contacted at any time."

"What was wrong with your friend that was so important when your husband was missing?"

"It's very complicated, but to make a long story short, Wendy was shot."

"Was this in Boston?"

"Yes."

"What is your friend's name?"

"Her name is Wendy Noble, she's an author."

"How did you learn your friend had been shot?"

"Dwayne Roberts, her attorney, called me from Florida about the accident."

"Florida? I'm confused. Why was the attorney in Florida and the accident was in Boston?"

"I'm confused by it all too, you'll have to call him. I don't know."

"I need to have the name of all the airlines you flew on from when you left Seattle, and the name of your land line and cell phone companies."

"Why? I haven't done anything."

"Maybe not. But we need to verify the information. Considering it's so late, we're going to let you go home to be with your family. You are not to leave town under any circumstances. You are to return here first thing on Tuesday morning. Is that clear?"

"Yes."

The officer stood up and said, "I'll take you home now Ma'am."

Brenda Lou walked out of the room and said, "Let her go, we don't have enough to hold her. I think she is full of bullshit. I want her back here on Tuesday morning."

"Why wait till Tuesday, Bea?" Sam asked. Bea had always been Sam's pet name for Brenda Lou when they were detectives in San Diego and it remained after they were married.

"Because we need to get information from Wendy Noble's attorney and Allison's flight schedule and phone records. Hopefully, we can have all that by Tuesday. Sam, remember when we were in the Boston Courthouse about six months ago with that pervert that had kidnapped the little girl?"

"Yah, what about it?"

"This woman, Wendy Noble, is the same one that was getting the divorce that day and her husband made that threatening remark. This is Wendy's friend, Allison was with her in court, and we have her sitting in the interrogation room. I thought she looked familiar."

"Sounds like Aston tried to make the promise a reality, doesn't it?"

CHAPTER 54

FBI agents continued their investigation and search for Trevor Aston. Trevor had pulled the rug out from everyone and was hiding underground somewhere.

There were no leads to Trevor's whereabouts. However, they verified the firm where he worked and more records were retrieved. Large sums of money had been withdrawn from two bank accounts and a third account in a different bank under Sheila and Billy's names. Credit card information had been obtained from both Trevor's office and his home. They had not been used.

Agents had been to the Aston residence more than once and asked the same questions repeatedly. Fran was like a Mama Bear protecting her cubs and wouldn't allow any questioning of the children. They were minor children, and at that point, she was the adult in charge.

One day, while Fran was at the store and Billy had stayed home from school, the agents dropped by, unannounced, and asked Billy a few questions. Having no information whatsoever about his dad's work, their line of questioning was of no value.

Fran came home just as the agents were leaving and she ripped them up one side and down the other. She made sure they understood there wasn't any information to be had that they didn't already know and they were never to return to that house again. Whether or not they would pay any attention to Fran's orders was only a matter of time.

Sheila cried herself to sleep almost every night, while Billy had become more somber and quiet. They'd left so many calls on Wendy's cell that the only message they got now was the 'mail box is full'. Calls to their dad's phone revealed it had been shut off and out of service. Fran tried to be as supportive and as encouraging as she could by repeatedly telling them 'Daddy is away on business.' It didn't help.

Meanwhile, in Seattle, Brenda Lou returned the call to Dwayne Roberts. "Mr. Roberts, I received a call from your office after my attempt to reach Alicia Browning. How did you get my number?"

"Ms. Browning is my client and I have her cell phone in my office, I was only returning her call to you. So, how can I help you?"

They were on the phone for over an hour trying to sort out all the pieces of the puzzle and getting the story in chronological order with Alicia Browning and Wendy Noble.

"Ms. Davis, under the circumstances, I see no reason why I can't send you copies of everything I have regarding Wendy. I realize privacy is an issue here, but I feel very confident Wendy would give her full consent. I'll have my secretary prepare the file by this afternoon. I can overnight it to you or fax, which is your preference?"

"Thank you very much. I would prefer to have the files emailed a.s.a.p. Have you heard how Ms. Noble is doing?"

"No, not lately. I have a voicemail from Josh, her boyfriend, but I haven't called him back. I've got to do that. How's everything going on your end? Did you get anything out of Allison?"

"Not really. I've ordered copies of her flight schedules and both phone records. Something stinks here, but I'm not sure exactly what it is. We have some conflicting information we got from her neighbor. So, who is this Josh?"

"Josh Townsend is a friend of Wendy's who helped sort out the Ponzi scheme that Trevor was involved in. I'll send his information along with the rest."

"Thank you, we'll get it all figured out."

"I'm counting on it. I would appreciate it if you could keep me in the loop."

"I'll do the best I can. Thanks again Mr. Roberts," Brenda Lou replied and hung up.

Dwayne sat in his office and knew legally he had made a mistake by volunteering to give Ms. Davis Wendy's files. However, it would've been only a matter of time until she would have subpoenaed the records. Someone needed to get to the bottom of all this for Wendy's sake and Detective Davis was certainly in a better position to do so.

Being out of the loop, Dwayne was curious if Trevor had been picked up yet. It was a mystery to him how Matt had gotten from Atlanta to Seattle without being picked up, but then criminals often slip through the cracks. There was a client waiting in the reception area, but he was going to take time to call Josh for an update.

Josh answered on the first ring. He was good at that these days, expecting a call from the hospital regarding Wendy.

"Josh, Dwayne here. I'm sorry I haven't called, but I've been up to my eyeballs with work. How's Wendy doing?"

"Glad you called. I just got back from spending a few days in Boston. Wendy is responding some and starting to come around, but it is really hard to know what is real to her. She still hasn't opened her eyes. The nurses are pleased there is some progress and so is the doctor. Anything new on your end?"

"I don't think I know any more than you, other than I did get a call this morning from a Detective Davis in Seattle who wants copies of Wendy's file, so I'll get that off to her. She was terribly confused with Alicia Browning and Wendy Noble, as were most of us for a while. Still no word on Trevor. The only one who would call me about him would be Leo Steele, he was the attorney in Boston for Wendy."

"There are a couple incidents that happened at the hospital after Allison got there. The first thing was she called me and said she was at the airport waiting for a cab. When she showed up at the hospital, she was in a black limo and the driver was in plain clothes. I didn't see her pay him and they seemed to have a short conversation. My first thought was that it was Trevor.

Then, I had stepped out of Wendy's room for a minute and when I walked back in it looked to me like Allison was about to put a pillow over Wendy's head and smother her. Allison said she was just fluffing the pillow and put it back under her head. Allison wasn't at all rattled by my appearance, but rather nonchalant. Might not have been anything, but it sure made me feel uneasy."

"Josh, I'm going to make note of this information and send it on to Detective Davis along with your name and phone number. She'll probably be giving you a call. Just fill her in on everything you know. Keep in touch and take care."

"Thanks Dwayne, I will."

CHAPTER 55

Josh talked with the hospital every day and most days, twice. He had talked with Dr. Boyer and it was encouraging to know Wendy was improving enough to go to a re-hab facility. It had been a week since Josh had been in Boston.

"Dr. Boyer, I know I am not a husband, family or legal guardian to Wendy, but can she be brought to Lexington for re-hab? Can her medical records be transferred to a doctor down here?"

"Josh, I can't answer that question. I personally don't see any reason why not, but legally I wouldn't have a clue. I think the best person to get answers from would be an attorney. Wendy's not quite ready to go, but she will be soon."

"Thank you Doctor, I'll see what I can find out."

Dwayne was the only attorney he knew to call. Placing the call, Josh explained the situation regarding Wendy's move to re-hab.

"Josh, at this point there is nothing legally preventing Wendy moving to Lexington, in fact, I think it would be a good idea. The only legality that needs to be addressed is her finances. Under the circumstances, I believe she needs to have a legal guardian appointed until she recovers to where she can take control again. I can assure you the court will only permit either the court or an attorney." Dwayne explained. "Let me do some checking and I'll get back to you. It sounds like she is doing much better?"

"Since I was there last, she has made some rapid improvements. I haven't heard anything about Allison since the police picked her up and took her back to Seattle. Have you?"

"No, I don't have any information other than a request for Wendy's file and anything else I had. I sent her file and the police reports. I'm sure they will get to the bottom of this very soon. Still no word on Trevor, though."

"That makes me nervous that he's still out there. As soon as Wendy is moved, will she lose the security or can that be extended?"

"That was a court order and I will check with Leo Steele about that. I've got to run Josh, talk with you soon."

"See ya."

Josh got the phone book out and searched for re-hab centers in Lexington. He made a list and started the phone calls. After repeating his inquiries to each facility regarding medical staffing, physical therapy programs, number of beds and explaining Wendy's medical condition, Josh eliminated quite a few. He based his decision first on the size; he didn't like the idea of a big facility. Some of them sounded like a nursing home for the very old and dying and that didn't appeal to him at all.

It finally occurred to him to call hospitals and find out which re-hab facility was recommended for their patients in a situation similar to Wendy's. He was happy with his findings and had three highly recommended facilities. At least he was prepared with information to give to Dr. Boyd.

Jim overheard part of the conversation in passing and asked, "Is everything alright?"

Since they had been busy all morning each doing their own work, they had not crossed paths until that moment. Spook had been following Jim around until he saw Josh and made a mad dash for him. Spook was such a cool dog and made friends with everyone. Still, there was the time when Spook thought Wendy was being threatened by Josh and grabbed his pant leg, that was soon forgotten.

Josh had told Jim about the trip to the hospital and how Wendy had progressed. He filled him in about Allison and his concerns, including the police coming to pick her up and escort her back to Seattle.

"Ya know Jim, I don't have any say in Wendy's life or her future, but, if there is any way I can convince her doctor to let her come to Lexington for re-hab, I would sure like to do that. She'd be so much closer, she could see Spook and no one has ever known about her being here at the ranch. I think it would be a great safe haven for her. Don't know if I can pull it off or not."

"That is a lot of responsibility for you to take on Josh. You might want to think that over for a while. I sure wouldn't know the first place to start with that process. Pretty big job."

"Yah, I know. I don't know how long they will keep Wendy in the hospital before they decide to kick her out and send her to re-hab. Oh well, time will tell. I got to get back to work."

Josh was a little irritated with Jim's reply 'to think it over'. Josh was feeling responsible for Wendy and couldn't bear the thoughts of her being out there alone without any protection. He felt very sure that as soon as she was discharged from the hospital the security would be canceled. Wendy's life had already been compromised in so many ways and would continue until Trevor was arrested and all of this was put to bed.

That evening, Josh received a call from Detective Brenda Lou Davis, "Mr. Townsend, we're working the case on Wendy Noble's behalf. What can you tell me?"

Taken back by the call, Josh told her everything he could think of, including the incidents at Massachusetts General with Allison.

CHAPTER 56

Detectives Sam and Brenda Lou Davis sorted through file folders from Dwayne Roberts. They had ordered the surveillance tape from the day of the shooting at the courthouse and hoped to receive a tape from the hospital that might reveal if Trevor Aston was the limo driver that delivered Allison.

Sam had discovered Allison had lost her job a month ago. That was the beginning of the demise for Allison.

"Mrs. Harper, since you have not been to work for a month, and we've verified you have been terminated, what were you doing in Las Vegas and who were you with?" Sam asked.

"I did attend the conference. My boss asked if I could go although I was not working. I was there alone."

"Really, why if you were terminated from your job, would your boss ask you to attend a conference?"

"She just did, because I had attended that conference before and she knew I was the best one to go."

"When was the last time you saw Trevor Aston?"

"I haven't seen Trevor."

"Why did your husband try to run down Wendy Noble?"

"I don't know."

"Did your husband meet with Trevor in Las Vegas?"

"Not that I am aware of."

"Did you meet Trevor in Las Vegas?"

"No."

Detective Brenda Lou came into the room and asked Sam to step out.

"Sam, I've just received copies of Mrs. Harper's phone records. I think you need to take a look at these. There is one number that is repeated on phones, her cell and landline, but they're untraceable. The calls were made from a prepaid phone. She is lying through her teeth."

"I'm not surprised. Have any of the surveillance tapes arrived?"

"Yes, they are going over them now. We've got to break her, she's way too cool in there. Let me go in for a while."

Brenda Lou was relentless, "Mrs. Harper, I have copies of your phone records, can you tell me who made these calls to you?" Brenda Lou had highlighted one particular number on each phone record.

"I don't know who that is. I get telex-marketing calls all the time."

"I get those calls too, but never do they last more than thirty seconds. Some of these calls are thirty minutes or longer."

"I don't know. Wendy and I talked a lot."

Ignoring the calls from Wendy, Brenda Lou continued, "I think you do. I think these calls are from Trevor. What was going on between you two? Were you having an affair?"

"Absolutely not! How dare you. Wendy was my best friend and I didn't like how Trevor had treated her, ever."

"When was the last time you spoke with your husband?"

"Matt called me from Las Vegas that he had a meeting to attend in Atlanta, it was unscheduled. He was not happy about it, he had already been gone five days and wanted to come home. I never spoke to him again."

"Show me when that call was made."

Allison looked over the two lists for several minutes, "I believe this was when he called me. I don't remember exactly. A lot has happened since then."

"How did you arrive at the hospital to see your best friend?"

"I don't know what you mean?"

"I understand you flew to Boston from Las Vegas. How did you get to the hospital, by taxi, bus, train, limo? What means of transportation did you use?"

"I called a taxi but there was an available limo service, so I took it."

"Did you know the driver? Wasn't that so-called limo driver Trevor Aston?"

"No."

"How much did that fare cost you from the airport to the hospital?"

"I don't remember."

"You don't remember? Ordinarily a limo service is quite a bit more than a taxi. Didn't you ask how much the fare would be?"

"No, I didn't. I just wanted to get to the hospital to see Wendy."

"I'm puzzled by something. If Matt was in Atlanta, how did he end up in the Duwamish Waterway in Seattle?"

"I don't know?"

"I think you do. I don't think Matt was ever in Atlanta and I don't think he was ever in Las Vegas."

"I don't really care what you think Detective. I've told you what I know."

Sam came in and motioned Brenda Lou to come out in the hall. "Let's take a break for lunch, and then I'll take over for a while.

Sam and Brenda took their time at lunch and discussed the kids and their schooling dissatisfaction. Brenda had always expressed her disapproval of public schools, since she had taught for a couple years in Idaho. She had wanted to enroll the kids in a charter school only to discover there were none in the State of Washington. Something she hoped to pursue.

After lunch, Sam went back into the interrogation room. "Mrs. Harper, how long have you known Trevor Aston?"

"I don't know for sure, I met him through my husband."

"Did your husband and Trevor work together?"

"They were in the same business, but Trevor was in Boston and Matt worked in Seattle. I don't think it was for the same company, Matt and I never discussed his work."

"Do you know where Trevor is now?"

"No."

"When was the last time you talked to Trevor?"

"The only time I talked to Trevor was right after Wendy, his ex-wife or soon to be ex, left him. He called the house checking to see if she was there."

"What do you mean by 'soon to be ex'? I thought you said Wendy had divorced Mr. Aston."

"My understanding is that in the state of Massachusetts it takes approximately eighteen months before the divorce is final."

"Who did you hear that from?"

"Wendy, right after the hearing."

"And you're sure you haven't spoken with Trevor since then?"

"Yes I'm sure. He talked with Matt many times when he called the house. Matt said it was too upsetting for me so he always took the calls. Wendy was my childhood friend."

"Was? Did something happen to Wendy?"

"No, well, yes, she's in the hospital in Boston. Wendy is still my best friend, I didn't mean to say was."

"I understand. Do you know anyone who would want your husband dead, any clients, Trevor Aston or anyone that you can think of?"

"I have no idea."

"Why did your husband try to run down your best friend Wendy? You are aware of that aren't you?"

"Yes, I'm fully aware that is what the police have reported. And I know nothing about it."

"Do you know of any reason why Wendy was shot?"

"I live here in Seattle. All of that was going on in other parts of the states, I was unaware of any of it. I didn't even know where Wendy was living. That was something she and I agreed on, that she wouldn't tell me."

"Why was that? Why didn't you want to know where your best friend was living when she constantly had to move because of her ex-husband?"

"We just felt it was an extra precaution."

"Precaution? From who?"

"Why are you asking me all these questions? I don't know anything other than what I have been told by Wendy's attorney and her boyfriend Josh, or whatever he is."

"Look Mrs. Harper, we are trying to get to the bottom of this. You can either cooperate and go home, or you can make it as difficult as you want to and stay. Your choice."

"I can't answer your questions because I don't know. I'm in the fog as much as you are. I don't know where Trevor is and I don't know why or who killed Matt. I was told I needed to come back to Seattle because of Matt's death. I didn't know I was going to be interrogated with a bunch of questions I have no answers to."

"Okay. I understand you have been terminated from your job. How long ago was that and where have you been?"

Allison skipped right over the part about being terminated. "I was in Las Vegas for a conference and then went to Boston to see Wendy."

"How long was the conference?"

"Four days, but I left after three."

"Who did you attend this conference with?"

"No one other than those that are in Family Services through their state." Brenda knocked on the door and Sam stepped out.

"The experts have gone over all the tapes. You are going to love this."

"Really? Then let's take a look." Brenda Lou was anxious to see what was on those tapes.

CHAPTER 57

Josh was busy with all the usual ranch duties. Spook had made the trip by air without a glitch and was excited to see Josh.

Spook took to the ranch routine as though he had done this before. Jim quickly grew fond of Spook and even tried to coax him to go out on rides with him, but Spook stuck close to Josh.

Every morning and evening Josh called the hospital for updates on Wendy's condition. She was improving slightly every day. Wendy was becoming restless and had involuntary jerking leg movements. She had opened her eyes very briefly several times. The nurses were trying to get her to eat and drink water through a straw, little bits at a time. Wendy had physical therapy twice a day in her room. With all the activity she had daily, Wendy was still not completely waking up. Doctor Boyd didn't seem to be real concerned yet. He relayed the message that this could last a while longer and not to get discouraged.

Josh had not heard from Allison so he had no idea what happened when she went back to Seattle. He tried to call once, but just left a message.

Dwayne Roberts had not returned his call, therefore leaving Josh in the dark. He had hoped he would be in the loop and be kept up on what was going on with the case.

Josh was making plans to go to Boston to see Wendy on the weekend. It would be a fast trip, but he needed to be there.

When Friday arrived, Josh was up early and got his chores done then started work for the other guys. Jim walked into the barn and dug right in and helped Josh with grooming the horses. "Hey, Josh why don't you knock off and get yourself ready and get to the airport. I can finish this up."

"Yah, I guess I didn't realize the time. So, I'll get out of here. See ya Sunday night."

The flight gave Josh plenty of time to think, not that he hadn't thought of Wendy almost every waking moment, already. A couple things kept creeping back into his thoughts. The incident that bothered him most was Allison with the pillow and what appeared she was about to smother Wendy. Even though she acted calm and said she was simply fluffing the pillow, it still haunted him. The limo driver who delivered Allison to the hospital remained a curiosity, could it have been Trevor? The fact Trevor hadn't been found and Matt being murdered also remained a mystery to him.

While Josh was waiting for a cab, his phone buzzed in his pocket. Recognizing the number from the hospital, he was ecstatic to hear the nurse say, "Mr. Townsend, Wendy has opened her eyes and is trying to talk."

"I just arrived in Boston and waiting for a cab. I'll be at the hospital as soon as I can get there. That is great news. Thank you for the call."

In the cab, Josh instructed the driver, "Get to Massachusetts General as fast as you can."

Josh literally ran through the hospital until he got to Wendy's room. He stopped outside her door, took a deep breath and walked to her bedside. "Wendy, it's Josh. Do you remember me?" He noticed the tennis balls were gone from her hands, some of the monitors had been disconnected, but she still had a hazy look when she opened her eyes.

"Wendy, it's Josh. Can you talk to me?"

Wendy stared at Josh with a puzzled frown and said in a weak voice, "Hi" then closed her eyes.

"What does this mean?" Josh asked the nurse.

"This is normal, she's been in and out all morning. But the ins are coming more frequently. Just sit and talk to her like you've done before. Something will bring her back."

Josh stayed most of the afternoon talking about the same subjects he had already repeated so many times. Occasionally she would respond with "Hi", but, most of the time Wendy just stared at him.

When Josh was leaving to check into his motel room and get something to eat, he leaned over and kissed her on the forehead, "I'll be back in a little while. Get some rest and eat all your dinner." Josh smiled at her and squeezed her hand and he saw a slight smile and a couple tears rolled down her cheek. "You do hear me don't you, Wendy?"

Wendy responded, "Hi."

Josh stopped by the nurse's station and told her what he had just experienced with Wendy.

"That's a really good sign. I'll go in and check on her and get her ready for her dinner. Every time we move her around, she seems to be more alert."

"I'm going to check into my room and get some dinner and come back. What time will the doctor make his evening calls? I'd like to be here."

"Usually around seven. I'll let him know you are here."

Josh met with Dr. Boyd and gave him the re-hab information he had from the Lexington facilities. Dr. Boyd assured him he would look into it.

The rest of the weekend was simply repetition of conversations. Wendy seemed more awake and stared at Josh. She would squeeze his hand on command and some subjects brought tears to her eyes, especially when he brought up Allison. Josh felt like she knew what had happened to some degree and Allison's name was very disturbing to her.

As Josh was leaving on Sunday, she smiled.

CHAPTER 58

Information was coming in by leaps and bounds that appeared to be making the case against Allison pretty easy to break.

Sam and Brenda Lou went to where the experts were viewing films from the Boston courthouse and Massachusetts General Hospital.

"Look at this." Brenda Lou said as she pointed to the film from the courthouse. "Stop and back it up, please. There, stop. Look at the passenger. Look at the hand coming out of the SUV window, this is a female, look at the ring on her finger. Plus, she is wearing a baseball cap. That is Allison. Print a picture of that ring, then one of the images with the baseball cap. Let's go to the tape from the hospital."

"I called Allison's supervisor, she told me Allison was not asked to attend a conference in Las Vegas and was unaware of a conference." Sam said.

"I'm really curious why Allison went after her childhood and supposedly best friend. What was she going to gain, certainly not her money and Trevor was divorced. Maybe Matt discovered the affair and was angry and threatened to blow the whistle on their scheme. I don't think Matt was ever in Atlanta." Brenda Lou added.

"Bea, remember it takes eighteen months in Massachusetts before a divorce is final. That still gives Trevor the rights to Wendy's assets if she were to die."

"Really, guess I don't remember that."

Viewing the video at the hospital and enlarging the image of the limo driver, it was clearly Trevor.

"Bea, I'm going back in and question Allison some more. We have her right where we want her, but I want a confession." Sam walked out and headed for the interrogation room where Allison was impatiently waiting and being obnoxious about it.

"Allison, how bout you coming clean with us? Matt was never in Atlanta, was he?"

"He said he was when he called. So where was he?"

"You tell me. Isn't it true that Trevor came to Seattle and together you and Trevor killed Matt?"

"Absolutely not!"

"Isn't it true that you and Trevor were in Las Vegas together and you were not attending a conference?"

"No. Detective, I have answered the same questions time after time. I want my attorney. I'm done and you have no grounds to keep me, only your sick imagination. I'm leaving." Allison stood and started for the door.

"I don't think so. Allison Harper, you are under arrest for the murder of Matt Harper and attempted murder of Wendy Noble." Sam handcuffed Allison and read her rights to her.

Allison became hysterical and started screaming, "You have no right to arrest me, you can't prove any of your accusations, and you have refused my request for an attorney. You have to let me go."

"I have not refused you an attorney, here's a phone. Make your call." Sam unlocked the cuffs.

Allison sat down, shaking and sobbing as she placed the call to her attorney. Sam re-cuffed her and told an officer to take her to the holding cell to wait for her attorney.

Sam joined Brenda Lou, "I didn't get a confession, but she is under arrest. She ain't going anywhere for a very long time. Now we just have to get Trevor Aston. Anyone have anything on him yet?"

"Good job, Sam. No, nothing has come in on Aston. He has gone underground somewhere and possibly not even in the country. The FBI has been to his residence several times, and it is very evident from the reaction of the nanny and children, he was not there, nor had he been."

"Thanks." Sam replied. "What happened when Allison's home was searched?"

"Nothing. Allison's daughters were there and assured them they didn't know Trevor or anything about him and had never heard the name. The search confirmed he wasn't there and no evidence that he had ever been."

"There has been an APB for the Canadian and Mexican borders and throughout the United States. That was ordered the day of the indictment. Who knows where he is now." Sam confirmed.

"Ya know, it is amazing to me that someone with as high a profile as Trevor Aston hasn't been seen anywhere. The FBI is pretty relentless with someone like him and now they have all this other information, I doubt it will be long until he is apprehended."

"Of course, they'll get him, I have all the confidence in the world in the FBI." Sam smiled.

"I feel so bad for Wendy. She has a lot to deal with when she returns to reality. Her re-hab is going to be more mental than physical. I can't even imagine how she will get through it all."

Sam took Bea's hand, "I hear she's a pretty tough cookie. It'll be rough, no doubt, but she'll make it. Let's get out of here and go home to our family." He stood up and gave Bea a kiss on the forehead.

Two FBI agents walked into the office as Sam and Brenda Lou were ready to leave. After appropriate introductions they sat at a table in an empty office.

Agent William was first to speak, "I understand Matt Harper's wife has been charged with his murder?"

"That is correct. She was arrested about an hour ago." Sam replied.

"I understand you suspect that Mrs. Harper and Trevor Aston were involved together for quite some time."

"Yes, that is our accusation."

"What information have you based this on?" the agent asked.

Brenda Lou responded, "We were called in by the Sheriff's Department to investigate Matt Harper's homicide. It was through questioning Mrs. Harper that we discovered her friend, Wendy Noble, was shot after a grand jury trial for fraud against Trevor Aston. It has all evolved from there. Connecting the dots was a no brainer. Finding Trevor Aston appears to be a bit more of a problem for the FBI." She concluded with a snide smile.

Resituating and adjusting his tie, Agent William replied, "It does appear that way doesn't it, Detective Davis? I can assure you we have a nationwide alert out for this guy."

"These guys." Sam corrected.

"Yes, Matt Harper was one of them, but he is no longer an issue. Two other men are out there that were also involved. Three have been picked up and charged in this Ponzi scheme. But now we have added suspicion of murder to Trevor Aston."

"What is your next step and what can we do to help?" Sam asked.

"At this point the FBI is taking over the case and we are asking for any information you have obtained thus far."

"Really? We have done all the leg work and have all but solved this case and you just waltz in here and demand our files without blinking an eye?" Brenda Lou said as she stood and placed both hands on the table and leaned forward towards Agent William.

"Yes ma'am, that's exactly what we are doing. You are now off the case."

Brenda Lou turned and slammed the door as she walked out of the office.

Sam stood, knowing very well the FBI had jurisdiction over them in this case. "I'll get the files."

CHAPTER 59

Two weeks had gone by and Josh was getting ready to make another trip to Boston. Wendy was improving every day and had even been able to talk on the phone very briefly with the assistance of the nurse. The nurse did a lot of relaying and deciphering the conversation and it was working, somewhat.

Dr. Boyd called Josh on Wednesday before he was to leave Friday afternoon. "Josh, I have been in contact with a re-hab center in Lexington and I believe it will suit Wendy's needs very well. They have all the physical therapy equipment that will help Wendy tremendously and they can handle all of her medical needs. However, she is down to very little medication at this time. I've talked with Dr. Ellen Riske and I'm comfortable with her credentials and experience. Having said all that, we are planning to air ambulance Wendy to Lexington on Friday. How's that fit with your schedule?"

"Oh, my God, Dr. Boyd, that is perfect. This is great news and I'll be there to meet Wendy. What time are they coming in?"

"It's hard to say exactly, but they are planning to leave here around one in the afternoon. I would suggest you make your introduction to the facility and ask that they call you when they have an ETA. I'll be keeping in touch with Dr. Riske just to keep abreast of Wendy's progress."

"Thank you so much Dr. Boyd, you have saved Wendy's life and I know she will be forever grateful to you and so am I. Thank you so much."

"You're welcome. Good luck to the two of you."

Josh was so excited he didn't know who to call first, naturally Jim was his first choice. He leaned down and patted Spook as he gave him the good news. Josh put Spook in the back of the truck and raced up to Jim and Cecelia's.

Screeching to a stop at the front of the house, Josh ran to the door to be greeted by Jim and Cecelia. "Is everything okay, Josh?"

"Everything is wonderful. Dr. Boyd just called and he is transferring Wendy to re-hab in Lexington on Friday. He has it all set up with another doctor assigned to her case."

"WOW! That is great news. Sure going to take a load off you. We're so glad to hear this Josh."

"Thank you, me too. I need to call Dwayne Roberts, see ya later." And off he went, leaving in as big a spin as he had arrived.

Jim and Cecelia smiled as they stood on the front porch, "I don't think I have ever seen Josh this excited. I'm concerned this is going to be more than he has bargained for. But, who am I to say?"

"He is a driven man, Jim, you know that."

"That I do."

Josh called Dwayne, but hadn't noticed the time until the recorder relayed the message 'the office was closed'. He rummaged through his desk papers and found his cell number. He got another message that Dwayne was unavailable.

"Dwayne, this is Josh, please call me as soon as you get this please. I have great news about Wendy. Dr. Boyd is transferring her to Lexington for re-hab. Call me."

Twenty minutes later Josh got the return phone call. He filled Dwayne in on everything Dr. Boyd had told him. Dwayne was equally as thrilled that Wendy had recovered to the point of going to re-hab.

"Josh, I'll let Wendy settle in for a few days then I'll make a trip up there to see her. Do you know how much she knows about all that has happened to her?"

"Not really. She has been told why she is in the hospital. I know she has sensed something was wrong with Allison, but I don't think she really comprehends it all yet. The doctors here will help her with all that. She's tough, but it is going to be devastating. It's sure going to be nice to have her here so close. I can see her every night and she can see Spook. This is great."

"It sure is, Josh. Keep me posted after she gets settled in and ready for visitors, okay? I'll give you a call in a few days."

Josh was so excited all he could do was walk in circles. Then he decided it was time to clean house, and clean house he did. You'd have thought Wendy was coming to his house for re-hab. Poor Spook, he just lay on his bed and watched Josh as though the man had just gone nuts.

CHAPTER 60

There seemed to be an extra amount of activity going on in my room this morning, but no one was saying anything.

Dr. Boyd came in and pulled a chair up beside my bed and leaned over, "Wendy, how are you feeling this morning?"

"Okay."

"Good. You have progressed very well, far better than we ever could have hoped for. I believe it is time for you to take the next step. Medically, you have made a great recovery. It is now time for you to go to a physical therapy hospital. There, they can concentrate on your physical and mental recovery. How do you feel about that?"

I stared at Dr. Boyd because I wasn't sure what he meant or where this other hospital would be.

"Do you understand what I'm telling you?"

My speech was still a little garbled and sometimes I didn't say the right words. "I not sure."

"Okay. Do you remember your friend Josh?"

"I think so."

"Well, that is where you are going. We have found a hospital in the city near where he lives. Is that okay with you?"

Still somewhat confused why I was leaving this hospital, I didn't know what else to say, "Okay."

"Great. You're going to have wonderful care and help to get you back where you were before. I believe you will make a full recovery, but, it'll take a while and a lot of hard work on your part. You're going to take a ride in a plane to your new hospital and Josh will be there to greet you. You'll have a new doctor, Dr. Ellen Riske, and I think you're going to like her. So, the nurses are going to get you ready for your trip. I know you're going to like this new hospital and doctors. Good luck and I hope you'll come back and see us someday."

As soon as Dr. Boyd left my room, the nurses came back and started their routine for the transfer trip in the ambulance to the airport.

A couple hours later, I was given a shot to relax me and then they put me on a gurney.

"We are going to miss you, Wendy. I hope someday you will come back and see us, just to say 'hi'. Okay, here we are. It is going to be very bright out here in the sun until we get you in the ambulance. Here are some headphones for you so you can listen to music. Good Luck." After all the situating inside the air-ambulance and fussing around, we were up in the air.

The ride seemed to be fairly smooth and the medication lulled me into a semi-conscious sleep. The nurse was waking me, "Wendy, we're about to land."

There was a grand reception at the Lexington re-hab center when the ambulance arrived. I had been slightly medicated just to take the edge off and make the flight easier.

Josh had made it a point to meet with both, Dr. Ellen Riske and Dr. Jon Flex, head of physical therapy, the day before I was transported from Boston.

My new doctor, physical therapist, a couple nurses and, of course Josh, were all waiting at the entrance when the ambulance arrived.

After I was unloaded from the ambulance, Josh trailed behind the four and the gurney. Dr. Riske asked Josh to come forward and speak with me so I would see a familiar face.

Josh leaned down and held my hand, "Hey there, how was your trip? I am so glad to see you."

I gave him a half smile, "Me too."

"Let's get you settled in your room and then we can visit for a little while." Josh walked along beside the gurney holding my hand until we got to the door. "See ya in a few minutes."

Josh followed an aide down the hall and was directed to a small waiting area. "I'll come out after we've checked Wendy and get her settled in. She appears to have fared the transport very well." Dr. Riske said and walked away.

After an hour, the nurse came out and told Josh he could go to my room. Dr. Riske and Dr. Flex were still there discussing my prognosis.

Dr. Flex spoke first, "Dr. Riske and I have thoroughly reviewed your medical records. We're impressed with your recovery thus far. We have arranged for a speech therapist two times a week, a psychiatrist twice a week in addition to physical therapy every day and sometimes twice a day. We believe, with a regimented program, we can bring you to nearly a full recovery. This isn't going to happen overnight, but we believe in a few weeks maybe you'll be able to go home and continue therapy there. How does this sound to you?"

Josh holding my hand, I said, "Okay."

"Good. We're going to let you visit for a little bit, then you need to rest. You've had quite a day. Welcome to your new home." With that both doctors walked out of my room.

Josh still holding my hand and massaging my fingers, he smiled, "It's so good to see you, Wendy. It has been a long haul for you, but you have come a long way. I hope you don't mind that I had you brought here so I could be closer and you can see Spook."

"Spook? What is that?" I didn't understand.

"Spook is your dog. Do you remember that you have a German Shorthair dog named Spook?"

"I don't know."

"It'll all come back to you. I'll bring Spook into see you as soon as the doctor says it's okay." Josh stayed for a while and talked about a lot of people, places I had no idea about. It was all so confusing to me. I was wishing this man would go, my eyes were starting to get droopy.

"I'm going to go and let you get some rest and I'll come back and see ya tomorrow. Okay?"

"Okay."

CHAPTER 61

The next two months were intense for me. I didn't have time for anything other than therapy or whatever they threw at me.

Jim and Cecelia came to visit several times and always brought me flowers. I was remembering them more with each visit. Tom and Rachel, the blue grass farmers, visited a couple times, I couldn't remember them at all, and Rachel talked, nonstop, and it made me uneasy. I think they may have sensed that and didn't come back anymore.

Dwayne Roberts came to visit after I had been in Lexington two weeks. "Wendy, it is so good to see you. Do you remember who I am?"

"Not really."

"I'm your attorney from Panama City. Do you remember living in Panama City Beach, Florida?"

"I don't think so."

"That's okay, it'll come back. The court has taken care of everything for you. While you were in the hospital, I had to have the court take over your finances. This was for your protection. You just need to get well then we can put everything back the way you had it." He stayed for a little while and visited about Rachel and Curly, people I didn't remember. He asked questions I couldn't answer. He seemed like a nice man and was very pleasant.

I was confused why the court was taking care of everything, but most things kept me confused. The doctors told me it would take time. I guess that was all I had, time.

Josh came to see me every day. On the weekends he brought Spook to see me and I could go out in the garden area. Spook was so glad to see me and it didn't take me long to remember I had had a dog. It was fun every time they came to visit.

Dr. Sara Syke, my psychiatrist, worked me in every angle possible to get me to remember my past. Bits and pieces were coming back, but some of it was totally blocked. Dr. Syke was forcing issues and it was painful remembering.

I was having nightmares with these bits and pieces, but I couldn't make any sense of these nightmares. Two children kept appearing, without faces, and I was sure I had never had children. These children would wake me up and I would be crying. Where did these children come from? Dr. Syke and I would work endlessly on these faceless dreams.

On almost every visit from Josh, I would ask questions. Some he would answer, but most of the time he just gave me minimal information.

Finally, one day, I had all the pieces and the doctor helped me put them in chronological order. It was heartbreaking to discover I had been betrayed by my best friend. Allison had been having an affair with Trevor long before I had ever met him. It was Allison who had actually arranged the meeting with Matt and Trevor. It was Allison and Trevor who were after my money and when Matt had discovered the affair, she and Trevor killed him and dumped him in the Duwamish Waterway. It was Allison that gave Trevor Matt's ID to rent the truck and try and run me down. Trevor and Allison had been in this together from the very start. And she was the one in the SUV that shot me and killed Jodi in front of the courthouse in Boston.

Depression hit me so hard when the puzzle was in place. It just wasn't believable to me. Allison and I had practically been like sisters, she was everything to me as I was to her, so I thought. It just didn't make sense how she could've changed, and when did she change? I never had any idea or noticed any difference in her whatsoever. I was devastated.

The faceless children became Sheila and Billy, now thirteen and fifteen. I knew I had once been their stepmother and I loved them very much as they did me. I was curious about what was happening with them now, but I didn't seem to have the emotional connection I was told I had before. That bothered me a lot. I had asked Dr. Syke if I could see the kids and she thought in due time it would be a good idea, just not now. They were in good hands and remained in the family home with the nanny. I had gone through enough and needed to process it all.

Josh never asked me any questions about my psychiatry sessions and let me work through it. He kept our conversations positive and never talked about what kind of a future we might have. I had this feeling there had been more to us than just being friends, but he never brought it up. Josh was comforting to me and I liked it when he came to visit. He was the gentle kind of man that just grew on me.

CHAPTER 62

Dr. Riske came in my room after I had been in re-habilitation for over two months. "Wendy, you have made such great progress. How would you feel about going home and continuing treatment as an outpatient?"

"Wow. That would be wonderful if I had a home here. Apparently I have been paying rent on a duplex in Panama City Beach, but I haven't been there since the accident. That will be quite the commute for treatment, wouldn't you say?"

"Yes it is." Dr. Riske said smiling. "Well, we'll have to work on this. We have time."

When Josh came to visit that evening, I told him about Dr. Riske's visit. "That is great news Wendy. When does she think you are ready to leave?"

"She didn't say, but soon, I guess."

"What do you want to do? Where would you feel most comfortable living?" Josh was remembering the previous conflict it caused every time he had mentioned to Wendy about living on the ranch. He thought she was way too fragile to bring it up again.

"I don't know. I don't think I'm ready to live alone right now. So I don't know what ideas the doctors will come up with. We'll see."

"Can I throw out an idea for you? Something to think about and talk over with your doctors."

"Sure."

"You could stay at my place at the ranch. I have a bedroom on the main floor with a bathroom adjoining. There is always someone at the ranch and Spook would be right there with you. Who knows, maybe you'll get back into writing again."

"I barely remember the ranch, but what I remember, I think it was a beautiful place. But, I couldn't impose on you like that, Josh."

"Wendy, it would not be an imposition. I'd love to have you there so I could take care of you. Just think about it."

"I'll think about it. Thank you. Josh can I ask you a question?"

"Of course you can."

"Did we ever have a relationship? Did you love me once?"

Josh sat down on the edge of Wendy's bed, held her hand, "Wendy, I have loved you since the first day I laid eyes on you. Yes, we did have a relationship for a short time, but I wanted too much too fast."

Wendy smiled at him. "I thought so."

"Does that frighten you?"

"No. It doesn't frighten me. I think it is something I can work on."

Josh leaned down and kissed Wendy on the lips, and with her arms around his neck, she kissed him back.

CHAPTER 63

Sam went into the office he and Brenda Lou shared to get the case files they had been working on. When he came out everyone in the office was standing around staring at a screen. The closer he got the noisier it got. Phones were ringing and the conversations were one solid buzz, non-decipherable by anyone.

Finally everyone threw their arms in the air and yelled, "They got him! They shot Aston."

Sam pushed closer to see the news reporter on the screen. The caption running across the bottom of the screen was 'NightHawk/Chopaka Border Crossing patrol kills Ponzi Scheme suspect, Trevor Aston'.

FBI Agent Williams looked at Sam, "Well, apparently, Mr. Aston tried to make it across the border. This is a pretty desolate, desert part of the state and not a highly traveled border crossing. I'm sure he thought he could just sneak over the border and no one would ever know. Didn't quite work that way."

EPILOGUE

Bea and Sam sat outside on the swinging chair they had brought when they moved from San Diego the year prior. "It never ceases to amaze me how the FBI can strut their stuff in fancy silk suits and take over a case. I know it is protocol, but I will probably never get over it," Bea said as she fanned a report.

"What have you got there?" Sam asked.

"Well, I just happen to have the final report and confession from Allison Harper. I find it so hard to comprehend how she could turn on a childhood friend the way she did. It's really sick that she allowed money to get in the way and betray Wendy who trusted her with her life and almost cost her just that, her life. You want me to read the whole thing or give you a brief summary? I have read it over more than once and I'm still overwhelmed."

"Just give me the brief version; I don't think I can stand to read what that 'sick bitch' has to say."

"Soooooooooooo, apparently, Allison has always been jealous of Wendy because she had two loving parents, and Allison did not. Wendy was single, attractive and free to travel with the comfort of enough money; Allison did not and had two little girls that confined her. Wendy was successful with her book publications and Allison only had her job until she met Matt. Matt was a great provider and certainly the innocent one in that partnership. Allison had met Trevor while she and Matt were in Las Vegas and that is when the affair between the two of them started. It was Allison that arranged the meeting between Wendy and Trevor and their plot to get rid of them both and get Wendy's money. As long as Wendy and Trevor's divorce was not final, her assets were his upon her death. I don't know how much money was involved, but the inheritance from her parents and what had been left from Wendy's grandparents was substantial. I guess enough to make murder worthwhile.

Anyway, it was not Matt that tried to run Wendy down on the beach. It was Trevor. They had already murdered Matt after he got suspicious of Allison and followed her to Las Vegas and found her with Trevor. When they got back home and Matt called her on it and conveyed his concern that Trevor was involved in a Ponzi scheme, she called Trevor and they set up the plan to get rid of Matt. Having Matt's ID, they disguised Trevor to look enough like Matt for the car rental.

Allison had even gone so far as to try and smother Wendy while she was in the hospital but was interrupted when Josh walked in on her. She was one gutsy lady and I'd say more than desperate. There are more details, but that is the long and short of it." Bea laid her head back on the chair, closed her eyes, "I can't even imagine."

"Have you heard how Wendy is doing? Does she know the whole story yet?" Sam asked as he put his arm around his wife.

"The only thing I know is that Wendy is in a re-hab facility and maybe going to Josh's place. They'll have a physical therapist going to the house and apparently she is doing quite well. I don't know if she knows the whole story yet or not. I talked with Dwayne Roberts, but he didn't know how much she knew. It had been awhile since he had seen her and he hadn't talked with Josh recently."

"We know one thing for sure; Allison will never see life outside of the bars on her windows. With Allison's attitude, I doubt longevity is on her side in prison. Trevor is a different story; he actually took the easy way out. Poor bastard." Sam sighed and lay back as they swung back and forth.

"Ya know Bea, in our line of work, there is seldom ever anything good that comes from our cases. The outcome is tragedy almost always from the get go. And, we'll move on to the next tragedy."

"I know."

Made in the USA
San Bernardino, CA
24 April 2014